He thrust up his visor.

'Children are not allowed in the tilt-yard. Where is your nurse?'

Cressida shook back her cloud of hair with an impatient hand. 'I am no child, sir,' she said frigidly. 'I regret that my sudden appearance frightened one of the horses.'

'I'm not so sure you should be out without a keeper,' he retorted grimly. 'Anyone with sense would know better than to interfere when men are practising at the quintain. Destriers are valuable.'

She was stung by his implication that she was less valuable than the horse. The rudeness of this stranger was not to be borne without retaliation!

Joanna Makepeace taught as head of English in a comprehensive school, before leaving full-time work to write. She lives in Leicester with her mother and a Jack Russell terrier called Jeff, and has written over thirty books under different pseudonyms. She loves the old romantic historical films, which she finds more exciting and relaxing than the newer ones.

KING'S PAWN

Joanna Makepeace

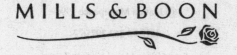

MILLS & BOON

For Eileen Evison,
in gratitude for over twenty-five years of friendship.
LOYAULTIE ME LIE.

*MILLS & BOON, the Rose Device and
LEGACY OF LOVE are trademarks of the publisher.
Harlequin Mills & Boon Limited,
Eton House, 18–24 Paradise Road, Richmond, Surrey TW9 1SR*

© Joanna Makepeace 1996

ISBN 0 263 79756 2

*Set in 10 on 11 pt Linotron Times
04-9608-90342*

*Typeset in Great Britain by CentraCet, Cambridge
Printed in Great Britain by
BPC Paperbacks Ltd*

CHAPTER ONE

PETER FAIRLEY paused with his hand on the door of his master's bedchamber. He looked down the stair to the winter parlour where their illustrious guest was waiting. Recently the Earl of Wroxeter had been given to retiring to his own chamber with strict instructions to his household not to disturb him for any reason whatever.

Peter knew, to his cost, that any disobedience was likely to receive dire punishment and he gritted his teeth determinedly. Whatever his master's reaction to this disturbance this morning, his wrath must be faced squarely. Such a visitor could not be kept waiting and certainly not sent away from the house without seeing its master. He lifted his hand again and knocked loudly.

There came no order to enter, nor any surly call to take himself off. Peter sighed, irresolute, but knocked again and pushed open the heavy oak door. He advanced nervously into the room.

Martyn Telford, Earl of Wroxeter, sat, legs stretched out before the sea-coal fire in his padded armchair. It was a chilly November morning in this year of Our Lord, 1484, and the mist from the river seemed to penetrate all the rooms of this fine town house in the Strand.

A book lay discarded upon the carpet near the Earl's chair as if it had slipped unheeded from his knee. He was staring through the glazed window over the secluded garden which backed up towards the river but Peter thought he was not seeing the mist-shrouded pleasance or the herb beds.

He turned suddenly as the squire's footsteps halted

some paces from the chair and snapped out ungraciously, 'Well, is the house on fire?'

'No, sir.' Peter did not dare to smile and nervously glanced down at the polished boards of the chamber floor.

'I told you earlier that you were not to disturb me unless there was an emergency. Since the house appears to be intact, is there a riot in the streets? I confess I have been aware of no outcry.'

'No, sir.' Peter's acute nervousness was growing by the moment.

'Then will you inform me of what dire need causes you to so flagrantly disobey me?'

The boy's brown eyes implored him for understanding.

'You have a visitor, my lord.'

Dark brows rose in sarcastic enquiry. 'Have I not taught you to deal with importunate visitors, boy?'

Peter swallowed and glanced uncomfortably back towards the chamber door as if he feared he might be overheard.

'The visitor will not give his name, my lord...'

'Then send him about his business.'

'Sir, I cannot. He is from Court and I believe... He is muffled against the weather, my lord, and two men-at-arms are waiting in the street as escort for him, but' he finished in a rush, 'I could not refuse him, my lord. I believe him to be on the King's business. He demands to see you urgently, sir, says he is aware of your need to seclude yourself from the world at large but—it is imperative he see you at once.'

The Earl's slumberous dark eyes stared into the boy's anxious brown ones. His lips tightened then he sighed, stooped and picked up the precious book and replaced it on the small table near him, stood up and stretched his tall frame. 'Very well. See that our important guest is plied with wine and offered what other refreshment he might require and say I will be with him in moments. I take it you showed him into the winter parlour?'

'Master Rawlings did, my lord. Like me, he thought...'

'Quite. Go down, boy, and see our guest is well served.' The Earl smiled a trifle grimly. 'I'll put to rights my dishevelled appearance since you are so keen to stress our unknown visitor's importance. All is well, lad; I'll not keep him waiting long nor...' he hesitated with a wintry smile '...nor will I prove too disagreeable despite my unamiable mood.'

The boy scurried out and the Earl moved towards a mirror on his dressing chest. He was still dressed in mourning black, unrelieved by ornamental chain. He wore no jewellery save two rings, one a cabochon-cut emerald deeply prized.

He hesitated after running an ivory comb through his ruffled dark hair then, sighing, slipped the golden chain with its gleaming Yorkist suns and roses, which had been lying, discarded, on the chest before him, over his shoulders, smoothed down the fine-cut velvet of his doublet and prepared to confront this court visitor whom Peter had considered so important.

As he entered the winter parlour, he saw that the man was seated before the fire still wrapped in his cloak. If he had come from Westminster, as Peter supposed, he must have got very cold indeed seated within the ferry boat which had brought him downriver.

Wroxeter spoke from the doorway. 'I see my servants have provided you with refreshment. I'm sorry to have kept you waiting. Recently I've lived a hermit's life but my squire tells me your business is urgent.'

The man in the chair rose and turned. He was wearing a low-crowned velvet chaperon with an enveloping scarf which swept round the throat and over one shoulder. Wroxeter saw the ruby glimmering sombrely in its grey velvet depths as its wearer put back the scarf and faced him squarely. He gave a great gasp of recognition and came on into the room at a run and dropped to one knee.

'Your Grace, you honour this house. Why did you not summon me immediately to Westminster if you had need of me? You had no need to suffer the inconvenience of travelling in this bitterly cold weather.'

King Richard smiled down at his friend and held out a hand to signal to the Earl to rise. He divested himself of chaperon, cloak and gloves, laying them by on a stool near him.

'Martyn,' he said, gently reproving, 'you have been hard to reach these last weeks. I know you had no taste for court ceremonial. To tell the truth, I have little heart for it myself, but I did wish to speak to you on a purely personal but important matter, one on which I did not wish to be overheard. It seemed appropriate that I should call on you without ceremony and, I hope, without undue notice from others.'

The King was gesturing for Martyn to seat himself in the second chair drawn up in front of the fire.

'No, don't summon your servant again. This burgundy is excellent. Take wine with me, Martyn.'

A table had been drawn up beside the King's chair and the Earl was relieved to see that Peter had provided the King's favourite wine in a silver flagon and two silver goblets, beside a platter of meats and fine white manchet bread. The King appeared not to have touched the food but was drinking appreciatively.

Martyn Telford smiled as he poured out wine for himself, as ordered, and took his seat beside his sovereign.

'I think Peter guessed your identity, Your Grace, and knew your fondness for burgundy. He was at pains to impress upon me the importance of my visitor but did not dare actually name you.'

The King chuckled. 'You are fortunate in that boy, Martyn. I hear he shapes up well in the tilt-yard, but his discretion is worth his weight in pure gold.'

'He is a good lad,' Martyn conceded, 'and he has had much to put up with lately.'

The King eyed him steadily. His shrewd grey eyes took in the dark shadows round his friend's eyes, the strained air and tight, hard line of the usually mobile mouth. Wroxeter was not handsome but personable. His tall, lean length was well proportioned and strong-muscled. The long-featured face, formerly good-humoured and sleepily attractive, with the strong, dominant nose and heavily lidded, dark eyes, marked by black, well-arched brows, had proved a favourite with the Queen's ladies.

The King knew that that sleepy, half-bored expression hid a mind both quick to grasp essentials and as shrewd as his own when needed to grasp the intricacies of court intrigue. His brother, the late King Edward, had instituted a system of scurriers and spy networks which had kept him well informed as to the propensities of those about him at court, within the realm at large and overseas.

When Richard had been offered the throne by Parliament, after the discovery of the bastardy of King Edward's children, Richard had found the need to continue that very useful organisation and had discovered in the young Martyn Telford a superior intelligence to oversee its work. He had come to rely on Wroxeter to make him aware of what his normal military scurriers failed to discover by usual means. Lately he had missed the presence of so clever and discreet an adviser by his side at Westminster.

He said quietly, 'I know what a terrible blow Elinor

Maudsley's death has been to you, Martyn. I've suffered a similar crushing pain myself.'

Martyn turned his grief-ravaged face full upon his sovereign and, for a moment, a hint of tears glimmered in his dark eyes. He too saw marks of intense suffering upon that narrow, clever countenance which he had come to love and admire.

The King had had much to face during this first year of his reign: the rebellion of his trusted, much loved cousin, George of Buckingham, intrigue at home and abroad, problems upon the Scots border where the thieving reivers were set to take advantage of the King's absence from the territories he had kept secure during the previous eleven years, as the late King's ruler in the north, from his fastness of Middleham Castle in Wensleydale.

He had also had to deal with more immediate concerns, not least the scheming of the French King, ever his enemy, determined to keep the presence of the last Lancastrian heir on French soil as a dependant, constantly a thorn in the English King's flesh.

Henry Tudor was scheming quietly and determinedly, surrounded by disaffected Lancastrian gentlemen who had fled the realm following the Yorkist victory at Tewkesbury, the principal supporter being his uncle, Jasper Tudor, the exiled Earl of Pembroke. It had been Martyn's work to keep a careful eye on any courtier or country squire who might be tempted to change allegiance and offer support to the Tudors.

All this as well as the King's most personal tragedy— the death of his only son and heir, young Edward, Prince of Wales, on March the ninth last, when the King and his Queen had been on progress. They had received the dread news at Nottingham and Richard had declared the fortress his 'Castle of Care'.

Only too well, Martyn was aware that the gentle Queen Anne was ailing and unlikely ever to be able to give the King a second child. He sighed, recognising his weakness in allowing his own loss to take him from his loyal attendance and duties at the King's side.

He said, chokingly, 'Your Grace, you must forgive me. What can be my loss compared to yours?'

The King shook his head. 'Every man's sorrow is as great to him as another. You have known Mistress Elinor Maudsley since you were both children, yet it is only a short time since you became reacquainted and your affection for her grew. You had great hopes of a happy life together stretching long into the future. It has been a terrible blow to you for her to become so ill so suddenly this summer and die with so little warning.'

Martyn said slowly, 'I could not believe it. She had a pain, she said, on her right side, and she was dreadfully sick. At first I thought of poison yet no one who knew Elinor could wish to harm her. The physicians could do nothing. She became worse by the evening and died early the next day in excruciating pain. I could do nothing. . . Thank the Virgin I was there with her—'

He broke off suddenly, noting the haggard expression which had deepened upon the King's countenance. 'Dear God, forgive me again, Your Grace, for my crass insensitivity. I know you were unable to be with the Lord Edward. . .'

'It was that which has gnawed at the Queen's peace,' the King said soberly. 'It was days afterward before we knew. She had missed him so much and then—to lose him like that. . .' His voice had become hoarse with emotion and, abruptly, he cleared his throat and began again. 'From what you tell me his symptoms were similar to those of the Lady Elinor. He too died in great pain and his illness developed as suddenly.'

They were both silent for moments, then Martyn said, 'If you have need of me, of course I will come to Westminster this very day.'

'That will not be necessary, Martyn. Your clerk,

Master Standish, is managing well, John Kendall, my secretary, informs me, though it is essential that a good watch is kept continually, particularly upon the Welsh Marches. It is on that very matter which I wish to consult with you.'

'Some insurrection, sire?'

'No, not yet, but some of the Marcher barons could be open to temptation. I know the Tudor's agents are constantly on the move, gathering information as to our strengths and weaknesses and offering promises of preferment should Henry gain his desire and ascend my throne.'

'We all pray that may never happen, my lord.'

Richard's lips twisted wryly. 'No more determinedly than I do, my friend.' His eyes were showing grim amusement now, the grey-green irises dancing in the firelight.

'Rumours are continually put about concerning the fate of my nephews. You know well enough that such deliberate mongering is false. The boys are safe enough where I have placed them and young Edward of Warwick is, at last, making some considerable progress in his arrested development under careful tutelage at Sheriff Hutton, but all this adds to the fuel of men's resentment.

'These southern lords have never been as ready to give me their trust and devotion so readily granted to my brother Edward. They do not know me well, or my officers from the north. Besides these, there are still men dissaffected since Tewkesbury, men who did not flee abroad like Pembroke and Oxford but who still hanker for the old Lancastrian cause, men like Daniel Gretton.'

Martyn's eyebrows rose and the King leaned forward in his chair. 'He is a close neighbour. You know Gretton?'

'I have met him,' Martyn said cautiously. 'I had not

thought his allegiance in question. He is married happily, I understand, and appears thoroughly contented with his lot.'

'I have received information that he has harboured men suspected to have been sent by Pembroke.'

Martyn frowned. 'You wish me to have him arrested?'

'No, nothing so drastic. The man is wealthy and influential on the Welsh border. He has a manor near Ludlow. Naturally he must have seen something of the young Lord Edward when his household was there with Rivers as his tutor.'

'Yes, sir.'

'Gretton and his father fought for Margaret of Anjou at Tewkesbury. Old Sir John Gretton was killed in the retreat. Daniel took refuge with Somerset and the other Lancastrian knights in Tewkesbury Abbey, and was released and allowed to disperse the day following the battle, after Somerset surrendered and he and the ringleaders were brought before me for judgement. As you will know, those ringleaders were executed in Tewkesbury market-place. Sir Daniel Gretton must still recall those grim days, as I do myself.'

He gave a brief sigh and gazed into the fire, as if remembering the terrible slaughter in the pursuit after Tewkesbury and his harsh task as Lord Constable of England, as he had been then, at only eighteen years of age.

Acting on his brother's orders, he had seen to it that Margaret of Anjou's principal captains had not lived to challenge the new Yorkist dynasty under Edward and soon after Edward's return to London with his brothers, Gloucester and Clarence, the confused, pathetic King Henry VI had died in the Tower.

Martyn thought there must have been many mourning the victims of that battle, Gretton amongst them, and that resentment could have festered. Would that man now risk his life and fortune by allying himself with some rebel force, devoted to the exiled young Lancastrian claimant, Henry Tudor? Martyn pursed his lips. Surely not—and yet he knew only too well that ambitious men were like to risk anything for the hope of preferment.

The King turned to face him again, his lips curving into a rueful smile. 'Gretton has, as you said, made a happy marriage, or so I hear, but he has no heir and is unlikely to get one now. He has a daughter, Cressida, almost sixteen and ripe for the marriage bed.'

Martyn stared back at him, astonished.

The King smiled again regretfully.

'I see you find it hard to accept that you know what I am saying.'

'Your Grace, you cannot mean that—that you wish me to consider marriage with this—child?'

'Yes, Martyn, that is exactly what I am saying.'

'But. . .'

'I ask too much, even from one so loyal as you are?'

Martyn had risen from his chair, half in surprise, half in anger, then, finding his sovereign's eyes on him, commanding his attention, he sat down again, drew a hard breath and subsided into sullen acquiescence.

'Believe me, I know what a hard sacrifice I ask of you.' The King turned away for a moment and his fingers drummed awkwardly upon the chair arm. 'Martyn, my Queen is sick. My physicians inform me she cannot improve, at least not permanently. I may soon be compelled to make this same sacrifice—for the good of the realm.'

'Your Grace, I confess I am confused. My brain addles with the newness of this suggestion, but I need to have it spelled out to me what you intend and how you think it will achieve your ends.'

'You are an earl, wealthy, Gretton's neighbour. Despite his wealth and standing amongst the Marcher knights and lords he could not aspire so high for his daughter and, I am informed, she is everything to him. If I could dangle before him the hope of so important a match I can bring him here waiting attendance upon me, under my eye, at least for the next months when the crisis is looming.'

Martyn was still silent, but the King could see that the thoughts were ticking over in that clever, astute mind.

'You need an heir, Martyn. The girl is young, malleable. I have it on good authority that she is more than presentable, but, that aside, I know men have different attitudes to beauty. By this marriage I would see you did not lose.'

'My lord, you have been more than generous. I would not wish—'

'Continue to hear me out patiently, Martyn. As I said, it is unlikely Gretton will have an heir. The girl will inherit extensive estates which will march well with yours. By all standards it will be an excellent alliance. Allow me one personal question, my friend. Is there amongst the ladies—are your affections in any way engaged elsewhere?'

Martyn gave one small, anguished cry of protest. 'By the Saints, no, Your Grace. I still can think of little else but Elinor. This is why I cannot concentrate on reports brought in by your scurriers.'

The King nodded serenely. 'It is as I thought. Will you consider this, Martyn? All I wished to do for the present was invite Sir Daniel with his wife and daughter to the Christmas festivities and the crown-wearing ceremony. I shall suggest to him that it would be my pleasure to try to arrange an advantageous marriage for his daughter. He will not dare refuse. We shall have opportunity to see the girl and assess her suitability. Should you still object to the match—' he shrugged '—then I will have to look elsewhere.'

Martyn had buried his face in his hands. He sat leaning forward, his body rocking slightly in the chair. The King touched his shoulder in a light, affectionate movement then rose to his feet.

'I must leave you, Martyn. I have a council meeting at the Tower. I do not demand an immediate answer. Think over what I've said. You will be present at Court over the Holy Season? You must begin to put grief aside, man. It is God's will that our loved ones are taken and we cannot—*must* not allow ourselves to become bitter or neglect our duties.'

Martyn had stumbled to his feet as the King had risen and he gritted his teeth against the justice of the gentle reproof. He bowed deeply.

'Your Grace does right to remind me of my loyalties at this uncertain time. If you have need of me, you have but to command my service...' He hesitated for a second, then added, 'In all matters, both official—and personal.'

Richard smiled. 'Thank you. Some of my southern lords may be tardy in their allegiance, but I know I can always rely on my very special friends.' His lips twitched slightly. 'Unfortunately, none but you is available for this very special service.'

Martyn lowered his head again in courteous acceptance of his King's command. 'I understand, Your Grace.'

He rang a small hand-bell for service and Peter Fairley came running.

'Peter, please escort our illustrious guest to the door. I take it you do not wish to be seen openly with me just at this moment, sir?'

'You have it exactly, my lord earl. It would be unwise, yet, for my intentions to be guessed at—by anyone.' The King assumed his chaperon and pulled the velvet scarf across the lower part of his face.

'Farewell, Martyn. I hope to see you soon at Westminster.'

Martyn bent to kiss the bejewelled hand and watched as the King left with his squire. He moved to the carved oak fireplace and, placing his two hands on the over-mantel, leaned down, staring once more into the flames.

He was twenty-three. In these unsettled times it was only sensible that he beget an heir. He had served as squire in the household of Sir Francis, now Viscount Lovell, until he had been knighted by Duke Richard of Gloucester, as the King had been then, for service with him on the Scottish border.

He had been then almost twenty and so busy with martial affairs that he had not thought to take a wife. His father had not pressed him and he had not been betrothed in childhood, a circumstance which he had come to believe fortunate, when faced with the evidence of mismatches he had seen in others of his acquaintance. Then Lord Wroxeter had died suddenly of an inflammation of the lungs and his heir had been hastily summoned south to be invested with his title.

The hasty necessity of his former duke ascending the throne in the past year, and the intrigues and rebellions which had followed, had demanded his loyalty and complete attention, and rendered him impervious to the bright eyes of suitable court ladies until Elinor Maudsley had arrived at Westminster to serve Queen Anne.

They had known each other in childhood and been close friends. That pleasure in each other's company had ripened into love. They had become betrothed with the King's gracious approval. Martyn had looked forward eagerly to an autumn wedding, then the cruel fates had struck without warning. Elinor had sickened suddenly and died four months ago.

He would not have believed that he could suffer so terribly from his loss. She had been gentle, yet intelligent and competent, an entertaining companion, and he had known she would make an excellent chatelaine for his castle and manors. He missed her constantly. She had come like a bright star onto his horizon and like a meteor had left it as suddenly. He felt unmanned by the depth of his grief.

Now the King was requesting that he face the possibility of marrying some child bride, a stranger, chosen for him simply by the necessity of welding an alliance in the Welsh Marcher lands. He tasted salt blood as his teeth bit down savagely onto his nether lip.

So be it. The King had need of him. He would not—*could* not love again. Why not this unknown girl? If by marrying her he could solidify Gretton's allegiance to the Crown, and achieve some measure of gain in lands and standing in his king's affections, then surely he would be a fool to refuse?

He straightened up in sudden determination and glanced down ruefully at his mourning black.

He would present himself this very afternoon at his office at the Palace of Westminster, then, perhaps tomorrow, he would summon his tailor to consult with him about more suitable attire in which to greet the youthful Mistress Gretton at the coming Christmas feast.

Cressida had watched the arrival of the messenger from the window of her bedchamber. Over this last year she had seen men arriving, sometimes clandestinely, being received by her father privately, then going off hurriedly about their business. She could not understand now why the arrival of this particular courier should arouse in her a feeling of vague unease.

The man had been dressed in the usual leathern jack, salet and breastplate, but she had glimpsed beneath the martial accoutrements the murrey and blue livery of the royal house of York. So the courier came from Westminster.

The doubt which had assailed her grew stronger. Was her father under suspicion? Yet surely if he was to be arrested there would have been an armed escort, not a solitary messenger?

She called to her nurse, Alice, now serving her as maid, to bring her a warm hooded cloak and to send down to the stables for a groom to saddle up and bring into the courtyard her favourite jennet.

Alice grumbled as usual. 'It's very cold this afternoon. Why do you want to ride out? I imagine you'll go alone as usual. You know I don't approve. Anything can happen to a young lady alone these days. You are too old now to risk insults from any peasant who might be around, or even worse. . .'

'Alice, not many months ago you were insisting I was too young. I'm only going into the copse. I shan't even leave our own desmesne land. What harm has ever come to me there? You know I hate to be watched over.'

'Aye, I know you've always had your own way in everything,' the nurse said tartly. 'One of these days you won't.'

Cressida was adjusting the fur-lined hood over the plain linen cap she preferred to wear about the manor, rather than the elaborate headdresses her father had recently ordered for her from the embroidress in Ludlow. She pulled on her riding gloves and looked up into her nurse's face, her brows pulled together into a frown of concern.

'Now, what ever can you mean by that?'

'You know what I mean right enough. Your father is already looking for a suitable husband for you, and husbands, let me tell you, do not expect or allow their wives to get their own way. They require them to be patient and obedient.'

'You are always issuing me deadly warnings like that. Father does not treat Mother as a slave. He loves her and often defers to her wishes.'

Alice gave an expressive sniff. 'And very fortunate she is, but there are times when she keeps silent about his declared plans, especially when she disapproves of them, and you'd best learn a trick or two from her—and soon.'

'Perhaps I shall learn the knack of leading a man by the nose without allowing him to be aware of it.'

'Aye, that depends on the man, my lady. Pray you'll get one as considerate as your sire.'

Cressida's amused smile vanished. 'I trust my father to find a man who will love me and be considerate of my wishes.'

Alice was silent as Cressida continued to stare at her challengingly, then she said, 'Your father will make the best match for you he can. His considerations as to that will hardly take in your prejudices. Fathers' wishes seldom do. You'll be a wealthy heiress, mistress. He looks high for you.'

'A royal duke, think you, or an earl?' Cressida bubbled over with laughter. 'I should be quite satsified with a plain country knight or squire, thank you.'

'Will you?' Alice moved away to close the heavy lid of the clothes chest. She said over her shoulder, 'Just take care while you're out and about, that's all I ask. Your father would have the skin off my back and half kill all the grooms in the household if anything were to happen to you because we allowed you to wander at will, but there, you'll do what you want, whatever I say.'

'I promise I will be careful.' Cressida touched the older woman's hand reassuringly. 'I shall be back within the hour. It is just that I feel stifled indoors today.'

Her jennet was ready as requested. The elderly

groom who lifted her into the saddle murmured the same warnings as Alice had done. Cressida dimpled at him prettily and uttered the same reassuring platitudes. The old man was genuinely fond of her.

Cressida was aware that the household servants indulged her as much as her parents did. She felt a little guilty sometimes for using their affection to obtain her own ends but her natural youthful spirits always returned quickly after such conscience-stricken moments and she found herself repeating the charms she had used previously to entice submission to her will.

She rode hard at first through the copse along the ride which led towards the ancient town of Ludlow and finally drew rein within a small clearing where a charcoal burner's hut had been built some years earlier and was now abandoned. From here, through the bare canopy of tree branches, she had a distant view of Ludlow Castle. It had been a favourite place since early childhood when her father had brought her here, and later when she had ventured even nearer and been delighted to observe the household of the young former Prince of Wales issue forth on hawking expeditions.

Cressida dismounted onto a convenient flat-topped boulder which made a useful mounting block, tied her jennent's reins to the low branch of an oak and walked up the small rise facing her for a better view.

She had never been near enough to see the young Prince clearly. He would now be almost her age, she thought regretfully. How life had changed for him! The disclosure of his father's, the late King's, secret marriage, first to the Lady Eleanor Butler, daughter of the great Talbot, Earl of Shrewsbury, then bigamously to the Dowager Queen, Elizabeth, formerly the widow of Lord Grey of Groby, had resulted in the loss of all his hopes. He and his brother and sisters had been declared illegitimate and his uncle, the new King Richard III, had ascended the throne.

Cressida knew that her father bitterly resented what he considered a usurpation of the throne. He had never discussed it openly, but had received the news tight-lipped. Her father was not Yorkist in sympathy. He had fought for Lancaster at Tewkesbury, but the Queen had been Lancastrian before her marriage and for the past years the young Lord Edward had lived amongst them, here, at Ludlow, and his supplanting had been a bitter blow. Now a King's courier had arrived at Gretton Manor.

Cressida leaned against the bole of a larch and frowned in concentration. Surely her father had not been foolish enough to speak openly of his reservations concerning the new King? If so, it could bring disaster to them all.

A familiar voice hailed her and she turned eagerly to greet the newcomer who had ridden into the clearing. Howell Prosser, the son of their nearest neighbour, was ascending the rise. He was of middle height, a square-made, brown-haired young man with an open, good-natured countenance.

'Little Mistress Gretton. What are you doing out in such inclement weather?'

Cressida had been so deep in thought that she had not really considered the icy chill which blew down the length of the ride. She was reminded of it now and drew her enveloping brown frieze cloak well around her.

'I am not so little, Master Prosser,' she said, tossing back her head. 'I shall be full sixteen next month.'

Howell Prosser laughed as he joined her, throwing back his own hood to reveal curling brown hair. She was not disturbed by his presence. Howell was only three years her senior. She had become used to his teasing over the years and often encountered him on

her rides. He was a frequent visitor to her home and
she knew that her father trusted both him and his
father implicitly.

'It is cold,' she admitted, 'but I needed the air.
Mother was busy checking the linen and father engaged
with his steward. I just felt in need. . .'

'Of pleasant company,' he finished and she laughed.

'And you consider yourself worthy?'

'I always consider myself worthy. As for describing
you as "little", you will always be so to me and quite
perfect.'

'Stop teasing me, Howell. You know my father
would disapprove of such talk.'

'Because you will be sixteen next month?'

Her face clouded and her expression grew grave.

'Is there talk of a betrothal?' Howell Prosser was
merely an esquire and he was aware that, despite the
easy camaraderie which existed between his own father
and Sir Daniel Gretton, Gretton was wealthy and
looked much higher for his daughter than the son of
his friend, however well Howell was liked.

She shook her head. 'Oh, no, nothing like that. I
suppose you are right; up till now I have really not
thought of myself as really grown-up, but now Alice
keeps warning me that. . .' Her voice tailed off
uncertainly.

'I suppose it must come soon and I shall have to
leave the Marches. Oh, I love it so, Howell; I have
been so happy here and that could all change, just as
the Prince's fortunes changed so abruptly. Whenever I
see the castle I think of him and wonder how he and
his brother are faring.'

Howell's countenance darkened. 'If they are faring
at all.'

'You mean they might have been—murdered?' The
distressed note in her voice was obvious and he gave
her a regretful smile.

'You must not let my gloomy talk alarm you, Cressida. Who knows what has happened to the Princes?'

He shrugged. 'There have been rumours, some emanating from the French Court, that the boys were done to death soon after the new King's coronation. Certainly they have not been seen in public since that time, but there is no proof that the boys are dead, certainly none that could involve their uncle in any *accident*.' He stressed the last word ruefully.

'But you are inclined to believe the talk?'

He looked hurriedly round the clearing to assure himself that they were alone together, then lowered his head and said softly, 'The fate of overthrown kings has never been good. King Edward II died a tragic death; so did King Richard II. Is it sensible to believe that King Edward V will fare any better at the hands of a usurper?

'Come, Cressida, you must not even think of these things. It is unwise to talk openly of these rumours even amongst friends. You cannot know who could be nearby and overhear. Do not question your father on the subject. Keep your own counsel.'

Cressida nodded thoughtfully. His grave words had not allayed her fears. She said hesitantly, 'A courier arrived at the manor house just before I left. I could swear he was wearing royal livery.'

Howell Prosser's brown eyes darkened and his brows drew together. 'He was alone?'

'Yes, there was no escort of men-at-arms.'

It seemed that Howell relaxed his tense stance slightly. 'I should not think there is any cause for alarm. The King fears armed insurrection since the Earl of Buckingham's rising of 1483. Richmond sailed for England and was almost trapped on that occasion. The King sends his minions to see that all is well about the realm, especially here on the Marches and on the Scottish borders.'

She nodded again, her blue eyes widening, lips pursed.

'I am sure my father has committed no foolish act. . .'

'Of course not.' He offered her his arm to lead her back to her jennet. 'I think you should return to the house. These November days are short. It will be dark soon.'

He lifted her into the saddle and sprang into the saddle of his own mount. She was glad that he was riding beside her for part of the way. She had always felt safe with Howell.

He pulled up his horse within sight of the Gretton manor house.

'You should be perfectly safe from here. I should not ride too much alone these days, Cressida. If there are King's men in the vicinity—' He broke off awkwardly. 'You might not be safe, even on your own land.'

She held out her gloved hand to him and he grasped it. A year ago he would have accompanied her right into the courtyard. She had noticed lately that he did not appear to wish to be seen with her alone, especially by her father. It was a tacit reminder that Alice's words were meaningful. She was no longer a child and should not be seen in the company of any man without a chaperon.

She lifted her ornamental riding whip in salute and he drew off slightly as she rode on ahead.

It was always a pleasure for her to come home to the manor house. It was constructed in honey-coloured stone, sturdy and welcoming against the background of fine pasture land with the vague shape of the Clee Hills in the distance. Her father owned several manors here on the Welsh border, but she loved this one the most and the family spent much of their time here.

As she entered her chamber, Alice rose hastily from

the window-seat where she had been repairing a small tear in one of Cressida's gowns.

'Your father is asking for you. He's in the solar with your mother. Best make yourself presentable.'

Cressida tugged at the strings of her cloak and Alice hastened to help her.

'I saw a courier arrive. There is no bad news, is there?'

Alice clucked impatiently as she drew off the cloak and stood back to eye her young mistress critically. The dark blue woollen gown was plain, but did not appear to be muddied or too crumpled. It would do rather than keep Sir Daniel waiting longer than need be. When he'd come up an hour ago he had seemed excited and more than a trifle impatient.

'How am I to know what news your father has had? He wasn't like to take me into his confidence. If you hurry, you'll probably find out.'

Cressida's parents were seated close to the roaring fire in the new side fireplace. The solar was luxuriously furnished, with tapestries on the lime-washed painted walls, even two fine carpets upon the floor. Even on this cold November afternoon it was warm and inviting.

Lady Gretton looked up, smiling, to greet her daughter as she paused in the doorway to give a quick curtsey. Cressida's mother was small, as Cressida herself was, but, in middle age, her figure had developed pleasantly rounded curves. Her features were less fine drawn than her daughter's but as yet unlined, possibly because her expression showed her nature to be generally serene and kindly and she frowned less than any other woman Cressida knew.

She wore a slightly outmoded gown in heavy cranberry velvet and, like Cressida, she had put off her veiled hennin in favour of a more comfortable embroidered linen cap, from which her still fair hair curled at the front and sides.

No one could have doubted that they were mother and daughter or that Sir Daniel Gretton, who towered over both of them, his arm around his wife's shoulder, loved both of them exceedingly and, unlike many of his contemporaries and equals, was not ashamed to display that deep affection openly.

He opened his arms now to greet his daughter and she hastened into them to be hugged to his muscular chest.

He put her aside gently. 'I have been worried. You have been from the house too long unescorted.'

'I met Howell in the clearing near the charcoal burner's hut.' Cressida dimpled up at him and came to seat herself on a small stool at her mother's feet.

Sir Daniel Gretton came from behind his wife's chair and seated himself opposite, his eyes regarding his daughter steadily. Even dressed as she was in that plain, unfashionable house gown she was exceedingly lovely, so tiny and yet exquisitely fashioned, her glorious golden hair streaming to her shoulders beneath her cap.

'I have had a visitor,' he announced without preamble.

Lady Gretton's hand rested lightly upon her daughter's bowed head.

'I saw a courier arrive.' Cressida looked up at her father questioningly. 'I feared there might be bad news, but you look quite happy, Father.'

'Indeed I am. The man came from the King at Westminster. He honours me with an invitation to the crown-wearing ceremony at the Christmas feasting.'

Cressida frowned slightly in doubt. 'Could not that be dangerous? You have not been to Court since the late King's coronation and your sympathies were well known. You have said as much when you talked of the slaughter following the battle of Tewkesbury. You said you only went to Court for the coronation because you judged it politic to do so and you received a safe conduct on that occasion.'

Sir Daniel smiled benignly. He was a big man, dark, square-featured, almost ugly compared with the beauty of his wife and daughter.

'I am convinced of his Grace's goodwill. He has instructed me to bring both my wife and daughter to Court. It seems he has heard of your coming sixteenth birthday, Cressida, and wishes you to be presented to his Queen, on the understanding that you might enter her household as a lady-in-waiting—until your marriage, that is.'

Cressida sprang to her feet, almost falling in her haste as her unwary foot caught at her hem. She righted herself, faced her father squarely, and gave a little stamp of her foot.

'Father, we cannot be from Gretton over the Holy Season. Every year our people look foward eagerly to the celebrations. We always invite the Prossers and our other neighbours to join in and the household servants so enjoy the feasting. . .'

Sir Daniel rose and took his angry daughter's shoulders in his two large hands. 'Child, I am sorry we shall miss the traditional celebrations, but our neighbours will understand. I swear you will not be disappointed. You cannot imagine the splendours of the royal festivities, and you will be able to wear your finest gowns. . .'

'Am I a doll to be dressed and displayed?' she raged. 'I do not wish to go. I want to be with my friends.' Her face was flushed with angry colour and her taut young breasts rose in agitation.

'Father, you don't understand. I know my sixteenth birthday marks a milestone in my life, that you have plans for me. This may be my last Christmas at home. Please, you must let me share it with my friends.'

His smile had faded now and his expression became

grave. 'Daughter, you are the one who does not understand. The King has issued a command. He cannot be disobeyed. He wishes to see me at Court and you and your mother with me. He has made a point of stressing that. You, a mere knight's daughter, will be one of the Queen's ladies. He has also assured me that he has your interests at heart and will make it his business to find a suitable husband for you.'

She broke from him and turned passionately to face her mother.

'This cannot be. I am no heifer to be sold at market to the highest bidder. I know I must marry soon, but to a man of your choosing, Father, not some elderly courtier of the King's household. I had so hoped I might find a husband from amongst one of our neighbouring families. That I should not have to leave the Marches. I want to be near you both.'

Tears were spilling down her cheeks now and her father's embarrassment deepened. Cressida had that rare ability to weep without tears marring her beauty in the slightest. Those violet-blue eyes sparkled like the flowers they resembled in colour, bedewed by the crystal drops from the spring showers. He always felt totally awed by her beauty, he, a man completely practical in nature, never before given to poetical thought. He could never resist her pleading when she was so distressed.

He cleared his throat in an effort to hide his own discomfort. 'Cressida, the King is scarcely above thirty years of age. Those nobles who form his household are like to be of a similar age or younger. Trust me. I will not allow you to be given to some doddering old man nor yet some dandified lecher, no matter how wealthy or high-born he might be.'

'Then you will send some excuse? Please, Father, I beg of you. Say I am ill. . .'

'That cannot be, Cressida. I have already accepted

the King's invitation.' Sir Daniel looked pleadingly
towards his wife for support. 'It would be unwise,
indeed dangerous, to refuse. Such a refusal would be
considered grave insult and I could come under suspicion—'

He broke off and looked into the fire. 'It is impossible, child. We have been commanded to Westminster
and we must go with all speed before worsening
weather makes it difficult to travel.'

His daughter's bleak expression of desperation made
him soften his tone as again he reached out and
squeezed her shoulder reassuringly.

'I promise you will find this journey a great adventure. Cressida, other girls in your position would be
delighted at this opportunity. I have heard Queen Anne
is a gentle mistress, beloved by her attendants, and we
promise we will remain with you in London until—' he
cleared his throat again '—until your future is
determined.'

Cressida rushed to her mother's side. Mildred
Gretton sighed heavily and enfolded this one beloved
child in her arms. Too well she knew what Cressida
was feeling. She had experienced the same doubts and
fears, only to find delight and fulfilment in her husband's arms. She prayed that Cressida would discover
a like joy.

'Nothing is determined yet, but your father must
obey the King. You would not wish to put him into
danger by your foolish fears?'

Cressida shook her head vehemently.

'No, of course not. Go and inform Alice Croft and
tell her to look out your finest gowns. She will go with
us, naturally.' She cupped her daughter's chin in her
hands. 'You are so lovely, child. The world will be at
your feet. There will be so much to do and see in the
capital that you will forget your disappointment at not
spending Christmas here at Gretton.'

She bent close so that her words were hardly more
than a whisper. 'It is the lot of us all, child. You must
make the best you can of life. Your father has high
hopes for a noble match for you. The King has hinted
at it. He needs your father's support.'

'And I am to be the price to be paid for the King's
favour?'

Mildred Gretton sighed again. 'We are all little more
than chattels, child, however highly prized.' She forced
a smile. 'You have a gift, Cressida, of getting others to
do what you wish. See that you use it well on your
future husband. It is more priceless than jewels or land.
Think about what I say. We'll talk again before we ride
east.'

Cressida turned and faced her father. She forced a
brave smile.

'I am sorry, Father. I am being foolish and childish.
Of course you must obey the King. I'll go now and
make some preparations for our coming journey.'

He nodded, relieved by her apparent compliance,
and shot his wife a grateful glance.

At the door, Cressida said softly, 'Will you send to
inform the Prossers of our imminent departure? I
would not have them think us ungracious.'

'Aye.' He nodded again. 'There will be several
neighbours to be informed. Be assured that Howell will
know why you leave in such haste without formal
farewell.'

She crimsoned and he grinned back at her. 'Don't
worry, lass. He'll understand. He's been a good play-
mate over these years, but he is not for you. He knows
that well.'

Her violet eyes clouded again. She had never
seriously considered. . . She drew a hard breath. Yes, if
she was honest with herself she knew that she had
vaguely considered the possibility of marriage with
Howell Prosser. It would have been highly convenient.

She would have continued to live here, near to her loving, indulgent parents.

She had never asked herself what her true feelings were for Howell. She knew she liked him, was always happy in his company. Yes, such an alliance would have suited well.

And now the King, that shadowy, sinisterly menacing figure, so far away in Westminster, had declared his wishes concerning her and the whole pattern of her life had changed disastrously. She would never forgive this unwelcome interference in her affairs.

CHAPTER TWO

FORTUNATELY, the weather did remain fair for their journey to Westminster. Despite her earlier forebodings, Cressida was excited by the new sights and experiences, though Alice grumbled almost every step of the way.

Like her charge Alice had not wished to leave Gretton so near to the Holy Season of Christmas. She had promised herself visits to her kinfolk, who lived close to the manor; now she faced arduous days of travelling and the prospect of dealing with a recalcitrant young mistress when they reached their destination, for Cressida had been in a foul temper when she had ordered her nurse to make preparations for their departure.

'As if it is not enough that we must make this journey at the worst time of the year and miss Christmas here at the manor, my father is already planning to wed me to some doddering old lord chosen for me by the King,' she had announced disgustedly. 'It is insupportable that someone who does not know me should have the power to so interfere in my concerns.'

'The King is the King,' Alice had returned stolidly, as if this explained everything, whereas, in fact, it had merely emphasised Cressida's growing sense of resentment against this man living so far from them, yet who exercised such dominance over her.

She determined not to allow her parents to know that she did actually begin to enjoy the adventure of this first long journey of her life. She had had a tearful parting with Howell, and her father in particular, whom she held totally responsible for giving way too easily to

the commands of his sovereign, was made to suffer her
constant show of displeasure.

Loving her dearly as he did, and suffering her
deliberate rejection of his displays of affection, Sir
Daniel found the travelling uncomfortable and tedious,
and the problems facing him when they arrived in
Westminster alarming. Lady Gretton accepted her
daughter's tantrums with her usual equanimity, though
she did scold her on one or two occasions for making
Alice's life difficult.

'Really, Cressida, you are behaving like a spoilt child,
which I fear you are. My father would have taken a
whip to my buttocks if I'd behaved as you are doing,
and there is simply no excuse for acting so churlishly
towards those who are only trying to do their best to
serve you.'

It was no help to Cressida's wounded sensibilities to
acknowledge to herself that her mother was speaking
the simple truth. They were all in the King's hands and
she must accept her lot more patiently. Often she
castigated herself for such shows of childishness, but
Cressida was no 'Patient Griselda' however often she
promised herself that she would make an effort to curb
this tendency towards waspishness.

She was an excellent horsewoman and did not find
the long hours in the saddle too trying. The roads were
hard-rutted and the weather chilly without excessive
frost, the sun watery on most days and low in the sky,
but, despite the barrenness of the brown earth fields,
and the stark, skeletal branches of trees arching over
their heads, Cressida rejoiced in the sights of the rolling
English country they passed through.

The towns were a special delight for she had considered Ludlow important until they passed through
Hereford and Gloucester, with their towering
cathedrals and bustling streets.

They broke their journey for several days near

Witney, visiting her mother's brother, Sir John Paynton, and it was here that Cressida celebrated her sixteenth birthday on the twenty-eighth of November. It was a joyous occasion and she was made much of by her burly uncle, who had longed for a daughter, his wife having given him four sturdy sons, two of whom were older than Cressida and the two remaining still too young to be sent into the households of neighbouring gentry to be trained as pages.

Cressida received fine presents of rich silks and brocades as well as jewellery from her devoted kinfolk. She forced herself to accept them with cries of delight, though they reminded her again of how she was to be displayed and sold in the marrige market at their journey's end.

Sir John escorted them into Oxford where Cressida stared entranced at the spires and walls of the magnificent, finely endowed colleges and marvelled at the unfamiliar sight of black-clad clerks and scholars scurrying about their business.

The weather broke at last as they were approaching the capital, and, with it, Cressida's bubble of optimism which had sustained her throughout the days of travelling. Her mother now began to exhibit signs of exhaustion and the six men-at-arms who had escorted them began to grumble amongst themselves and look eagerly ahead to their destination, which now seemed almost within reach.

Alice, riding pillion behind one of the men, expressed her profound relief when they clattered finally into the stinking, crowded streets of London.

'Thank the Virgin. I think my aching bones can endure no more of this junketing about. I can only pray we find comfortable accomodation, for I hear it is in short supply in palaces.'

Alice's forebodings proved unjustified, for Sir Daniel found that the rooms set aside for his use in the Palace

of Westminster were far more commodious than he
had dared to hope, considering the fact that many other
of the country's greatest nobles had arrived to witness
the age-old custom of the Christmas crown-wearing
ceremony and the rambling old palace, with its outbuildings and extensions, was solidly packed to the
rafters.

Cressida and Alice were to share a small chamber
off that of her parents and Alice clucked her satisfaction at the sight of it. Cressida was not so pleased. Her
own apartment at Gretton was far finer. She had no
experience of the cramped conditions under which
most of the Court lived and did not realise that to be
granted private rooms within the palace at this time
was a signal mark of the King's favour to her family.

She was astonished by the size and frantic hubbub of
the place and wrinkled her nose against the river stinks
which assailed her nostrils when she thrust open the
small glazed window of her bedchamber to look down
upon the bustling activity of the King's steps below,
beyond the small pleasance, then to the brown depths
of the Thames, crowded with barges carrying sea coal
and market goods, and the ferries which constantly
conveyed nobles and officials to and from the city
downriver.

'Oh, Alice,' she said despairingly, 'how long do you
think we shall have to remain here in this dreadful
place?'

Alice looked up from a travelling chest from which
she was lifting Cressida's finest gowns to shake out
their creases. Somehow she must find one which would
be suitable for her mistress to wear during supper
tonight in the great hall.

'This is Westminster,' she said flatly. 'The city itself
near the great bridge and the Tower is much more
crowded and insalubrious. Your father brought your
mother to the capital when he came to pay his respects

to the late King Edward. We lodged then near the Chepe and I thought I could scarce breathe for the stink from the open kennels, but, there, it was summer then. We were all glad to get back to the clean fresh air of the Marches.'

Cressida plumped down upon the narrow bed. 'Did you see the King, Alice? They say he was the handsomest man in Europe—quite unlike his brother, the new King, who is said to be dark and small and not in the least attractive.'

'Aye, Edward was bonny, tall and huge and fair. "The Rose of Rouen", they called him. He was born there, you know, and I saw young Gloucester, as the King was then. He was certainly smaller and darker, less impressive, I suppose, but I thought him personable enough. He was little more than eighteen then.' She sighed. 'He's seen a mort o' trouble since. I reckon he'll have aged considerably.'

'Some of the trouble he brought on himself,' Cressida snapped. 'He should not have usurped the young Prince of Wales's throne.'

Alice rose, rushed to her charge and caught her fiercely by the wrist. 'Hush, you foolish child! Would you put us all in danger by such parlous treasonable talk? The King is the Lord's anointed and when you are presented you will behave with true humility, do ye hear me? Have I taught you no respect for your elders and betters?'

Cressida smiled ruefully. 'Alice, I'm sorry. I'm just tired and over-excited. Mother has explained over and over how I must be respectful and grateful—though for what I cannot say.'

'Well, plenty of girls would give their eye-teeth for the privileges offered to you. I suppose the King must be in great need of your father's support to honour him like this.'

Cressida leaned down to whisper mischievously in Alice's ear, 'Now who is talking treason?'

Alice's round red face expressed almost comical alarm and she covered her mouth with her hand, but Cressida laughed, shaking her head in real amusement at sight of her nurse's discomfiture.

Lady Gretton dispatched her maid, Bronwen, to fetch Cressida to her. Sir Daniel had gone from their chamber on some errand of his own, possibly to see that his men-at-arms were suitably lodged.

'Well,' she said, smiling, 'it seems all has been done to ensure our comfort. Now, Alice, find a suitable gown for Cressida. Sir Daniel was informed that the King will sup privately tonight so she will not be formally presented. Keep her finest gown for the feasting, but we must not be outshone by these court nobles. Do your best.'

She eyed her daughter critically. 'You should lie down and rest for an hour or two. It wants some time before supper is served and you need to look your best.'

Cressida curtsied formally, then impulsively hugged her mother and returned to her own chamber. Already the excitement of their arrival was leaving her, yet she was still too wrought up to sleep at this hour in the afternoon.

Restlessly she watched from the window while Alice pulled out the truckle after laying out a blue velvet gown for the evening's first appearance in the great hall. The older woman then thankfully removed her shoes and lay down on the truckle, patting Cressida's bed invitingly.

'Your lady mother talks sense, child, as ever. You are over-tired and excited still. I can read the signs in your heightened colour. Great ladies do not behave like children. Rest and calm yourself. Your father will wish to be proud of you when he takes you down.'

Reluctantly Cressida left her post of vantage where, at least, she could watch the novel sights below, and came to remove her travelling gown and lie down, as her mother had recommended.

Alice had already settled to rest and Cressida did not want to bother her with the back lacing of her gown, but she experienced some difficulty in trying to manage it unaided. Worn out by the journey and flurry of arrival, Alice was already snoring softly, lulled by the warmth of the two braziers set for safety, one near the window and the other near the door.

Cressida paused, undecided. She hated to disturb Alice, whom she loved dearly for all the care the older woman had bestowed on her since her babyhood, but, at the same time, Alice's strictures and continual murmurings against Cressida's natural need for independence as she grew older had developed a mild sense of resentment too.

She did not want Alice to wake and begin reminiscing about her former visit to Court, or to listen to her admonitions about Cressida's behaviour and how fortunate she was that some noble husband was shortly to be found for her.

She looked longingly towards the outer door. This palace would be a wonderful source of new discoveries and experiences. Tonight she would be escorted by her parents to the great hall. They would not take their eyes from her for a moment. She felt stifled by their protectiveness. She had a little time before supper. She would explore for a short time alone.

The corridor outside her chamber was deserted. Cressida could hear voices in the distance, laughing, shrill—women's voices? Possibly pages, too, had opportunity now to go about their own pursuits before they were summoned to wait upon their masters and mistresses at table.

She had slipped on her travelling cloak and pulled

up the hood. It was cold in the unheated passages and she shivered, yet the freshness of the air after the brazier-scented atmosphere of her chamber was welcome and she made for a passage she thought would lead outside. The river terrace had appeared infinitely interesting and she had seen from her window that both men and women seemed to be walking there unchallenged. She would not be noticed, she felt sure.

The palace was a veritable warren of passages. She passed rooms, some deserted, some where clerks pored over rolls of parchment, some inhabited by finely dressed courtiers chatting together near the huge hearth fires. Cressida did not enter but hastened on, seeking for a doorway to the courtyard outside.

When at last she saw the great oaken door open before her, granting her a vista of cobbled courtyard, she had to pass a small guard chamber where men-at-arms were drinking ale and dicing. As she tried to emerge into the open air she was challenged abruptly by two guards who crossed their bills before her face, pulling her up sharply, winded and frightened.

She tried to stutter some excuse for leaving the palace, but one of the men saw that she was young and a woman, and thought perhaps that she was some maid on an errand for her mistress. He signalled for his comrade to lower his bill and nodded for her to proceed, grinning broadly and making some lewd comment which brought a bright flush to her cheek. Cressida scrambled by the men, thankful that she had not been forced to identify herself.

The broad courtyard was bordered on two sides by long, low outbuildings which Cressida judged to be stables and mews. She could hear men whistling inside one of them, and the fluttering of hawks on their perches and their shrill, angry cries. There was no one to whom she could ask directions, but she made for a gateway and turned to where she was sure she would find a path leading to the pleasance she had seen from her window and, ultimately, a way to the river quay.

Obviously the many corridors within the palace had confused her, for she found herself in another court-yard, where the sound of hammering and sawing from the buildings contained within it told her that this was the quarter of the smiths, armourers and carpenters.

The cold was intensifying now that darkness was approaching and no one lingered here, outside. Cressida was in two minds about proceeding further but she disliked the idea of returning to her chamber and the enforced rest she must take there. She was too restless in spirit for that, so she forged on, hoping to come across another way which would eventually lead back to the palace pleasance.

As she passed through the second entrance she heard the sound of laughter and the clatter of horses' hooves. She paused for a moment, hesitating, then she recognised the place as the tilt-yard.

Her father had no squire and there was not one at Gretton, but she had heard her father and Howell's father discuss often how they had been trained to arms in their youth. A mounted knight had to control his mount by knees alone, handling either a lance or other weapon in one hand while he protected his body by his shield in the other. He learned to aim well for jousting by striking a wooden shield mounted upon one arm of a quintain and riding forward steadily.

She saw the wooden structure now some yards from her across the courtyard. Two mounted men prepared to try their skill and Cressida's blue eyes widened in astonishment as she saw a heavy weighted bag on the second arm of the structure. One unbalanced thrust would cause the crudely painted shield to swing wildly and, if the knight riding beneath was not skilful, the full weight of the bag would strike him and thrust him from the saddle.

Cressida was utterly fascinated. She had never seen a tournament, had imagined the colour and splendour of the occasion, the thrill of watching, breathless, as a gallant knight charged down the lists towards his antagonist and their lances splintered in the impact. How exciting it would have been to have some knight wear her favour bound around his sleeve and ride to risk himself, his aim to achieve victory for her delectation!

These men were practising, she knew that; both wore armour and the visors were lowered so that neither could be injured in the passes. They were clearly not rivals, for their laughter and friendly banter proclaimed them companions.

The destriers pawed the ground impatiently and Cressida saw that the men needed all their skill to control the powerful beasts. Cressida's lips parted in sheer delight at the sight of these glossy-coated creatures.

Neither man appeared to see her and, with a warning shout, the taller man rode towards the swinging quintain. He struck the centre of the shield unerringly, dead centre, and rode through as the weighted bag swung harmlessly over his head and he skilfully reined in his mount for the turn.

The second man prepared to follow, but Cressida must have made some sound or movement for he turned sharply in her direction. The brief break in his concentration brought him to the shield too soon. He had no time to strike it clear and as he rode on, in the impetus of the practice charge, the bag struck him full on the shoulder. He gave a startled shout and fell heavily from the saddle.

Cressida stood transfixed with horror as his mount charged on riderless, then neighed shrilly and reared. It seemed that the frightened horse would turn and come crashing back to trample his helpless master. Without waiting to consider the second knight and the probability of his coming hastily to the rescue, she gathered her skirts and dashed to the fallen man. She must either drag him clear or try to snatch the reins of his frenzied mount.

She crouched by him, horrified by the sounds of frantic hooves pounding inexorably towards her. There came an infuriated shout, and the neighing and screaming of the riderless courser. Too late she realised that her intervention had merely served to frighten the beast further. She could hear it snorting and scrabbling and stamping in fury.

There came several more shouted commands and what sounded like war-like oaths muffled by the helmet's visor, then, abruptly, she found herself lifted from the ground and swung across the second knight's saddle bow as he rode clear to the end of the courtyard.

Cressida struggled wildly. She was lying ignominiously, like a sack of grain, face down, with a powerful male hand holding her firmly in position and resisting every effort she made to lift her head. She was finally forced to give up her frantic fighting through sheer loss of breath and, equally, was unable to make any protest when she was as unceremoniously dumped upon the ground, upright, when the far end of the courtyard was reached.

Her stance was precarious indeed, and she waddled inelegantly a few steps forward in order to keep her footing. Her rescuer's destrier was snorting and prancing as fiercely as the other courser and only superb horsemanship on the part of the rider successfully held him in.

Head held down and panting, Cressida could do nothing but try to regain her breath. Even so, she was aware, though furious with the knight who had seized her so precipitately, that she was in no danger from his mount. The mailed hands forced the beast to stand compliantly while he swung himself out of the saddle.

He thrust up his visor. His voice was low-pitched, deliberate, but with the bite of hard steel.

'Children are not allowed in the tilt-yard. Where is your nurse?'

He stood, one hand on hip, a tall, dominating figure, looming over Cressida.

She lifted her head and glared back at him. The light was fading now and she could not see his features clearly, shadowed as they were by his helmet. She was painfully conscious that her hood had fallen back and her tangled hair was streaming free of its pins. Desperately she hoped that he had as little a clear view of her as she had of him.

She must not be identified. Her mother would be furious if the tale of this misadventure were to be repeated within the court circle. She knew well enough that it would be politic to apologise quickly and make her escape before this man took further note of her appearance, but such a cowardly retreat was foreign to her nature. She shook back her cloud of hair with an impatient hand.

'I am no child, sir,' she said frigidly. 'It is long since I needed the care of a nurse. I regret that my sudden appearance frightened one of the horses. I was afraid the rider would be hurt and tried to go to his help.'

'I'm not so sure you should be without a keeper,' he retorted grimly. 'Anyone with sense would know better than to interfere when men are practising at the quintain. It needs full attention. Destriers are valuable. Your foolish intervention could have caused the animal to damage itself.'

She was stung by his implication that she was less valuable than the horse. Throughout the course of her short life Cressida had come to believe that she was quite the most valuable creature within her parents' vicinity, and all the servants on the manor had treated her with the care they accorded the priceless Venetian

glass which her father had imported to glaze the solar
windows at Gretton.

No one had dared to afford her less respect than
would have been offered to her father. The rudeness of
this stranger was not to be borne without retaliation!

'I'm sorry that you should consider the horse more
valuable than that of a mere human life,' she said
haughtily. 'I repeat, I acted merely in an attempt to
save the rider from being trampled.'

'Destriers are trained to command, but a stranger
arriving on the scene so abruptly could have spelled
disaster. Don't you know they are also trained to
trample and bite enemies underfoot? You could have
been killed.'

He was leaning forward slightly now and staring at
her. He was puzzled. At first he had thought the
intruder one of the palace pages, but the cumbersome
skirts had told him that his first surmise was incorrect
and he had wrongly assessed the sex of the newcomer.

It was dusk now and he could not see the girl clearly,
but her voice was cultured, so she was not one of the
serving maids. Her dignified bearing, despite her terrifying ordeal, showed him that she was not the child he
had thought her, yet she was quite small of stature,
very young still, although the softness of her curvaceous
young body as he had held her close momentarily
before setting her down revealed the fact that she
would soon ripen into womanhood.

By God's wounds, what was she doing unattended in
the palace environs? Wasn't she aware that she could
be molested, even here, so close to the palace
buildings?

He called imperiously, 'Peter, see this young person
safely into the palace.'

His squire hastened to his side. He had been momentarily shaken by the heavy fall but was now quite
recovered. He'd listened, not without an awareness of

concealed humour, for he would not have dared to laugh outright, to the exchange between the Earl, his master, and this youthful but insolent stranger.

'Certainly, sir.'

She flashed an instant answer. 'Must I repeat myself yet again? I do not need a keeper and am perfectly used to looking to my own safety.'

'Mistress, I have seen little evidence of that ability this even.' He turned his back on her and gave his attention to his mount. 'Peter, regardless of this young maid's assurances, do as I order.'

Gently the squire offered his mailed arm to the rebellious stranger. 'Truly, mistress, you would be wise to take care, especially at this hour of the day. There are rogues and beggars nearby, some emerging from the sanctuary at Westminster Abbey, who would cut your throat simply to acquire the good cloak on your back. Allow me to escort you into the palace.'

She turned once to stare after the retreating back of her erstwhile rescuer, then turned and placed a hand, now somewhat grubby after her encounter with the dust of the ground and the knight's horse, upon his proffered arm.

'Thank you, sir,' she said quietly, mollified by his courtesy. 'I shall be glad to accept your offer, for I fear I am new to this palace and have missed my direction.'

The knight took the reins of both destriers and moved towards the stable-block. Cressida was further irritated by his decision to relinquish care of her to his inferior, for his mode of address to the second rider had suggested that he was the master and this more kindly and considerate escort his man.

She sniffed her displeasure. Once more he had shown a preference for his so valuable horses over his more obvious duty of courtesy to her. She bestowed upon her escort her brightest smile and allowed him to lead her towards the courtyard entrance archway.

Alice was awake and already panicking when Cressida reached her bedchamber. It had been difficult to find again. The corridors of the palace seemed all alike and now that the light had almost gone serving men were hastening to light the sconces, their air of urgency indicating that preparations were being made for the evening's supper in the great hall.

Cressida began to unfasten the strings of her cloak as Alice hurried forward, her eyes widening in alarm as she saw her charge's state of dishevelment.

Cressida did not wait to hear her complaints but said sharply, 'Have you informed my mother that I have been absent from the chamber?'

'No, of course not,' Alice said in a horrifed whisper. Even now she was afraid that Lady Gretton would be made aware that her charge had been out of her sight for some time.

'Good,' Cressida replied crisply. 'Come, prepare me for this supper tonight.'

'Where have you been and—' Alice hesitated almost fearfully '—what ever have you been about? Your parents will be furious. . .'

'If they find out, undoubtedly,' Cressida replied imperturbably, 'and it would be unfortunate for you, Alice, were they to do so, so let us get on. My mother will demand to see how I look any moment now.'

Alice had been Cressida's deeply loved nurse and attendant and she was too sure of herself to be truly rebuffed by her charge's sharpness; nor was she to be deflected by Cressida's evasions. If anything untoward had occurred during her excursion, unescorted, into the palace environs, she must know about it, and at once. She stood, arms akimbo, facing Cressida, who was struggling with the refractory laces of her travelling gown.

'Now, mistress, I want to know, now, just what mischief you have been at and, I warn you, trouble or no, I shall inform your lady mother if I think there is need.'

Cressida bit her lip uncertainly. On the one hand she did not want to tell anyone of her mortifying and embarrassing encounter with the stranger knight in the tilt-yard; on the other hand she did not wish Alice to magnify the possible consequences of any adventure which had befallen her. She sighed briefly.

'Alice, I was just restless and anxious to explore. I wanted to go to the river terrace but lost my way.'

'And?'

'I found myself in the tilt-yard by mistake and—and almost got trampled. . .'

'What?' Alice was almost incoherent with alarm.

'No, no, I came to no harm, as you can see. A knight snatched me up on his horse and got me safely out of danger.'

'He knows who you are?' Alice was scandalised.

'No, certainly not. We exchanged few words. His— squire, I think, showed me the way back to the palace door. I doubt either of them would know me again were they to see me at Court.' She gave a little stamp of her foot, though her manner was pleading rather than imperious. 'Please, Alice, come and help me or my mother will suspect something is wrong.'

'I shall want to know more about this man and what was said, mistress,' Alice said tartly. 'For now we must hasten to get you ready. Really, child, I turn my back for just one moment and you do something foolish— and dangerous. I am responsible for you, Cressida. Don't you care about what might happen to me should your parents cast me out?'

Cressida smiled winningly and placed her arms fondly round her maid's neck. 'Silly Alice, as though I should let them do such a thing—ever. I love you, you old tyrant, and you know it. Besides, soon I shall have a household of my own and you will be the most valued member of it.'

'Not if you carry on like this and earn a reputation for yourself,' Alice chided, but her homely face flushed with pleasure and she was already weakening from her concerned anger.

By the time Cressida was ready to be viewed by her anxious mother Alice had accomplished a total transformation. From the girlish, untidy hoyden, Cressida now stood revealed as an elegant court lady. To complement her eyes, Lady Gretton had insisted on a gown of deep blue velvet, edged with grey fur both round the hem and the cuffs of the modishly tight sleeves, as well as the deep V of the neckline. The modesty vest and covering of the small truncated hennin was of blue and silver brocade.

One single band of smoothly combed golden hair showed at Cressida's forehead, for Lady Gretton had decreed that the fashion of shaving the front hair to enhance the depth of the forehead was unsuitable for so young a girl and, besides, Cressida's unusual, bright burnished hair colouring was so lovely that she felt it should be glimpsed.

The complicated folds of the wired butterfly veiling shaded the youthful features and gave merely a hint of the beauty of her unblemished complexion. Lady Gretton grunted her satisfaction that her daughter's pale skin was not wont to freckle in the summer's sun, for no amount of warnings persuaded Cressida to anoint herself with fards and creams before venturing out in it.

She herself wore a gown of deep burgundy velvet and was convinced that it would not be discovered to be far from the present fashion. Sir Daniel joined them, fussing with his ornamental gold neck-chain over his green velvet doublet. He opened his eyes in astonishment at the sight of his daughter.

'Well, well, you look very fine indeed. See that you behave with decorum, daughter, for at Court, believe me, every foible is noted and remarked on.'

Cressida ate very little at supper, although she had not eaten since mid-morning, but she found the hubbub, colour and confusion in the great hall completely absorbing.

They were conducted to their seats near the high table by an officious, elderly steward, splendidly dressed and flourishing his white wand of office. Her father did not appear to be recognised by any of the nobles, knights and their ladies seated near them, though their presence was acknowledged by nods and half-bows of greeting.

It was obvious that their presence here was expected by the steward and places had been laid for them. Cressida was seated between her parents and, for once in her life, was almost nervous of peering too closely around her.

The moment they were seated the noise around them began again, as servants appeared at their side to provide them with plates and cutlery and two youthful pages also came with a bowl of rose-scented water for the rinsing of fingers, a ewer and clean napkins.

Cressida watched as her mother dipped her fingertips into the water and took the napkin from the boy who proffered it, kneeling on one knee. They wore the Yorkist colours of murrey and blue, ornamented with the King's personal device of the white boar.

Sir Daniel and Cressida followed Lady Gretton's example, and Cressida peered cautiously from beneath her shadowing gossamer veil to see if any other lady was watching closely, ready to laugh if she was clumsy or made a mistake.

There were no homely bread trenchers here and gingerly Cressida handled the newfangled two-pronged fork provided. Since she was not squired by husband

or attentive suitor she was content to be served by her
father with various delicacies and shared his cup with
her mother.

The removes of food were many and varied, but too
rich and heavily spiced for Cressida's taste. She ate
sparingly and found the malmsey wine over-sweet, so
drank little. The places of the King and Queen in the
centre of the high table beneath the richly embroidered
cloth of estate were unoccupied, though several other
lords with their ladies were seated in their places on
either side of the royal chairs.

Her father pointed out to her the King's chamberlain, Viscount Lovell, whom, he said, had been the
King's friend since boyhood and had served him loyally
for many years on the Scottish border and on the
Council of the North. The haughty lady beside him,
whom Cressida thought to be his lady, appeared to
have more time for her neighbour than her lord, for
she constantly engaged him in conversation.

Lady Gretton was soon chatting with a lady beside
her and Sir Daniel tucked heartily into his food,
oblivious of what was going on around him.

Cressida looked round anxiously in case any man in
the hall was regarding her with too much attention, but
surely the knight she had encountered in the tilt-yard
would not be able to recognise her, dressed so totally
differently, and it had been half-dark then—yet she
continued to look covertly into the faces of those men
near her to see if she might notice anything in manner
or demeanour which would convince her of his identity.

No one appeared to give her the slightest notice after
the first curious glances and after a while she sat back
with a little sigh of relief. Alice was seated with her
mother's maid at the far end of the hall with other
servants, so she was free for a while of her constant
vigilance.

The gossip was continual but subdued, as if the

courtiers were conscious that they could be overheard and their remarks noted and informed on. The palace must be a hot bed of intrigue, she thought ruefully. Her father would have to be constantly on his guard here and watch his tongue. So must she.

She was more than a little startled when the steward appeared at their table near the close of the meal to summon them to the King's chamber of presence.

'If you will follow me, Sir Daniel, with your wife and daughter, the King wishes to greet you personally.'

Cressida's father rose at once, dabbing hastily at his mouth with his napkin. There was an instant hush in the talk near them and they found themselves the focus of all eyes.

Sir Daniel uttered some conventional polite response and offered his arm to his lady. Cressida half stumbled in rising, stared resentfully at the long-nosed elegant lady opposite whose lips were curved in a contemptuous smile, then swept after the retreating backs of her parents, who were too bemused by the signal honour afforded them to even look round to see if their daughter was following.

The King's private chamber was guarded by two men-at-arms in Yorkist livery with crossed bills. They stood aside as the steward fussily gestured for them to do so. The doors were flung open and the steward marched before them, announcing their identities in loud, ringing tones. At first Cressida was too concerned that she might fall over her own feet to look curiously around her.

Her father was dropping to his knees and her mother stooping in a deep curtsey. Cressida approached and curtsied low, as she had been instructed so many times during the course of their journey. She had been instructed repeatedly on how to behave, what to say and what not to say, how to look modestly down at the ground until she was commanded otherwise, so that she ought to have felt fully confident about this moment, but she found that that was not to be.

She was so terrified of disgracing herself before this man, who was the cause of this sudden, frightening alteration in the course of her life, that she found her limbs trembling and had to tighten her leg muscles lest she collapse before his feet.

A kindly, mellow voice greeted the visitors.

'Ah, Sir Daniel, my lady, Mistress Cressida, please rise. I regret I was unable to greet you earlier in hall, but it was necessary to consult with officials over supper tonight so we ate apart. My Queen and I wish you heartily welcome to Westminster. I trust apartments have been placed at your disposal and you are relatively comfortable? Palaces are so crowded, I find, and often less pleasant than one would wish, and at this, the Holy Season, more uncomfortable and thronged with visitors than usual.'

Cressida's father rose and bowed, then stepped forward slightly to kiss the beringed hand offered to him.

'Your Grace, I am honoured by your invitation and assure you that everything is to our complete satisfaction.'

Cressida rose from her curtsey to see that the King had risen from his high-backed chair and was offering his hand to her mother. Lady Gretton kissed the King's fingers and stood back to allow her daughter to approach.

Sir Daniel said quickly, 'May I present my daughter, Your Grace? She is overwhelmed by your kindness in offering to arrange a suitable marriage for her.'

The King's voice sounded almost teasing. 'Perhaps she is, Sir Daniel, or would Mistress Cressida prefer to speak for herself in this matter?'

Cressida kissed the strong brown fingers, her eyes dutifully lowered. There was a slight silence while her anxious parents waited for her to make some dreaded outburst.

She could not see the King's features clearly yet. She was too concerned by her need to obey protocol correctly.

She said in a hurried half-whisper, 'Your Grace honours my father by this interest in our concerns, sir, and I must be duly grateful.'

There was a faintly ironic note in the mellow-voiced answer. 'Well spoken, mistress. I see you have been suitably schooled.'

She looked up then sharply, straight into a pair of mocking grey-green eyes which were dancing with amusement. She tightened her lips and shook back threatening tears of embarrassment. Had she, in spite of all her care to be dutiful, said the wrong thing?

He was gesturing to her mother to take a stool nearby and turning to the woman seated in a chair near him.

'Anne, this is the young lady whose future we have been discussing recently. I trust she will prove a loyal and trustworthy attendant.'

A gentle voice bade Cressida approach the chair and quickly she curtsied low once more, this time to the Queen.

'Your Grace, I will strive to please you in every way I can, but I am a country mouse and unaccustomed to court ways.'

'Come, child, we shall not expect too much of you. You must not be timid. Come and stand by me.'

Cressida gazed helplessly towards her mother, who nodded imperceptibly for her to obey the Queen.

She went to the Queen's side, while her father took up his stance behind her mother's stool. Now, at last, when the King began to enquire about affairs in the Marches and the Queen engaged her mother in talk about the suitability of their Westminster apartment, Cressida was able to really look about her.

This presence chamber was not unduly large, though comfortably, almost luxuriously furnished. There were glowingly colourful tapestries on the painted walls— one depicting Christ as a child before the elders in the Temple, the other some pastoral, Classical subject, showing in the foreground a beautiful woman carrying a bow and arrow sheaf—possibly the Greek goddess Artemis.

A bright fire blazed in the hearth and the polished oak floor was strewn with fine carpets from the East. Wax candles in sconces on the wall and set in silver candlesticks on a low table near the Queen's chair gave a rich, comforting glow to the room. There were two high-backed, cushioned chairs for the King and Queen's comfort, fald stools and, in one corner, a cushioned prie-dieu.

Cressida's quick eye glimpsed signs of the interests of the pair. There were printed books upon the table, several devotional and one on hunting, and a rush velvet-lined basket containing embroidery silks and wools. A tambour containing what Cressida thought to be a half-completed altar cloth in white silk had been laid aside by the Queen at their entrance.

There was a movement near the shuttered window and an elderly brachet hound emerged from the shadows to flop down heavily beside the King's chair. Cressida was surprised to see the royal pair unattended. Even in this private chamber Cressida had expected to see courtiers and ladies-in-waiting. Evidently the King and Queen preferred to spend their quiet hours together in an atmosphere of pleasant domesticity. Cressida thought these hours must be few in number and valued the more for that.

The Queen had never been beautiful, Cressida decided. Her features were regular, her complexion pale and unblemished, though there were high spots of colour upon her cheekbones. She must be little more than thirty, Cressida supposed, but she looked older, ill. Once or twice in her talk she broke off to cough and apologised.

She was dressed in a dove-grey gown trimmed with sable and Cressida recalled that this last year she had lost her only child, Prince Edward. Her hair, beneath the black velvet frontal to her simple cap hennin, was fair and looking faded. Despite the gentleness of her demeanour, Queen Anne had a determined chin and Cressida believed that she would not allow sloppiness in her attendants.

She was aware suddenly that the King had paused in his talk and was regarding her sardonically. She coloured hotly and lowered her gaze in an attempt to evade the cool appraisal in his grey eyes.

'Your father assures me you have been well schooled in household management, though you love the Marches and like to be about country pursuits. Do you ride well, mistress?'

Cressida swallowed nervously. 'I am told I do, Your Grace.'

'So you enjoy hawking and the chase?'

Cressida considered. 'I enjoy the challenge and the thrill of the hunt, sire, but not the kill.'

He nodded, as if approving her answer. 'Can you read?'

'Yes, Your Grace. Our local parson was sent to tutor me.'

'Good. I like to see a woman who is educated to think and know her own mind. My own nieces are well read. I like to discuss literary matters with the Lady Elizabeth.'

Cressida thought, fleetingly, that the two princes had been well schooled by their other uncle, Anthony, Lord Rivers. He lay now in a cold grave after his execution at Pontefract. Where were his charges now? This domestic scene had momentarily diverted her from her natural wariness towards the King.

He was, as Alice had said, of middle height, spare of build but well muscled. He had been a doughty warrior, she knew. He was not unattractive, with a clever, narrow face, the Plantagenet nose dominating the even features. His eyes were fine and luminous, but his mouth rather thin. She thought he held it in too tightly when struggling to control moments of tension or inner pain.

Like the Queen, he appeared older than his thirty-two years and Cressida considered that the problems and suffering over these last months had left their marks. For all that, there was something very winning about this man when he smiled, as he was doing now, inviting openness in her and without the suspicion of tantalising humour at her discomfort that she had noted earlier.

Like the Queen, he was dressed soberly in a doublet of very dark blue, but the jewels in his ornamental shoulder-chain and on his long brown fingers glowed richly.

Her parents had remained silent throughout this questioning and Cressida blushed hotly as she realised she was being assessed as a suitable bride.

There came a respectful knock upon the door and the King called permission for the newcomer to enter. A young page appeared, behind him a noble, for Cressida's shrewd eyes summed up the worth of his fine violet velvet doublet and well-fitting grey hose. He remained just within the doorway and bowed low.

'Your Grace requested that I present myself at this hour.'

The King rose at once, smiling.

'Come in, my lord. You come well in time. I was talking to you recently about my intention to invite Sir

Daniel Gretton to our Christmas revels this year,
knowing him to be a neighbour of yours. Allow me to
present also his wife, Lady Gretton, and their charming
daughter, Mistress Cressida, whose father informs me
she has only days ago, during their journey to
Westminster, turned sixteen.'

He addressed Sir Daniel, who also had risen. 'My
Lord Earl of Wroxeter, a trusted member of my council
and one whom I rejoice to acknowledge as friend.'

Sir Daniel bowed to the newcomer deferentially as
his title required. He glanced swiftly back towards the
King, who smiled almost conspiratorially. With a tre-
mendous shock, Cressida understood that this man had
been commanded to the King's presence especially to
view her. She watched, bemused, as her father and the
Earl clasped hands and the Earl bowed low to the
ladies. Feeling her mother's anxious eyes upon her, she
too sank low in a curtsey.

The Earl turned to acknowledge her and, for a
fraction of a second, stood perfectly still, his lips slightly
parted in astonishment.

He had never encountered before a creature quite so
divinely lovely as this girl. She was small in stature,
almost diminutive, a fairy child, yet he knew instinctively that when she moved it would be with the natural
grace and regality of a queen. Though she was so
young, he could glimpse the budding curves of her
high, rounded breasts and sweetly swelling hips and
belly outlined against the soft blue velvet of her gown.

He started abruptly, aware that huge, luminous blue
eyes shaded by dark golden lashes were regarding him
curiously, almost hostilely. Her face was heart-shaped,
her complexion and features flawless. Her nose was
well shaped, with the slightest tendency to tilt upwards
at the tip, and he could not resist a faint smile at the
delightful air of impudence it gave her features, for her
mouth was unsmiling, the full, sensuous underlip held

in tightly, as if in an effort to prevent her thoughts from revealing themselves too readily.

Only one small band of hair showed demurely from beneath her hennin, but he almost gasped at the splendour of its colouring. Golden was a totally inadequate description; it was the deep, dark gold of the most precious Welsh metal prized above all other gold, the colour of ripe corn shining in the sun's full glory.

He was stunned and felt sharp desire stab at his loins. Immediately he was ashamed. How could he be so stirred by this child, and so soon after the loss of his adored Elinor?

He forced himself to bow again, stiffly, and lowered his gaze from that intense blue stare of hers.

'Mistress Cressida,' he murmured formally. 'Your parents I have had the good fortune to meet before. This is the first time I have set eyes on their lovely daughter. I trust and hope you will enjoy the Christmas festivities to the full.'

'Thank you, sir.' Her voice was lower than he had expected, pleasantly pitched and clear without being in the least strident. 'The King honours us and, though I shall miss the revelries we enjoy at home at Gretton, I'm sure I shall find the feasting here at Court very splendid and not a little overwhelming.'

His lips twitched slightly. 'I cannot believe you would be overwhelmed by anything, mistress.'

The small pointed chin jutted faintly, as if she was conscious that he was teasingly addressing her as if she were a child and resented it.

That movement, slight as it was, and the earlier suggestion of a rebuke for his assumption that she would be blinded by the unusual glitter and pageantry of court procedure, stirred his memory and he turned once more and stared full at her.

It was unbelievable—yet undeniably true, for all that. This fashionably attired creature, who behaved with as much confidence as if she had been present at Court since babyhood, was the same young woman whom he had snatched from impending death in the palace tilt-yard. She did not appear to recognise him, though he could not be sure.

He glanced enquiringly at her father and thought better of any prior acknowledgement of having met his daughter. More than likely the parents were unaware of her peccadillo. She would undoubtedly be angered if he were tactless enough to let such a secret slip.

Queen Anne was addressing him warmly. It was clear to Cressida that the Earl was a favoured friend to both monarchs. He was stooping over her chair, flattering her shamelessly, and Cressida saw the tired eyes light up in pleasure.

When, at last, they were graciously dismissed, Cressida was silent as they returned to their allotted quarters. Her father was clearly overjoyed by what had transpired at the interview.

The King had made it plain enough. He would be pleased to approve a match between herself and the Earl. Why? She was totally astounded. This man was so far above her in station. Why, she would become a countess! The understanding was no sweetener for her acute resentment.

Sir Daniel embraced her and her mother smiled her very real pleasure. Cressida knew she should be grateful. The Earl was young, personable, she supposed, wealthy and powerful within the King's Council.

She stood docilely while Alice prepared her for bed. Her maid must, in some way, have got wind of the honour soon to be afforded her charge for she chatted incessantly about how wonderful life would be for Cressida as the wife of so important a noble.

Cressida made no tart rejoinders. She was too busy considering her next move. How could she convince her parents, and, most important of all, the King, that she had no desire to be a countess and live so far from her beloved Marches?

As she lay in the darkness, Alice sleeping contentedly nearby on the truckle, she reviewed her first opinion of the Earl.

He was quite young, younger than the King, perhaps twenty-five or -six? He was so tall that he towered over her, making her feel a veritable manikin. She had not liked to stare, though he had at her. He had dark hair worn to his shoulders, slightly wavy and brushed back from his long, high-cheek-boned face. The eyes had been heavy lidded, almost sleepy, she thought, when he had not been so intent on appraising her.

No, he was not handsome, though well formed, his body slim but muscular, highly presentable. Why, she wondered, had he not already married? Was he a widower? If so, they had not informed her. She considered those eyes. At parting they had displayed a distinct twinkle. An angry flush dyed her cheeks. If he thought her a child to be mollified and managed he was decidedly mistaken.

Then, suddenly, she shot to a sitting position, her heart thudding wildly. Those eyes—and that voice—Sweet Virgin, he had been laughing at her because—because he had only hours before rescued her from the hooves of a frightened horse in the tilt-yard. So he knew! And she had been pert with him—would he continue to keep such an amusing and titillating tale to himself?

More and more it was going to be difficult coping with her father's desire to wed her to this man. Perhaps it was just possible that he had conceived a dislike for her? Her behaviour had certainly not been appropriate to one who aspired to become his countess. She sank back, breathing heavily. Matters might well be left in the Earl's hands and prove quite satisfactory to Cressida herself, after all.

CHAPTER THREE

IT WAS not to be as she had hoped. In the middle of December, Cressida was summoned into the King's presence once more to formally give her consent to a betrothal between herself and Martyn, Earl of Wroxeter. During the intervening weeks negotiations had been put in hand concerning the terms of the wedding contract. Sir Daniel appeared to be in excellent humour and had agreed, with good heart, to all the proposals.

He was prepared to give his daughter a fine dowry in exchange for the happiness of knowing that she was soon to be a countess and the privileges she would obtain by this exalted position, not to mention the advantage he himself would gain by pleasing his sovereign with this match which the King appeared to favour.

Cressida had hardly been consulted. Her mother had chatted on happily about how proud they were of her and it would have been pointless to object. Though he loved her dearly and had greatly indulged her, Cressida had known only too well that her father would insist on her consent.

The Earl, it seemed, had no apparent objection to the match. She'd seen him rarely over the days following the unpleasantness in the tilt-yard and, when she had, it had been in the company of her parents, and on several occasions in the presence of the King and Queen. Her parents had made no reference to the matter and Cressida judged that the Earl had decided to keep the knowledge to himself. Only once had she referred to it, when they were momentarily alone

together on the river terrace, Alice walking some paces
to the rear, ever watchful.

'My lord,' Cressida said, a trifle stiffly and more than
a little nervous, 'I trust neither of the horses took hurt
from my unfortunate sudden arrival in the tilt-yard the
other afternoon?'

He checked slightly in his walk, his sleepy eyes
regarding her coolly. 'Ah, I see you have recognised
me as the knight who snatched you up so unceremoniously. I regret that I may have hurt your feelings, but,
you know, you were in grave danger.'

She lowered her gaze. 'I think, my lord, that you
have made no mention of this to—my parents—or the
King.'

'Indeed not.' His long lips were twitching at the
corners in amusement. 'It shall be our secret, Mistress
Cressida. You would prefer it so?'

'Yes—oh, yes,' she said hastily. 'I mean—I think my
mother might be distressed. . .'

'Hardly distressed, surely? Nothing untoward took
place regarding your honour.'

She shot him a challenging glance. She was sure he
was laughing at her, but his expression was perfectly
grave again now.

'Nothing whatever,' she snapped. 'Surely you cannot
believe my presence in the yard was to. . .?'

'To observe the men at their martial play?' His lips
twitched again. 'No, no, of course not, mistress. As you
explained, you lost your way in the unfamiliar environs
of the palace.'

She was strangely uncomfortable in his presence.
Though she had been informed that he was but twenty-
three years of age, she was aware that there seemed
aeons of difference between them in maturity. He had
been trained in the houses of the great, served the
present King as household knight and lived constantly

both at his northern court and here in the intrigue-ridden atmosphere of Westminster.

He was ever courteous, even when alone with her, exaggeratedly so, as if she were a child to be cherished rather than a woman of flesh and blood. That, she thought, venomously, would most likely change when they were wedded and bedded.

It would probably suit him, once he had pleased the King by this match, to return her to his principal estates near Shrewsbury, where she would see him but rarely. She thought that in many ways she would prefer such an existence. She would, at least, be where her heart was, in her beloved Welsh border land.

She said hastily, looking away from him, 'I thank you for your discretion, sir. I—I am unused to court life and do not know how such an innocent adventure would be received here.'

He laughed out loud then. 'I assure you, no one would think ill of you. . .'

'But they would laugh,' she said bitterly.

He shook his head slowly. 'They will not have the opportunity, though, Mistress Cressida, I have judged you not incapable of dealing squarely with any man, woman or child who dared to laugh at you.'

There it was again, that note of humour at her expense. She ground her teeth in impotent fury and made him a curtsey when she took her leave of him.

They were betrothed on the seventeenth day of December in St Stephen's chapel in the presence of the King and Queen. Cressida wore a gown of rose-coloured velvet and was glad of its warmth, for the day was icy cold.

Before he took her hand the Earl said quietly, 'I would ask Mistress Cressida two questions, please, Sir Daniel.'

'Certainly, sir, but my daughter—'

'Is ever dutiful. I am quite sure of that, sir, but please allow me this boon.'

Sir Daniel glanced uneasily at his wife, who smiled to reassure him. She had already spoken with Cressida this very morning, early, and had obtained from her a promise that she would behave well during the ceremony.

Cressida looked up at the Earl, who was towering above her and so very close, a little uncertainly. He had not so much as broached the subject of this arrangement to her and she had assumed that he was completely satisfied. Now she was not so sure.

'First, Mistress Cressida, is your heart engaged elsewhere?'

'My lord, my daughter is very young. She would never be foolish enough. . .'

Again the Earl silenced Sir Daniel's bluster with an upraised hand. 'Let her answer for herself. Though she is but sixteen she may well have developed a closeness to someone she has known well for some time. I would not have her forced.'

Cressida's thoughts flew, fleetingly, to Howell Prosser. She liked him well enough. He would have proved a convenient partner to keep her where her heart lay, but she had never really considered him as a possible husband. She blushed slightly. Indeed, only now was she thinking of any man in that light, sharing hearth and board—and bed. Soon this man would be beside her, determining her way of life.

She shook her head and said firmly, 'There is no one, my lord.'

Behind her she heard her father utter a deep sigh of relief, only to give a slight gasp of alarm again as the Earl asked his second question.

'Have you, Mistress Cressida, developed any real antipathy for me?'

Cressida, too, gave a little startled gulp and looked

up again sharply into his face. The usually hooded eyes were looking into hers intently and there was no sign of sleepiness or humour in them.

Her lips trembled a little as she said softly, 'Why, no, my lord. Why should I? You have offered me no discourtesy.'

He gave her a little bow, took her chilled hand in his, and turned back to the waiting priest.

'Then we will proceed.'

Afterwards, as they moved towards the door of the chapel and she felt the unfamiliar weight of the betrothal ring upon her finger, he said clearly, 'I shall wait impatiently for the marriage ceremony which will truly bind us together, Cressida, and I know you need some weeks, at least, to get to know me, but Lent will come all too soon, forbidding all unions, so we should marry before that.'

She nodded hurriedly and withdrew her hand from his grasp. As ever, she felt uncomfortable in his presence, his fingers conveying to hers a faint tingle at contact, his eyes now sleepily hooded again, dominating her gaze as a stoat did a rabbit, forcing it to stand completely still for the kill. Why did such a thought occur to her now? She had told him she had no dislike for him, nor distrust—but fear, that was something quite different.

Yet he had never, by the slightest word or gesture, given her reason to be afraid of him, not even in the tilt-yard. No, this fear came of herself—fear that her life was changing inexorably, that childhood had gone for ever, and that, in her plighting of her troth to this man, she had accepted her own fate, for she knew instinctively that he would not have allowed her to go through with the ceremony if she had given a positive answer to either of his questions.

At the feast which followed he plied her with delicacies attentively, and she found herself drinking more of the sweet malmsey than she had ever previously consumed. Once she gave him an uncertain glance and found a strange, sad expression upon his features which caused her some misgivings. Was he, too, being forced into this match against his will for some political reason?

But the Earl of Wroxeter was a decisive man, powerful in the King's Councils. She had already discovered that, despite her newness to court circles. No man would force his hand had he determined otherwise. Her dowry was considerable. Had he embarked on this marriage to enrich his coffers? Yet she knew that his own holdings and estates were great enough to cause her own father some envy.

The King was smiling genially upon them. She was aware that he was now utterly triumphant and a little spasm of anger surged up in her that all of these noble persons seated at the table should be governed by his whim.

Despite her anger towards the King, Cressida enjoyed her work in attendance upon Queen Anne. There was nothing onerous about her duties and Anne was gentle though firm. Cressida soon saw that she was, indeed, quite sick. The Queen tired easily and suffered bouts of coughing which left her even more exhausted.

It was obvious, too, that she adored her husband. Cressida often saw her gaze across at him yearningly when he was busied about his court duties and sit disconsolate when he was absent from her side. Her older ladies loved her dearly, but some of the younger ones sometimes gossiped about her lack of energy behind her back and her seeming inability to bear the King another child.

'She must have another son,' Cressida heard Lady Mary Bolton say to her companion the day after Cressida's betrothal. The three of them were in one of the garde rooms, engaged in sorting out and airing the

Queen's most elaborate gowns, ready for the coming
Christmas feasting. Cressida had left the other two for
moments to take out one of the gowns and shake it in
the open air. Her companions were momentarily
hidden from her by the half-open door to the garde
room as she returned and they did not hear her
approach.

'She'll not do that,' Lady Joanna Scrope whispered
back. 'I heard Dr Hobbes talking to the King the other
day and both their faces were very grave. It's my belief
she won't live very long, poor lady, though, truth to
say, her passing would leave the King free to marry
again and sire an heir.'

'My uncle insists he loves her now, even after her
beauty has faded. If she dies I think it will nigh break
the King's heart. He'll not wish to replace her, even for
the good of the realm.'

'People marry for other things than love, as you
should know,' Lady Joanna asserted waspishly. 'Yesterday's ceremony showed us all that. Wroxeter has soon
put aside his feelings for Lady Elinor to marry that chit
with the sing-song Welsh accent and everyone knows
he cannot love her. She's still just a child and they have
only just met. It's being said it is to please the King and
she has a considerable dowry, I'm told.'

Cressida gave a little gasp of hurt surprise. Until now
she had not realised there was any resentment levelled
against her for gaining the Queen's favour, though she
might well have understood that, as she was so newly
come to Court, yet the real spite in Lady Joanna's voice
was only too obvious. She drew back a little, unwilling
to face the pair until she was sure she had regained her
air of tranquility.

A clear, authoritative voice spoke from the corridor
behind her so that Cressida turned, startled.

'I should have thought you two would know better
than to stand and gossip when Her Grace has need of

your services. As to accents, Lady Joanna, your vowels
are broad enough, clearly revealing your upbringing in
the wastes of the north. You would know that well
enough, if you paused in your own foolish prattling
long enough to hear the sound of your own voice.
Hurry, both of you. The Queen needs you in her
chamber.'

The speaker was tall and slim, her stance regal,
despite the fact that her purple gown, which had once
been splendid, was now slightly rubbed and worn and
the braid tarnished.

The two ladies addressed hastily put down the garments they were holding, turned and made low
curtseys.

'Lady Elizabeth, we—we had no idea...' Lady
Joanna stammered. 'The Queen instructed us to do
this...'

'She is not feeling well now and is anxious to lie
down for an hour. Lady Mary, go for a towel and
scented water to bathe her forehead and you, Joanna,
turn down the bed in her chamber.'

Again the two curtsied low, with hurried glances at
Cressida, before hastening about their designated
duties. Cressida was about to join them when the Lady
Elizabeth placed a restraining hand on her arm.

'Mistress Gretton, you stay with me and help finish
hanging these gowns. They can manage perfectly well
without you.'

Cressida had seen the newcomer once or twice about
the Court, had heard her father's whisper to her mother
concerning her identity. This was the Lady Elizabeth
Plantagenet, the King's eldest niece, sister of the
deposed King Edward V. Cressida curtsied a trifle
nervously as she advanced into the garde room in the
Princess's wake to place the heavy gown upon the
waiting press.

Elizabeth, like her celebrated mother, the Dowager

Queen, who had been first Elizabeth Woodville, then
Lady Grey, and lately King Edward IV's Queen, was a
decided beauty. Her face was heart-shaped, her features good, though she did have the slightly over-large
Plantagenet nose.

Cressida caught only a glimpse of her hair, smoothed
decorously back behind her velvet frontal, and judged
it fair, almost silver fair. Her mother was famed for
that hair and men said, unkindly, that she had spun
with it a web to catch the late King. The Princess
turned large grey eyes upon Cressida and the full
mouth widened into a smile.

'Do not let their malice disturb you. You have won
the prize that all the young ladies at Court desired—
Martyn of Wroxeter.'

'Oh.' Cressida was a trifle winded by the discovery
that she had carried off the most eligible bachelor
knight. 'I—I did not know my voice was so. . .'

'Liltingly Welsh?' The Princess said, smiling. 'I
assure you it is very pretty. Since it speaks directly to
Wroxeter of his own border lands, he must find it so
too.'

'Your Grace. . .'

'I am Lady Elizabeth now, since the bastardy of my
father's children was confirmed. Those who know me
well call me Lady Bessy.'

Cressida was even more embarrassed, but the
Princess had spoken so simply and without any trace of
rancour for her changed status that it was hard to know
what to say in reply.

Lady Elizabeth said quietly, 'I have accepted my new
position and since we left sanctuary and came to Court
life has become again much pleasanter, but I do know
the ladies gossip behind my back as I found them doing
about you. Court is a hard place to learn the lessons of
assuming indifference. You will manage it in time and

soon you will be Wroxeter's bride and immune from such malice.'

'They—they spoke of Lady Elinor. Is she—is she Lord Wroxeter's mistress?'

'She was his betrothed. She died,' the Princess explained bluntly. 'Lady Elinor Maudsley and Martyn, Earl of Wroxeter, had planned to marry this last autumn, but she developed some internal disorder and the doctors could not save her. He has been absent from Court for some months during his time of mourning.'

Cressida's brow creased in an alarmed frown. A discarded mistress she could have dealt with, accepted, but a promised bride whose memory might continue to haunt her betrothed husband was a more serious matter altogether.

'No one told me,' she said slowly. 'I saw at the feast last night how sad he looked when he thought himself unobserved. He must have loved her very much.'

The Princess sighed. 'Indeed, I think he did. They had been childhood companions. She would have made an excellent chatelaine, I'm sure, though who is to know how deep his passion for her was? At all events, we cannot live with the dead. Their passing changes all our circumstances.'

Her voice was calm, but conveyed to Cressida the sadness she was still feeling for her own father's death and the terrible change it had wrought in her life.

'Wroxeter has chosen you and I am not surprised. You are very lovely, Cressida Gretton, which is cause enough for those foolish girls to be jealous of you. He is a wealthy man, and generous. I have always had respect for him. You are fotunate. All we womenfolk must accept the fate chosen for us and make the best of it.'

Cressida nodded. 'My mother has said as much.'

The Princess laughed merrily. 'If I am beginning to

talk like a mother, things are come to a sore pass indeed.'

Preparations for the Christmas festivities soon began in earnest and Cressida found herself fully engaged. She was delighted to discover that many of the traditions she had enjoyed at Gretton were kept up here at Westminster.

The festive yule logs were dragged into the palace and holly and laurel boughs were appearing in all the state and presence rooms. The Queen's ladies giggled over the mistletoe hanging conveniently from many boughs, an open invitation for kissing. The chaplains frowned on such pagan customs but on these joyous occasions were totally ignored. Even the King and Queen, known to be pious in their religious observances, much more so than the late King Edward, turned blind eyes to the general merriment.

Everywhere courtiers and ladies were refurbishing their finest clothes for the several feasts of the twelve-day season. Cressida was thankful that her mother had insisted on the careful packing of her own gowns, for she was confident that her wardrobe would prove more than adequate.

Her friendship with Lady Elizabeth prospered. Her feelings had been deeply hurt by the malicious gossip she had overheard and the Princess's kindness was balm to her soul. From Elizabeth's information she came to recognise some of the most important nobles of the realm and, though the subject of the recent usurpation was never mentioned, Cressida was aware of the undercurrents of treasonable talk rife in the chambers and corridors of the palace.

In her discussions with the Lady Elizabeth she never once dared to refer to the fate of the two young Princes, Elizabeth's brothers. It occurred to her that the princess's ease of manner in the King's presence was strange, but also reassuring.

The Court and common folk were known to be concerned about the health of the Queen. Anne herself knew it and was determined to lay some of the worst rumours to rest by appearing at her most splendid and radiant over the days of the feasting.

She enlisted the Lady Elizabeth to help her choose her finest gowns and jewels. Elizabeth was constantly at her aunt's side and Cressida was struck by the shocking contrast the two made when together. Both had inherited the Neville fairness of hair and complexion but in Elizabeth they shone like a beacon and, despite her brave efforts to appear youthful and lively, the Queen's faded looks and lack of energy were only too evident.

Once Cressida caught the Earl of Wroxeter watching the two bent heads close together while Queen Anne was purchasing new velvets with the advice and help of her niece. His expression was thunderous; for once those sleepy dark eyes of his were hard with disapproval.

Cressida said nervously, 'The Lady Elizabeth is a great comfort to the Queen, always attentive and kindly.'

'Is she?' he said almost brusquely. 'Yes, I imagine it is good for the Lady Elizabeth to be about in court circles again after her long months in seclusion.'

'The King constantly shows his gratitude to her for her devoted care of the Queen.'

The Earl turned his hard gaze on Cressida. 'Yes, I have noticed it. It would be better if he were to find a husband for her—and soon.'

Cressida considered that thoughtfully. Yes, the Princess was past the age when most girls were given in marriage. She knew Elizabeth had once been promised to the French dauphin, but the alliance had come to nothing. Now she was a penniless dependant of her uncle.

Despite the fact that the Queen, her mother, had taken sanctuary in Westminster and resisted all persuasion to give her second son, Richard of York, into his uncle's care until forced to do so, an obvious declaration of her fear and distrust of the new King, she had finally emerged with her daughters, apparently reconciled, and Richard had treated her well, promised her suitable marriage arrangements for the young Princesses, and Elizabeth, the eldest, had been made most welcome at Court.

No wonder she was glad to wait upon her aunt and show her devoted gratitude to the King. Yet Wroxeter seemed suspicious of her motives. Why? In what way could a defenceless girl possibly hurt the King's cause?

Cressida had not prepared herself for the actual splendour of Christmas 1484. The palace had throbbed with excitement for days before, but the reality was beyond all expectation.

Cressida sat with her parents and Wroxeter, very close to the royal table where Richard and Anne sat below the cloth of estate. Both monarchs wore their most elaborate, fur-trimmed and jewel-encrusted garments, and Anne had forced herself to an outward display of gaiety, despite the fact that her heart was aching still for her dead son.

Remove followed remove each day at table, throughout the twelve days of feasting, as no expense was spared. It seemed that the King was determined to show his Court and the common people that no rumours from France concerning Henry Tudor's intention to contest the English throne could destroy his peace.

Cressida found herself being helped to rich delicacies by her betrothed; pike in rich sauces, roast haunches of venison, tench served in jelly, rabbit, larks' tongues and, following, an assortment of sweetmeats. The subtleties, composed of spun sugar and marzipan, were magnificent sculptures of castles and carracks, birds and animals, the King's personal device of the white boar taking pride of place on the high table. Though she was becoming used to the richness of spiced dishes served at Court, this over-abundance was too much for Cressida and the prolonged festivities gradually made her wish for simpler food.

Throughout, the minstrels played from the gallery on flute, flagelot and vielles. The King had declared his intention to be patron of the arts and kept a company of musicians by him constantly. When the trestles were removed the hurdy-gurdies, trumpets and sackbuts played for dancing.

Cressida was intrigued to see that the King rose to lead the Princess Elizabeth onto the floor. They danced well, moving with grace through the complicated patterns, and there was hearty applause at the conclusion of the dance. Elizabeth was laughing happily, flushed and rosy from the exertion.

Cressida had once heard that the King was slightly deformed—malicious rumour had said, unkindly, that he was downright crippled—but she had seen for herself, long before this, that that was all nonsense. He was crook-backed, they said, but she saw no sign of it. If he had one shoulder higher than another, the discrepancy was very slight indeed, and no greater than that of many men who practised hard with sword and axe and developed the muscles of one arm and shoulder more greatly than the other.

Now she saw that he was very skilled in the dance, nimble-footed and able to lift his partner high into the air, which set to naught all such foolish speculation. The Queen applauded with the others, but took no part in the dancing. Cressida, who had seen her coughing and panting, exhausted in her chamber, well understood that she was not fit for such a show, but Anne had proudly accompanied Richard onto the balcony of the palace at the crown-wearing and received much good-humoured clapping and bantering advice from the crowd as to her duty in setting about providing another heir. Only too well did Cressida know that to be unlikely.

She glanced now sharply towards her betrothed, who had been watching the Lady Elizabeth with the King.

'The King dances very well,' she said softly. 'It is good to see him enjoy himself so much—a respite from the many cares of State.'

Wroxeter nodded. He did not seem so concerned tonight with the Princess's closeness to the royal pair, or, if he was, was disinclined to show it.

He turned to her father. 'Have I your permission, Sir Daniel, to dance with my betrothed?'

Cressida's hand trembled upon the stem of her wine cup. She had danced at court but never so publicly. She was not sure she would acquit herself well.

Sir Daniel was smiling expansively and readily gave his permission, and Lady Gretton smiled at her daughter fondly.

'Certainly, my dear. Go and enjoy yourself.'

Cressida rose and took the Earl's proffered hand. She noticed in passing that her two former tormentors were watching her progress with avid interest.

He danced well, as she had expected. She had learned, from the talk about her over recent days, that he did all things well. He was popular with the Queen's attendants for his courtesy and good humour. Cressida thought wryly that apparently no one but she had seen glimpses of him when really angry, as she had seen him in the tilt-yard and when he had commented adversely on the Princess Elizabeth's constant presence at Court.

He was skilled in the joust, she had heard. That did not surprise her. He practised hard for that, she thought with some asperity. What did amaze her was his known prowess on the battlefield. The King's favour had been won during combat on the Scottish border.

Somehow, Cressida had not seen her betrothed as a doughty warrior. That sleepy expression had lulled her into a false understanding of his nature. She had thought him too fond of luxurious living to face the rigours of a battle camp, let alone the actual danger of face-to-face encounters, when more was at stake than the possible loss of horse and accoutrements.

The Lady Elizabeth had told her that her fellow ladies were envious of her good fortune in winning the hand of the wealthiest and most admired bachelor at Court. Now she felt many pairs of eyes fixed upon her, willing her to perform clumsily or even trip over her gown. She was, after all, the country maid, come but recently to town.

As in all things, he guided her with expert skill, smiling down at her encouragingly as the minstrels struck up a merry tune. Her fingers felt icy cold in his grasp and her heart was beating so fast with nervousness that she felt he must see her agitation, but the steps of the dance were fast and furious and she was forced to give all her concentration to them.

He drew her along the lines of dancers, swinging her expertly, then his hands were about her waist, strong and supportive, as he lifted her high into the air and brought her down safely, laughing and gasping. The great hall, with its colourful throng, moved madly round her as again she was swung into the elaborate patterns, till the music stopped and they halted at last, out of breath but triumphant.

He bowed and led her from the group of dancers to a side bench beneath a flaming flambeau.

'Wait while I fetch you wine. The room is growing over-hot from the throng of revellers—' he glanced round with some amusement '—getting drunker and more bawdy by the moment. I fear your lady mother will soon be withdrawing you from the company.'

Her breathing had slowed by the time he returned with a goblet of wine and she sipped at it gratefully.

'Thank you, but I think I, too, am taking more than I should tonight.'

'To give you courage?'

She glanced up, startled by his half-amused challenge, then lowered her gaze hastily. 'Yes, you might well be right, sir.'

'You seem over-anxious tonight. Why, Cressida? I assure you you are the object of admiration from all quarters.'

'I do not think that is true. Many of my companions think me very boorish. They comment often upon my accent.'

He glanced down at her fairy-like beauty. She was dressed tonight in a gown of softest blue brocade and tendrils of that extraordinary fair hair had broken free from the confines of her veiled butterfly hennin and brushed the rosy glow on her delicate cheek. He was not surprised that she faced spiteful criticism. What girl in the room could hope to match her ethereal beauty?

'I was not thinking of the ladies present,' he returned drily.

'Oh?' She was surprised by her own state of confusion. She had never felt so downright stupid and churlish in Howell's company, but then, he did not pay her fulsome compliments which put her out of countenance.

'Do not avoid my gaze. You are my betrothed and I am proud to lead you in the dance, to show the world you will soon be mine indeed.'

The half-veiled reference to what would follow the marriage ceremony caused her to colour again hotly and she turned away to look anxiously for sight of her parents.

He gave a good-humoured laugh. 'You will have no need to fear me, Cressida, I promise you.'

'I fear no-one, sir,' she snapped, riled into a return to the spirited responses she had given him at their earlier encounters.

He laughed again. 'No, I do not think you do fear any man or woman—except, perhaps, yourself.'

'What ever do you mean, sir?' Her startlingly blue eyes were very wide now, challenging his dark ones.

'I think all maids look with apprehension—to what is unknown.' His words were very gently uttered and the hard line left her mouth and she smiled so sweetly that his heart almost turned over. How childishly vulnerable she was, and determined that no one should know it.

She was again looking towards her parents and he took her fingers prisoner for a moment, concerned to reassure her, as he would any child looking to him for succour.

'I will treat you kindly, allow you to get to know me better before pressing my demands. I think it best if you remain for a while here at Court in attendance upon the Queen. I have duties in the Council, but later, if you wish, we can go for a while to the Marches and I shall take you frequently to see your parents.'

She gave a little relieved gasp. Many women, she knew, were totally separated from all kith and kin once the marriage knot was tied, a future she had secretly feared. She loved Gretton so much that she knew her heart would be broken if she rarely saw it.

He seemed kind, this man who would soon command her obedience. They all insisted that she was fortunate, from the King to the Lady Elizabeth. Why, then, did she feel this strange presentiment that he was not as he seemed outwardly; that, if she were not compliant, he could prove a tyrant? She had felt a wild excitement when he had placed his hands about her waist and again when their fingers had touched as he had handed her the wine.

She forced a brave smile. 'You are kind, sir. Your words convince me of your goodwill. I hope — I shall be able to please you, as you deserve.'

The corners of his mouth quirked oddly. 'Why do I feel that that is a more politic answer than an entirely sincere one?'

'I know my duties and —'

'Will perform them with punctilious regard for my approval. I think not, my Cressida. I do not wish for a mouse of a wife.'

He took the empty wine goblet from her nerveless fingers and drew her to her feet. Within moments he had restored her to the care of her mother and strode off to lean attentively upon the arm of the chair in which the now exhausted-looking Queen sat.

The Christmas festivities continued until Twelfth Night, with all the traditional games and entertainments.

One evening a company of mummers performed the play of Sir Gawain and the Green Knight. Seated between her father and the Earl of Wroxeter, Cressida shivered with premonitory fear when Sir Gawain cut off the Green Knight's head with one savage stroke. The Earl turned to her, his amused expression, as the actor stooped to recover the stuffed head from the floor where it had fallen from its high woven supports upon his shoulders, changing quickly to one of alarm as he noted her unwonted paleness.

'Cressida, you are upset? I thought you must have heard the tale many times before and would be prepared for this scene. The Green Knight represents the dying winter while Gawain represents the burgeoning powers of spring.'

She shook her head. 'No, no, of course I know the tale, but have never seen it actually performed before.

It—it made me think of real executions. My blood ran cold for the moment.'

Her father tutted his disapproval of her unconsidered words. 'Hush, Cressida. Westminster is no place to speak of executions.' His voice was cautiously lowered as he regarded the King, seated some paces from them, laughing uproariously at the bawdy adventures of the hero, Gawain, as he attempted to find the sinister Green Knight and, true to his sworn oath, stand firm while the Knight took a retaliatory blow at his own head.

Cressida shivered again as she thought how frightening a place the Court was, despite its assumed atmosphere of merriment this Christmas. Collingbourne had died horribly not so many months ago at Tyburn for daring to write a scurrilous verse concerning the King and his closest councillors, and the King's cousin, George of Buckingham, had lost his head in Salisbury market-place after his failed rising of 1483.

She had seemed so very far from these terrifying events at home at Gretton. Soon, as Wroxeter's bride, she would be forced to live far closer to these men who waited attendance on their sovereign with murder in their hearts and smiling lips.

She wondered if Martyn of Wroxeter was as truly loyal to the King as he seemed. Could she innocently find herself embroiled in such a plot? The thought appalled her. Again she longed with all her heart to return safely to Gretton after these festivities and to remain there safe and protected from all poisonous intrigue and danger.

Twelfth Night was to be the culmination of all the Christmas activities. The Queen dressed with special care and showed a forced jollity as her ladies fussed around her for this final state occasion of the season. Privately Cressida thought that Anne would be glad to rest for a while in her own apartments after all this, when many of the summoned lords and their ladies had returned to their own manors.

As Cressida stepped back with her companion ladies to view their handiwork, she felt that their efforts had been fully justified. The Queen looked magnificent. The material of the undergown of purple cloth of gold, with its woven design of suns and roses, was the King's Christmas gift. Over this Anne wore an ermine-trimmed white velvet overgown sewn with seed-pearls.

She wore her golden hair unbound to her waist beneath her golden crown, and when the King came gallantly to her chamber to escort her to the great hall Cressida saw his grey-green eyes light up with the glory of his love for his wife. Truly, tonight, she looked like a bride adorned for her husband.

He stooped and kissed the palm of her hand.

'You are so beautiful. No woman will outshine you tonight, my Anne.' He seemed totally unconcerned that his open adoration was observed and noted by all his wife's ladies.

She laughed gently. 'You look very fine yourself, my lord.'

He too was attired for the splendour of the occasion, in a scarlet velvet doublet over which his golden Yorkist collar gleamed beneath the candlelight, setting the ruby eyes of the pendant boar device glinting with artificial life.

The great hall was more crowded than ever tonight, and Cressida felt quite suffocated by all the noise and the greasy, spiced smell of the rich dishes. She had had more than a surfeit of such food over these last days and would have been grateful for more simple fare. Wroxeter, it seemed, was of a like mind, for he ate but sparely, though he was assiduous in placing the choicest morsels upon her plate.

The merriment seemed more bawdy and forced, as if

the general company was making the best of this last
chance to feast at the King's expense. Throughout it all
the Queen sat resplendent beside Richard's side as a
host of courtiers paid them both a wealth of fawning
attention.

It was almost at the close of the banquet when the
chamberlain announced the arrival of the Lady
Elizabeth Plantagenet. Cressida craned her neck to see
her friend approach the high table. Elizabeth had not
been present in the Queen's chambers over the last few
days and, only three days ago, Cressida had had only a
hasty conversation with her on the river terrace before
rushing back to serve the Queen.

There was a sudden silence which cut across the
high-pitched laughter and chat in the hall. For a
moment Cressida's view of the King's niece was
obscured by taller people between her and the chairs
of State. She felt Wroxeter give a little gasp beside her
and turned to see an expression of pure fury etched
upon his features.

Then Elizabeth moved into view and Cressida herself
gave vent to a half-suppressed cry of shocked surprise.

The Lady Elizabeth was curtseying before her aunt
and uncle, and when she rose Cressida saw immediately
what had caused that sudden hush to fall upon the
packed company.

Elizabeth's gown was almost a copy of the Queen's.
The purple brocade undergown was not so fine, true,
as Queen Anne's, but the cut of that and the white
velvet overgown with its ermine trim was almost an
exact facsimile. Whereas Anne's was starred with
pearls, Elizabeth's was scattered with crystal drops
which sparkled in the torchlight.

More shocking than the similarity of the gowns
chosen by these two royal ladies was the fact that
Elizabeth's youth and air of eager enthusiasm con-
trasted so starkly with the Queen's sudden pallor and

wearied posture in her chair. It was as if a shaft of
sunlight had appeared and totally eclipsed the moon's
beauty.

As soon as it had hushed the company hastily
resumed its assumed gaiety again as the King bent over
the table to welcome his fair young niece and place her
near to him at the high table, where, again, her position
next to the tiring queen showed only too clearly the
differences between them, despite the similarity of
garb.

Cressida stole a hasty glance at her betrothed and
found him watching the by-play at the high table with
intense interest. Soon the trestles were cleared and the
dancing began. Cressida sensed rather than heard the
gossiping innuendo of talk as the King led his lovely
young niece onto the floor, while Anne remained
quietly in her chair, outwardly engaged in watching the
dancers, sipping occasionally from her bejewelled wine
goblet, while, even from a distance, Cressida saw her
free hand tighten upon the carved arm-rest of her chair.

Suddenly Wroxeter appeared before Cressida holding out an imperious hand to lead her into the dance.
His expression was grim. He did not even stop to ask
permission from her father as he usually did.

Tonight she was too concerned about the grimness
of her betrothed's expression to be worried about any
ineptness on her part in the dance. They moved
through the complicated patterns without problems,
largely due to the Earl's expert guidance. Cressida was
not surprised, nor in the least relieved, when at the
dance's end he led her from the floor towards one of
the doors into the corridor.

She glanced back anxiously to where her parents
were seated and then back to a little knot of superior
attendants where Alice was gossiping with a middle-
aged, over-dressed lady of considerable girth.

Wroxeter was tugging at her wrist impatiently, urging

her onward, and she thought she would have a bruise
to show for it later.

'Where are we going?' she panted. 'We cannot leave
the company without a chaperon. I'll call Alice. . .'

'No need,' he said calmly. 'You are my betrothed.
No one will comment. We shall be gone only a short
time. I wish to talk to you and with no third person
present.'

She was pulled, willy-nilly, along the corridor and
into a small chamber some yards further on. Wroxeter
passed inside, still holding Cressida's wrist firmly. The
light from the sconce opposite the door showed her a
small room, furnished with a desk or table, two chairs
and a stool. The place was bare of comforts, with no
fine rugs on the floor or arras on the walls. It was clear
that this was used only for business, possibly by one of
the King's clerks or a secretary.

Wroxeter slammed the door to after lighting two
candles with tinder and flint placed ready. He shot
across the heavy bolt. He had released her wrist and
she was rubbing at it angrily. Then he indicated a chair
facing the desk.

'Sit down, Cressida.'

She obeyed him sulkily, glancing round the office
with a little shiver of unease. She could not rid herself
of the notion that this place was used for interrogation
purposes, and though there was no indication of any
sinister means of compulsion she was further uneasy.

Wroxeter appeared perfectly at home here. He sat
back in the chair opposite and eyed her gravely. For
once the hooded lids were drawn back clear of the
dark, compelling eyes.

'The Lady Elizabeth,' he said coldly. 'When did you
last speak with her?'

'What?' Cressida stared up at him in amazement.
Was this what had aroused his temper? He did not like
the Lady Elizabeth for some reason, and had stated

that he would rather she was far from Court, yet he had no means to influence so important a lady as the Princess Elizabeth, nor to object to Cressida's association with her. She set her lips and jutted her chin angrily.

'I don't understand all this. Why have you withdrawn me from the company? My mother will be alarmed. . .'

'I think not. She saw you were with me. Now, do not fence with me, Cressida. When did you speak with the Lady Elizabeth and talk about what the Queen intended to wear tonight?'

Cressida's lips parted in shock. 'You hold me responsible for. . . I know it was unfortunate that she—the Princess arrived in a gown so like the Queen's, but—'

'It was not unfortunate, it was deliberate,' he said harshly, 'and I wish to know if you informed the lady of what the Queen intended to wear. Answer me.'

Cressida's blue eyes widened. 'Deliberate? Oh, no, no one would. . .' Then she blazed, 'This is nonsense. How dare you question me so. . .?'

He leaned across the desk again and once more gripped her injured wrist so that she winced sharply.

'Cressida, did you or did you not describe for the Lady Elizabeth exactly what the Queen was to wear for this Twelfth Night feasting?'

Her heart was now thudding against her ribs. That genial, good-natured expression had completely vanished from his features and she recognised the fact that this man could prove a very dangerous enemy indeed.

'Yes,' she confessed at last, in a subdued voice. 'The material was so very beautiful and we had all enthused about it. The undergown was the King's Christmas gift, but. . .'

'Did she question you about it?'

'Yes. . .'

'When and where?'

'She—she has been away from the Queen's apartments for some days. I—I wondered if she was ill and then I saw her walking on the river terrace and we talked...'

She swallowed uncomfortably, vaguely disturbed by the cold opacity of those dark eyes fixed intently on hers. 'Yes, we did talk of the plans for this last Christmas feast. She asked what I was to wear and—and did ask after the Queen's health and—and which gown she...'

Cressida's voice trailed off miserably. 'I did not think it a secret. The Princess is the Queen's niece and—'

He released her wrist abruptly and sat back in the chair, frowning, the fingers of one hand drumming upon the polished oak of the desktop.

She waited uncertainly. Gradually her sense of pique eclipsed her previous vague fear. What right had he to tell her what she should say and what she should not? She had said nothing unwise, voiced no criticism of the King...

She said suddenly, 'Is that all you wish to say to me? If so, I would like to return to my parents. All this has been a great pother about nothing, if you ask me. It is embarrassing if one lady appears at a feast in attire like another's, but no great matter.' Her lips closed together tightly, revealing her anger at his unjust attack on her. 'The Queen did not swear us to secrecy.'

'She would think there would be no need,' he said wearily. 'No one but Elizabeth would dare to do such a thing.'

'Why are you so angry? The Queen has a right to be upset, I suppose, but—'

'No matter,' he said hurriedly. 'As you say, I must return you to the great hall, but—' he had risen from his chair and was now leaning down over the desk, his weight supported upon his two arms '—hear me well. You are soon to be my wife and I expect you to obey me. You will associate no more in private with the Lady Elizabeth.'

Cressida went pale with fury. 'The Lady Elizabeth has been undue kind to me when other ladies have not. I value her friendship. She honours me. You have no right. . .'

'I have every right,' he said harshly. 'I have an official position in the King's household—but, no matter, we will not speak of that. As your future husband I have authority to say with whom I do and do not wish you to associate. You will treat the Princess with courtesy, naturally, as you are bound to do, but you will offer no confidences. Do you understand me?'

She nodded unwillingly and rose from her chair as he took his hands from the desk and stood upright. He came round to her and took her hand, more gently this time.

'There are happenings at Court you do not understand, Cressida. This seems a small matter to you, but in reality actual harm has been done tonight and with your complicity—innocently, of course. Comply with my wishes. See as little of the Lady Elizabeth as possible. You have been used—and that could spell danger for you—and for others.'

She released a hard-held breath, her eyes widening again. She looked up into his eyes, seeking his understanding.

'I would not have willingly hurt the Queen,' she murmured at last. 'I know it looked—I mean, when we all saw them together. . .'

'Exactly,' he said grimly. 'Now you are beginning to understand. The Queen is unwell. She needs all our love and care. She should not be open to unkind speculation or rumour. You must respect all her confidences.' He sighed. 'You are such a child. I must learn to be more patient.'

He unbolted the door and turned to extinguish the

candles. Cressida experienced an overwhelming relief that she was to leave this chamber, not unmixed with growing irritation that he regarded her so slightly. She tossed her head resentfully as he bowed to her, once more the courteous suitor, and allowed him to lead her back along the corridor towards the babble of talk and loud laughter issuing from the great hall.

CHAPTER FOUR

'I CANNOT marry him. I will not marry him.' Cressida stood before her parents in her own small apartment, her voice shrill with unshed tears, almost hysterical.

Sir Daniel and Lady Gretton turned helplessly towards Alice who stood stolidly by the door. They had been hastily summoned to their daughter's chamber by her and had come at once. Alice shrugged equally helplessly. Her gaze went to her young mistress, standing there, looking so vulnerable, a child still but chin jutting rebelliously, determinedly defiant.

'You cannot tell us of anything alarming which has happened?' Lady Gretton sounded totally bewildered.

'No, my lady. Mistress Cressida seemed somewhat edgy when we left the great hall, then when we got back here I started to undress her but she suddenly began to cry. I could get nothing out of her and I thought at last I should send for you.'

Sir Daniel waved testily to the two women to be silent. He seated himself on the edge of Cressida's bed and folded his arms.

'Now, child, what is this nonsense? You say you can't marry Wroxeter? Why ever not? You went out of the hall with him. Did he attack you, offer you insult?'

Lady Gretton started forward angrily but again he waved her back.

Cressida gulped back tears. 'No,' she said, so softly that he had to lean forward to hear her answer.

'Then, in the Virgin's name, what is all this pother? Come, Cressida, I thought you had more spirit than to be taken by a fit of foolish womanly vapourings.'

Cressida turned away, plucking restlessly at the fine silk of her gown.

'I tell you I will not marry him. He—he frightens me.'

'Frightens you?' Sir Daniel looked even more bewildered. 'You tell me he did not touch you nor offer you insult, now you tell me he frightens you. The man appears courteous and considerate. The King thinks highly of him. . .'

'Oh, yes, the King,' Cressida snapped. 'The King must be right, and obeyed whatever the consequences. . .'

'Of course the King must be obeyed, Cressida,' Lady Gretton said worriedly. 'I cannot understand all this. Before the betrothal ceremony Lord Wroxeter asked if you had any misgivings. You told him you had none. Do you tell us now that you have become attached to someone here at Court. . .?'

'Of course not,' Cressida said desperately. 'I would do nothing to make you ashamed of me. There is no one, but—but Lord Wroxeter is such a powerful Lord, with a position of authority here at Court, and he overwhelms me. He—he has already given me commands as to whom I am to befriend and whom to avoid. . .'

'You are his betrothed wife,' Lady Gretton said quietly. 'He is well within his right. If there is some man. . .'

'There is no man. I have said as much.' Cressida found herself childishly stamping her foot. She stopped the moment she realised how foolish she was being as she caught Alice biting her lip in disapproval. 'There are—ladies—one lady in particular—with whom he does not wish me to be associated. I will not be so commanded. He will not tell me to deny affections. He will want me to dispense with Alice's services next.'

Lady Gretton pursed her lips. Only too well she was

aware that many bridegrooms indeed preferred to
dismiss their young wives' attendants. She herself had
been ever fortunate in that her husband had willingly
accepted her beloved elderly servants and welcomed
them into his household. She had hoped that such
would be the case for Cressida.

Sir Daniel grated, 'Of whom do we speak? Wroxeter
must have some reason for misliking one of your
companions. Mayhap she talks immoderately of married life and frightens you. If this so, you must accept
Wroxeter's ruling. Soon enough you will be wed and
away from Court.'

Cressida was about to speak of her interview with
her betrothed, then something froze the intended
words on her lips. 'You have been used,' he had said,
'and that could spell danger for you—and for others.'
She could not forget her fears for her father's safety
the very day the King's messenger had arrived at
Gretton.

Why was Wroxeter the Lady Elizabeth's enemy? She
had been kept from Court for some days. Had that
been due to his orders? Cressida gave a little shudder.
How powerful Wroxeter must be, indeed, if he could
dictate to those about the Queen so that the King's
royal niece was denied her presence at Anne's side.

She said stubbornly, 'I do not wish to proceed with
this marriage. Father, if you love me. . .'

Sir Daniel exploded into sudden, raw fury. 'Have I
bred a rank fool? You are solemnly betrothed in the
royal chapel. It would take a papal dispensation to
break such a binding pledge. You are all but wed, but
for the bedding—'

He broke off as he caught his wife's warning glance
directed at him balefully. 'Troth was plighted in the
King's very presence. Do you think for a moment that
he would countenance such a plea on my part to apply
to the Curia? What excuse could I give but a maid's

foolish pre-marriage fears? Make up your mind to it, Cressida. The match is made, contracts signed. You will go to the altar with Wroxeter and that is an end to it.'

Sir Daniel stood up decisively and her mother moved to embrace her. Cressida stood docilely, but withdrew a little stiffly as soon as she decently could. She curtsied dutifully as her parents withdrew to their own apartment, then said through clenched teeth, 'Alice, go fetch a warmed brick. I am frozen to the marrow.'

Alice hesitated only a moment, then hurried off about her errand. Cressida stood, hands clenched into small fists at her sides, then, slowly, she began to undress. Alice had already unhooked her elaborate gown and removed her hennin before summoning Sir Daniel and his lady, so Cressida found she could manage well enough. In fact she felt flushed, almost fevered, and her need of a warming device for the bed was merely a ruse to rid herself of Alice, if only for minutes.

She needed, desperately, to be alone. She was not really angered by her father's reaction to her plea. She had not expected him to behave in any other way, yet she had needed both her parents to understand her need.

Logic, however, told her that that was an impossibility, since she had been unable to explain to them just how she felt. She could not explain it to herself. She only knew she was experiencing a state of helpless panic. From the moment that messenger had arrived at her home her fate had been sealed, and she could not help but fear the fates of others she loved could be sealed also, yet she did not know how or why.

Her travelling mirror revealed her body in misty outline in the soft glow of the two dips in her chamber. She stared at herself critically for the very first time, turning this way and that to observe the features of her

naked form. He had said she was but a child. Was that
how she appeared to him? She did not feel like a child.
Her doubts and fears were anything but childlike.

She was very small. Had Wroxeter's lost love been
tall and stately? Cressida tossed her head, allowing the
mass of her golden hair to fall free from its pins and
cascade over her shoulders, down to her waist and
beyond. She was slim — too boyishly slim for a man
with sophisticated court tastes like Martyn, Earl of
Wroxeter? Her breasts were small but firm, the tips
rosy in the golden half-light. She stood on tiptoe,
arching her back, lifting her breasts with her two hands.

He had said she was fairy-like, but that was the stuff
of myths and dreams, tales told by the border folk and
Celtic peasants. A man like Wroxeter would want
something more substantial in his arms.

The false warm glow which had suffused her body
during the exchanges with her betrothed and her father
was fading. She shivered and reached for her fur-
trimmed bedgown and by the time Alice returned her
need for the heated brick had become a reality. She
snuggled down at last beneath the fur covering of the
bed, glad of the blanket-wrapped brick's retained heat.

Alice stood by the bed, arms akimbo, looking per-
plexed and somewhat alarmed still.

'You are angry that I sent for your mother? I did not
think your father would come, but I was worried. . .'

Cressida reached out a hand towards her maid,
patting the bedside welcomingly.

'I know why you did it. You are not used to seeing
me in a bout of hysterical tears. Faith,' she added
disgustedly, 'I am unused to the frightening sensations
myself.'

Alice sank down and enfolded her former charge in
her arms. 'You mustn't blame your father, chick. He
does what he thinks is necessary for your well-being.

You were not very explicit in telling him what you fear. Cannot you tell old Alice?'

Cressida gave a little laugh. 'Do not try those old tricks on me. You are not old, Alice, neither are you a foolish countrywoman, but wise in the ways of the world—probably far more so than my mother, who has been adored and sheltered throughout her married life.'

'Aye, well, won't you tell me what truly ails you?' Alice's eyes had narrowed shrewdly.

Cressida sighed. 'I'm not sure I know. Part of it is having to grow up so suddenly, face the dread of this coming marriage and all it entails—but,' she cut in quickly before Alice could hasten to reassure her with all the usual platitudes about women's lot in life, 'it is the atmosphere here about the Court. I am concerned that my father could be drawn into danger—and I know Wroxeter's loyalty is to the King and only to the King. He would sacrifice us all, if needful, to that cause.'

She told Alice what had taken place between her betrothed and herself and his final warning.

'I do not understand quite why he was so angry,' she said thoughtfully. 'Of course, it was a tactless thing for the Princess to do and I feel partly to blame for having divulged the secret of what the Queen was to wear, but the Earl was unnaturally disturbed—indeed, beside himself with fury, and he held me responsible.' She paused for a moment, thinking the incident through again.

'Do you think the Princess was making some point of her own? Does she now believe her brothers to be truly dead—and, if so, considers herself the rightful heir, her father's eldest daughter, Queen in her own right, and so dressed herself accordingly to show the assembled nobles at this ritual crown-wearing?' Cressida's lips trembled. 'If that were the case,

Wroxeter would consider it a challenge to the King's right and it could encourage others to take sides...'

She gave another shiver, knowing as she did her father's Lancastrian sympathies. He must not ally himself openly with any faction at this intrigue-ridden Court which was avid for scandal.

Alice was silent, then she shook her head. 'It seems more likely she was but making a bid for attention,' she said at last, then, before Cressida could question her further about her opinion on this matter, she bent and tucked in her charge and rose to her feet to seek her own bed.

'Never you mind about your betrothed. Like most men, he'll have got well over his temper in the morning.' She was frowning, though, as she turned away, having noticed the darkening bruise on her nurseling's wrist. The man was more of an enigma than she had taken him for, and she gave a heavy sigh at the thought of Cressida's coming dependence on her future husband's moods.

Cressida dreaded to see her betrothed after their quarrel, but, as Alice had promised, when she did encounter him within the Queen's apartments the following day he greeted her courteously, as if nothing had happened to cause him annoyance.

'How is Her Grace today?' he enquired quietly.

Cressida glanced hurriedly back to the open door of the Queen's bedchamber. 'She—she is exceptionally tired.' She had noted with concern the dark shadows beneath Anne's eyes and her seeming reluctance to rouse and face the day.

'That is to be expected after the gruelling pace of all these past celebrations.' His tone was normal, without any hint of anger, but Cressida could see that he was frowning. The Queen's condition concerned him deeply.

They were standing quite close, the other ladies giving them an opportunity to talk in private. He looked down deliberately at her bruised wrist, which she was nervously holding in her other hand.

'Was I responsible for that mark?'

Cressida flushed somewhat miserably. 'It is nothing. I'm sure you had no wish to hurt me. I suppose it happened when I was anxious to leave you.'

He inclined his head gravely. 'Certainly I had no intention of giving you pain. You will forgive me if I was attempting to make my point somewhat forcibly.'

She nodded and looked down at her feet without comment.

'Be careful, Cressida, with whom you gossip at Court. Repeat nothing of a doubtful nature.'

She looked back up at him quickly. His tone was regretful still but his dark eyes were unhooded and she knew he was anxious to impress upon her the gravity of her position.

She nodded again.

There was a little stir near the Queen's door and Cressida heard the cool, clear tones of the Lady Elizabeth cut across some polite murmur from one of the more senior ladies.

'If, as you say, Her Grace, my aunt, is unwell, then I should be admitted to her presence at once. I am sure His Grace the King would approve of my determination to wait upon her. She may well have need of my services.'

Cressida gave Wroxeter a hasty glance to see what his reaction would be to this move, but he merely watched thoughtfully as the two ladies near the door were swept aside and the Lady Elizabeth entered the bedchamber. His eyes were once more hooded as he bowed to the attendant ladies and excused himself. Cressida watched him walk away somewhat relieved.

She wondered if he had gone to the small, somehow daunting chamber where he had questioned her.

Over the next days the Queen's health continued to decline. The weather worsened and the cold, damp air from the river caused her to cough badly. The attacks were so prolonged and weakening that Cressida was often alarmed when on duty alone, but the Queen would frequently refuse to allow her physician to be sent for.

The King seemed busy once more with affairs of state, but when he did come to the Queen's side she forced herself to appear better for his benefit. In her presence he assumed a cheeriness which Cressida saw vanish when the Queen could not see his expression and, despite her reservations about the King's nature, Cressida was forced to acknowledge that he loved his wife dearly and was daily becoming more concerned about her.

The doctors were summoned and prescribed cough remedies and noxious potions which the Queen swallowed valiantly and without complaint, but nothing seemed to do her much good.

'I shall be better in the spring,' she averred confidently, her eyes far too bright and the hectic pink flush darkening her cheeks. Privately Cressida wondered if the ailing Queen would live until the spring.

The Lady Elizabeth came daily to her aunt's apartments and Anne valued her ministrations. The King himself drew his niece aside on several occasions to thank her for her services. No one referred to the unfortunate incident on Twelfth Night, at least not in Cressida's hearing, and the Lady Elizabeth was once more ensconced in the small coterie of the Queen's attendants.

She continued to single out Cressida for confidences. Cressida was stoutly determined to ignore her betrothed's former strictures and was warmed by this display of royal friendship. The Princess talked of her younger sisters, their hopes of a rosy future, and that the King would provide for them handsomely and find them youthful and wealthy husbands. Rarely did she speak of her mother, the Dowager Queen, whom Cressida had never seen at Court, and never was any mention made of the Princess's younger brothers.

Mary Bolton was overheard to remark that she had heard her father say that the infamous pretender Henry Tudor, Earl of Richmond, skulking at the French Court, had dared to declare his intention of wedding the Princess Elizabeth when he came into his own and sat on the English throne, rightfully his as the true Lancastrian heir.

'My father told my mother he thinks the King should hasten and marry her off to some gentleman of his household, so there would be no more of this nonsensical talk circulating about the Courts of Europe.'

'And what did your mother reply to that?' Her companion inclined her ear to gain the answer.

Instead of whispering, as might have been more sensible, Mary tossed back her head and declared so that Cressida, some yards away, could hear only too clearly, 'She says the King will not do that since he loves his niece well and is chary of parting with her company.'

The other girl broke into a spasm of soft giggles and Cressida frowned her disapproval.

'Her Grace the Queen would miss the Princess sorely if she were to marry now,' she said as she drew level with the gossiping pair.

Mary Bolton favoured her with a calculating smile. 'You think so? Perhaps she would be relieved to have the Lady Elizabeth gone from the vicinity of the Court.'

'The Queen always rallies when the Lady Elizabeth is present. I know she is glad of her company, which cheers her mightily.'

Mary Bolton shrugged and flounced off, her companion in tow. Cressida looked after them uneasily. Wroxeter had warned her not to become embroiled in this scandalous, almost treasonable talk. If Richmond was offering openly for the Lady Elizabeth's hand, it could only be to put one more thorn beneath the saddle of the King's peace, and such talk, here at Westminster, was not to be encouraged. It could only further distress the Queen were she to hear of it inadvertently.

Cressida's parents had delayed their return to Gretton until after her marriage and had taken lodgings behind an apothecary's shop in the Chepe in the city while Cressida, with Alice in attendance, remained at Westminster in the Queen's service.

Cressida was glad of a respite from the poisonous air of the Court when, one morning in early February, the Queen excused her from duty in order to allow her to visit her parents, and she and Alice set off downriver in one of the barges used to transport members of the royal household into the city.

Cressida was always relieved when they alighted safely at the steps near London Bridge, since the current beneath the Bridge piers was known to be very strong and dangerous. A servant in the royal service wearing the device of the white boar escorted the two women to the shop in the Chepe. Cressida courteously dismissed the man at the door, knowing her father would see to it that she was safely accompanied back to the palace when the time came.

The apothecary, a dry little stick of a man in a dark gaberdine gown, his sparse hair standing up wildly round his bald crown, greeted her obsequiously, rubbing his hands together as he stood back for Cressida to mount the stair to her father's lodging.

Alice knocked loudly. They were kept waiting for some moments. Cressida could hear the sound of two

male voices, then the door was jerked open suddenly
and she was startled to see Howell Prosser standing on
the threshold.

He looked as surprised as she was, then he broke
into a delighted smile.

'Sir Daniel, here is joy indeed; Mistress Cressida is
here to see you.'

Sir Daniel hastily joined him. He looked, Cressida
thought, more than a bit startled, as if this sudden
arrival of hers was not to be welcomed at this time,
then he too smiled and opened his arms wide to
embrace her.

'Daughter, come in, come in. I had not expected. . .
Well, as you see, Howell is here in London and in good
time for your wedding day.'

Cressida moved into the private solar, her astonishment at the unexpected news preventing her, for the
moment, from acknowledging the presence of her
childhood companion. Her father, too, realised that he
had babbled out the announcement too suddenly for
he gave a forced laugh.

'There, what am I thinking, girl, breaking the news
like that, before your mother has properly prepared
you. . .? Wroxeter was here last evening, requesting
that the ceremony be performed within the next month
since he cannot tell when the King will require his
services to travel, possibly to the north.

'I had intended to send for you and inform you, but
here you are unexpectedly and I blurted it all out
inadvisedly. Your mother will scold me, for sure. Sit
down, child, near the fire; you must be chilled to the
bone. Did you come by river?'

He was talking much too quickly, uncomfortable in
her presence. Why? Had the occasion when she had
argued against the marriage alarmed him so that he
feared her reaction to the news? Yet she had known it

must come soon, had prepared herself, while still hoping that it might be postponed for months yet.

'I see,' she murmured awkwardly. 'I saw the Earl at dinner yesterday, but he did not speak of this to me. Doubtless he wished to consult with you first.' She was determined to keep her tone level, especially with Howell here. She would not have him know how she dreaded the final moment when she would become truly Wroxeter's bride. She looked round anxiously. 'Where is Mother?'

'She went out into the Chepe, shopping for the final items for the wedding day. It is a wonder you did not see her on your way.' Sir Daniel brought her a tankard of spiced ale which he had mulled for her by thrusting in the glowing iron from the hearth. 'Drink, child, and warm the cockles of your heart.'

Howell had moved in closer. She smiled at him and he lifted her free hand and raised it to his lips. 'You cannot know how pleased I am to see you looking so well and happy, Cressida.'

She wondered that he thought she looked happy. She supposed she was rosy from the hasty walk in the cold air. Alice was fussing with her cloak and hood, and she sank down in the chair her father had vacated. Alice caught Sir Daniel's eye and slipped from the room. Downstairs there was a small back chamber where the few servants the Grettons had brought to the capital spent their waking hours until summoned.

Howell was anxious to question Cressida about her work at Court and she was glad to reassure him that she was happy under the benign rule of the Queen.

'We all worry so about her,' she said sadly. 'She seems so listless these days and the doctors are present constantly. It's said...' She hesitated, recollecting hurriedly that, perhaps, she should not complete the sentence, but, on seeing Howell's and her father's gaze fixed on her with interest and concern, she continued in a whisper, 'It's said that they are counselling the King to keep from her bed for fear of contagion.'

Howell frowned and Sir Daniel tutted in sympathetic concern. 'Poor gentle lady.'

'The Princess Elizabeth is by her side constantly and proves a great comfort to her.'

There was a sound of doors opening below and brisk exchanges between Lady Gretton and her maid. Cressida stood up eagerly to greet her mother as she bustled into the solar.

'My dear, we hadn't expected you for days.' Lady Gretton embraced her daughter warmly. Her skin was icy cold from the frosty air outside and she beamed expansively upon the company. 'Isn't it wonderful that Howell is here and can carry tidings of your wedding back to the manor and to our neighbours?'

'Ye-es.' Cressida was less enthusiastic and her eyes went to the numerous small linen-wrapped packages which her mother had brought upstairs with her, having dismissed her maid with the bulkier purchases to join the rest of the staff downstairs.

Lady Gretton appeared not to notice Cressida's lack of appreciation for her endeavours on her behalf. She gratefully accepted from Howell a tankard of spiced mulled ale after Sir Daniel had helped her remove her cloak and hood. She chatted brightly about the high prices in these London shops, though was delighted by the variety of goods on offer, and, at last, carried off Cressida to her chamber to show her the new materials and ribbons and called to her maid to bring the half-completed wedding gown that Cressida must try on and stand patiently while it was fitted.

It was Howell who offered to escort Cressida and Alice to Westminster and Sir Daniel smilingly agreed. As they walked to the Bridge landing stage Cressida waited nervously for Howell to question her about her betrothed. Other than asking her quickly, with a hurried glance at Alice, who was slightly behind them, if she was satisfied by her parents' choice, he made no more attempts to embarrass her. They both knew that had matters stood otherwise they would have now been discussing plans for a marriage between them.

Cressida said between her teeth, 'Wroxeter is young, personable and well thought of at Court. As for my parents' choice, that is beside the point. King Richard has chosen my husband for me and my parents are naturally flattered by his attentions.'

'But you are not,' Howell said bluntly.

'I have to admit I wish it had been differently arranged,' Cressida said quietly.

'Wroxeter will make you a countess,' Howell whispered with some trace of bitterness.

Cressida did not add, Far too soon now, it appears, but she was thinking it as Howell summoned a ferryman.

Seated within the boat, she asked, 'What does bring you to London—not my wedding, I'm sure?'

He grinned. 'No, no, business for my father. He wishes to know firsthand the prices of wool, for one thing—believes he is being cheated by the Ludlow merchants—but, of course, he knew I would be delighted to contact your parents in the hope that I would catch at least one glimpse of you.'

'Will you be long in London?'

'I go to Southampton tomorrow, but I shall be back within the week—and present for your marriage feast.'

As Howell was assisting her from the ferry boat at the King's steps at Westminster, Cressida saw Wroxeter with Peter Fairley in attendance alighting from a second boat. Immediately he came to her side and she introduced Howell Prosser.

'Master Prosser is a good neighbour of ours near Gretton. Fortunately he is in London on business and was present at my father's lodging and available to escort me back to the palace,' she explained. Her mouth was unaccountably dry. Though Howell's attentions were in no way excessive, she would have preferred her betrothed not to have seen her with him. Perhaps Howell's expression revealed all too clearly his opinion of this hastily arranged marriage.

Wroxeter bowed to him. 'How fortunate that you are here so near to our wedding day. Will you be able to delay your return so that you might honour the occasion with your presence?'

Howell bowed in return. 'Indeed, I may do so, my lord. Our friends on the Marches will be eager to know the details. Mistress Cressida is held in high esteem amongst our friends.'

Wroxeter's lips curved in a smile. 'I'm sure she is, as she is already here, at Westminster. Thank you for your care of my betrothed, sir, and now, if you have no business within the palace, I will take over my duty and escort her to the Queen's apartments.'

Cressida turned for a last sight of Howell as he was so summarily dismissed, but Wroxeter's light grip upon her arm was imperative and she was unable to gauge Howell's reaction to the lordly manner of her betrothed. She stopped at last outside the doorway to the Queen's apartments, breathless and angry. Wroxeter nodded to dismiss Alice, who had followed stolidly behind them. The maid moved off some distance along the corridor, but kept her charge in view.

'Why did you have to be so rude?' Cressida demanded furiously. 'I have not seen Howell for weeks and he was kind enough to escort me home.'

'Rude?' Wroxeter's dark brows rose in surprise. 'I do not think I was in the least rude. I invited the fellow to our wedding feast.'

'He did not need your invitation,' she snapped. 'My parents had already invited him. Howell is a very dear

friend and his father and our other neighbours will
want to hear about the proceedings and—'

'A dear friend?'

'A childhood companion,' Cressida reiterated.
'Trusted by my father and—'

'Often alone with you?'

She stopped open-mouthed at the sharp question as
she had been about to go once more into the attack.

'Certainly alone, though rarely,' she snapped again.
'I say again, we were children together. Howell has
never once said anything out of place. He regards me
as a sister.'

'Indeed? Does he?' Wroxeter's brows drew together
and his voice had resumed its habitual sleepy tone.
'And you think of him as a brother, I suppose?'

Cressida was brought up short again by the perceptive awareness of his question.

'Yes, of course.' She was somewhat embarrassed by
his sleepy but steely suggestion that she felt more for
Howell than she was prepared to admit. 'I have never—
thought. . .' Her voice trailed off awkwardly.

'I see.' He was smiling now, but wryly, and she felt
that he was not convinced.

She was goaded again into attack, feeling uncomfortably defensive.

'My lord, if you feel at all concerned about my
former friendship with Master Prosser, perhaps you
should seek a dispensation to allow you to withdraw
from our betrothal and not go forward with the marriage arrangements.'

He turned steadily to face her. 'Cressida, we shall
marry on the day appointed. Nothing will change that.
Afterwards it will be for me to decide just what
friendships I am prepared to allow you.'

He was still holding her wrist and she jerked at it
angrily to free herself, tears very near the surface and
cheeks and throat reddening in frustration.

He smiled deliberately. 'I trust your parents informed you of my wishes concerning the day?'

She nodded sullenly.

'The King will honour us with his presence. I expect you to behave circumspectly and not disgrace me or your parents.'

'You continue to treat me like a child,' she spat.

'You *are* a child still and a spoilt one into the bargain, but the contract is signed, and I am not entirely dissatisfied with the arrangement. There will be time in plenty for you to mature and come to terms with the outcome.'

He released her and called to Alice, then turned and walked away. Cressida conquered the urge to give way to tears. She must resume her duties and at any moment a page or servant might come along the corridor. She had no wish to be the subject of gossip, particularly as some of her companion ladies continued to treat her with some disdain.

Cressida's marriage to Martyn, Earl of Wroxeter, took place on the very last day of February within the royal chapel. Her wedding gown was magnificent, of heavy cloth of silver and trimmed with white fur. It was early evening and the candlelight glimmered on her slight form so that she appeared a veritable frost-faery creature as her father led her forward to the altar where the Earl waited, attended by his squire, Peter Fairley, the King by his side as sponsor.

Cressida's mother waited near the door of the chapel with the Queen and the Lady Elizabeth. Alice, her eyes shining with pride, stood behind them.

There was a little gasp as Sir Daniel appeared at the door of the chapel with his daughter. For the first time courtiers outside in the corridor had the opportunity to glimpse the unbelievable gold of her hair, which hung loose to her waist. There were few flowers at this winter season and she wore a simple circlet of silver adorned with pearls—the Queen's gift.

It was very cold. Even in the corridors of Westminster, breath froze whitely in the air as men spoke and there were braziers set near the door of the chapel and close to the altar. They did little to dispel the icy chill within Cressida's heart, yet she felt one stab of pure triumph at the sight of the King's niece. Wroxeter had not dared to protest at her presence.

In this one thing, at least, she had had her own way. She had continued her association with the Lady Elizabeth, despite her betrothed's strictures. This was a very private ceremony and St Stephen's chapel very small, so only immediate family members were present beside the sovereigns, but she would see Howell soon at the wedding feast within the great hall and she doubted that afterwards she would have an opportunity to speak with him freely again.

The scent of incense was so overpowering that she feared she would faint, but she stiffened her spine and tilted her chin and unprotestingly allowed her father to place her numbed hand within the Earl's. She took little note of the priest's exhortation and only turned when the ring was placed upon her fingers and the Earl recited his vows in his clear, ringing tones.

She saw now, for she had not dared look fully at him before, that he was clad in saffron velvet over dark green hose and the colour suited his dark colouring well. His tall form looked spare and elegant. Beside him the King, in blue, appeared small of stature, yet no one could ever have deemed Richard Plantagenet insignificant. His very demeanour and stance revealed his military prowess and his innate air of royalty.

She spoke her own vows woodenly and, as she knelt before the altar to receive the nuptial mass, realised, wonderingly, that she had given herself to this man whom she both disliked and feared without outward protest.

At the chapel door, the Queen embraced her and the King came to give her a hearty kiss upon the cheek. She forced herself not to recoil from his touch.

He was clearly delighted by the success of this match he had made.

'My lady,' he said gently, 'I wish you all happiness. I could not have found you a husband who pleased me more, for he is loyal and true of heart. I trust he will prove himself to you as he has to me.'

She curtsied dutifully and was hugged by her mother while Sir Daniel looked on, grinning expansively. He was hugely relieved that it had all gone so smoothly. He knew he had always indulged this beloved daughter of his and had secretly feared that she might, even at the last moment, refuse to pledge herself and disgrace him before his sovereign. Now it was over. She looked so very beautiful beside this tall, personable man who was her husband.

For one second his heart misgave him. Would Wroxeter treat her well, his Cressida, to whom he had never taken a switch in all her youthful happy life at Gretton? She was all unprepared to deal with a demanding, dominating husband.

He stole a hasty glance at that sleepy, inscrutable countenance. Surely there was no cruelty revealed by that long, sensitive mouth, no wanton sensuality either, for all he could see, and he had heard no undue, bawdy gossip about the man. No, the match was a good one. He must believe that since he had little choice in the matter. The King had been so determined on it from the beginning.

Cressida was placed upon the King's right at the nuptial feast, her parents near the Queen. She sat at the high table, still half-bemused after the ceremony, above the salt, her new husband beside her. She looked down from the dais at the courtiers and their ladies who had come to do the Earl of Wroxeter honour. She saw Viscount Francis Lovell, the King's chamberlain and friend since childhood, in laughing talk with her father. He was a handsome man, witty and charming.

Her father had hinted once that the King's household, which had come south with him from Middleham, was not completely accepted at Court. There too were Sir Richard Ratcliffe, Sir Robert Percy and William Catesby, who had turned his allegiance from his former master, the executed Lord William Hastings, more recently.

She remembered with a frisson of horror that William Collingbourne had died horribly only months ago at Tower Hill for penning the satirical rhyme which epitomised the opinions of many southern lords.

> The Cat, the Rat, and Lovell our dog,
> Rule all England under a hog.

Was Martyn, Lord Wroxeter, one of their company? Yes, she believed so. Fortunate for him that his personal device of a silver saltire on a green field, since he was related by marriage to the great Neville family, had not lent itself to being so lampooned.

She caught her mother's eyes upon her. They were troubled, she could see even from this distance, and she smiled back reassuringly.

Her husband was addressing her and she turned back nervously to meet his gaze. He was smiling and for once those brooding dark eyes of his were not hooded.

'I was saying,' he remarked pleasantly, 'that all that joyous company are envying me my wondrously lovely bride.'

Was he mocking her? Her fingers clumsily tilted the golden plate set before her and he put out a steadying hand.

'The page waits for you to rinse your fingers, my love.'

The word jarred, but there appeared to be no mockery in his expression. She turned hastily to the kneeling page, dabbled her fingers in the rose-scented water he proffered in a golden bowl and dried them upon a fine linen napkin. The King had spared no expense to honour his friend and loyal servant. The finest of jewelled plate was arrayed upon the snowy white drapery of this festive board and the food was excellently served and delicious.

Cressida had become used now to the Court custom of allowing her partner to choose the choicest morsels for her, but she almost baulked at the traditional ceremony when she was handed the loving cup filled to the brim with malmsey. With the eyes of the full company upon her, she took a hasty sip and handed it to Wroxeter, who gallantly placed his own lips upon the place where hers had rested and drank deep.

A hearty cheer rang out as courtiers rose to pledge bride and groom with good red wine. Turning away slightly, Cressida encountered the gaze of Howell Prosser, who was seated some way down the lower table. Her own eyes brimmed with sudden tears as she saw the yearning sadness in his.

She was glad when her mother came to lead her from the hall, Alice anxiously hovering behind her. It had to be faced, the final trial of this terrible day. As she passed the smiling courtiers with their ladies Cressida knew there were several of their number who envied her this moment. One man, she knew, felt quite differently. Howell Prosser deliberately did not look her way as she passed him.

A luxurious chamber had been put at Lord Wroxeter's disposal for his wedding night. Tomorrow Cressida would leave for his fine town house in the Strand. She would continue to attend on the Queen for

the present, though now, naturally, she would not take
her place at night within the Queen's bedchamber.

A roaring fire in the great hearth filled the room with
heat and light, but, like the braziers in the chapel,
failed to warm Cressida. She felt icy cold as her mother
and Alice helped her off with her finery and into the
simple white gown of embroidered lawn. She prayed
that the shaking of her limbs would not be put down to
pure terror but to the chill of the night.

She looked round at the great bed, which was
covered with furs and the scarlet velvet coverlet. She
noted, surprised, that it bore the embroidered device
of Wroxeter's house and must have been brought from
the Strand.

There was a goblet of wine upon the bedstand and
the candles were of the finest wax and scented. The
linen of the bed smelt of sweet herbs, marjoram,
rosemary and rose petals. The scarlet velvet draperies
on the testered bed gave the impression of enclosing
her within a scented prison and she tried not to
shudder.

Her mother whispered in Alice's ear and her maid
kissed her and left. Cressida thought her cheek was
moist with tears and hoped her own were not also.

Lady Gretton said softly, 'You said—you were afraid
of him. I—I have been gainsaid in this arrangement.
Child, all has been ordered, so it was impossible for
your father to object. You must forgive him if. . .'

Cressida impulsively hugged her mother. 'I do not
blame either of you. I know how it is.'

'Your father was known to be formerly allied to the
House of Lancaster. Now that rumours of treason
abound in the land, especially in the Marches, he dare
not be seen to oppose the King's will.'

Cressida smiled bravely. 'I know. Tell him I
understand.'

Lady Gretton gave a great relieved gasp for her

understanding of the difficulty of their position. 'This man—he has not shown you violence?'

'No.' Cressida's whisper was faint. 'He is just so very—lordly. I am used to a less ordered life—and—and I wanted so much to come home.' There, it had come out in a rush, the foolish childish words which could not be held back.

Lady Gretton caught her daughter close to her heart and smoothed back the luxuriant golden hair. There was a great lump in her own throat. It had all happened so suddenly. One moment this so dear child had been theirs completely, so much so that she had found it hard to contemplate her leaving them—and then the summons to Westminster had come and now this marriage had followed on so frighteningly fast.

She feared for Cressida—she could not help it. She drew back slightly, gave a little crooked smile and bent to kiss her daughter in gentle blessing.

'Be brave, my Cressida. You have been well prepared. Give your husband no reason to discipline you. I know,' she said, with a little catch in her voice, 'you will not find it easy to be obedient and biddable—but try. It is necessary for your own chance of happiness.'

She rose, leaving Cressida seated on the bed, and hastened out of the chamber. She knew that if she stayed longer she would give way to tears and she must not.

At the door she encountered the Queen and two of her ladies with the royal chaplain come to bless the marriage bed. Lady Gretton curtsied low as Anne went in to smile down at her youthful attendant.

'Stand up and let me look at you. Yes, you are so very lovely, and so young. I was scarce older than you when my lord took me to bed. I could not know then how happy he would make me, and after a terrible time in my life. I want you to be equally happy, Cressida. Martyn Telford is a good man and worthy of you.'

The Queen bent and kissed Cressida gently upon the forehead as her mother had done. 'Martyn cannot but be overcome with your beauty, my dear. I wish,' she said brokenly, 'I had had a daughter to bless on her wedding night but, today, I look upon you in this light. Be blessed, my dear, as I am with my dear lord.'

She was not alone long. The King accompanied the groom to the chamber door and Cressida heard his laugh of pure pleasure, but did not catch his last, pleasant exhortation to his friend. The chamber door was jerked open, then she was alone with her husband.

She sank back into a half-crouched, half-sitting position on the side of the bed as he came towards her. His squire had disrobed him and he wore a brocaded green and silver bedgown. The garment was magnificent and in it he looked huge and almost menacing. She caught her nether lip in her teeth, determined not to break into tears and reveal her apprehension.

He stood for a moment, looking down at her, and, despite herself, she shrank back a little. He cupped her chin in his hands and smiled down at her. 'So, they left you alone. I hope it has not been for too long.'

She shook her head mutely.

He moved to the other side of the bed and drew back the covers.

'If you sit there much longer you will freeze in that flimsy gown, even in this firelit room.'

He averted his eyes as she obeyed him and slipped beneath the coverlet. She was so overwhelmingly lovely and so vulnerable. He felt a stab of hot desire in his loins. She was his and he had every right to take her—indeed he would be a fool not to do so—yet he must not.

He had agreed, reluctantly, to please his sovereign in this. In time she would learn to accept his rule, be less afraid, for he could feel like a palpable thing her abject desperation and fear of him. No, he must wait until he could bring her to a more receptive mood. To take her now would be a violation.

She heard the stiff brocade of the bedgown fall to the floor as he discarded it and slipped into bed beside her. Her heart was beating so fast that she was sure he must hear it and she took deep, steadying breaths to calm herself. His body was so close to hers. It felt warm and hard beside her unyieldingly chill form.

He said quietly, 'You need have no fear, Lady Cressida. I have no intention of touching you at this time. You have a deal of growing up to do before you become truly my wife.'

She could hardly believe the words, the relief had come so amazingly. She swallowed hard.

'My lord?'

'Learn to address me, in private at least, as Martyn.'

'Yes, my lord—Martyn. I...'

'Now try to sleep. You must be very tired.'

'Yes, my lord.'

He smiled in the darkness for he had turned and extinguished the candle before settling beside her.

'I must, naturally, in order to avoid gossip, remain in your bed tonight. Later, at the Strand house, you will have your own chamber for the present. I have considerable pressure of work which brings me late to bed often and I would not disturb you at such hours.'

She made no reply, thinking through his words and attempting to come to terms with the knowledge that her most desperate fears had been groundless. At last she said through gritted teeth, 'My lord, my maid, Alice, said—said that the sheets will be noted and—and—'

'No one,' he said coldly, 'will dare to question or oppose my will. You may sleep easy on that, my wife. Nor will the validity of this marriage ever be doubted.'

She could find no words to answer him. She was deeply relieved that she would not yet be forced to give her body to him—yet she could not prevent a niggling disappointment from clouding her heartfelt gratitude for his forbearance.

She thought, resentfully, that he considered her a child still and this jibe hurt and thrust deep at her inner pride. Worse than that, she knew that the ghost of his former betrothed had once more come between them. He would not have been so restrained and considerate had Elinor Maudsley lain by his side.

She felt immediately guilty. How could she be jealous of a dead woman, especially since she had no love for her new husband?

Could she ever be a true wife to Martyn Telford, Earl of Wroxeter? She was his Countess, had seen evidence already of her new-found nobility in the way she had been treated at that splendid feast, even by those ladies who had formerly been seen to despise her. The Lady Elizabeth had not accompanied the Queen to her chamber. She would have liked to have her good wishes too, but perhaps Elizabeth knew of Wroxeter's dislike of her and had decided not to embarrass Cressida within his presence.

She moved restlessly beside him but he did not stir. She must prove herself worthy of the title, must learn to rule his household wisely, prove a welcoming and efficient hostess to his noble companions. It would not be easy. Would he always compare her best efforts with those of his lost love, so clearly better suited to be his bride? She gave a half-suppressed sigh in the darkness, turned on her side and tried to compose herself to sleep.

CHAPTER FIVE

CRESSIDA had expected the Strand house to be more commodious than her father's lodging in the city, but she was totally unprepared for the luxurious splendour of her husband's town property. She was conveyed there from Westminster in the Earl's private river barge, rowed by four oarsmen wearing his livery. In the stern was a covered area to protect the noble travellers from the elements.

She sat by his side, warmly wrapped in a cloak lined with squirrel fur, his squire, Peter Fairley, facing them, while she watched the smooth muscle-play of the oarsmens' backs as they plied their oars against the salt-laden fierce wind. The water was pewter-grey and the sky leaden. Cressida thought that the weather reflected the depth of her spirits on this miserable day when she moved to her new home.

She had taken a tearful farewell of her parents, only slightly comforted by the knowledge that they intended to stay a while longer in the city. At all events, the bad weather would prevent them from making the long journey back to the Marches for some days yet. She had received from them a promise that they would visit her before leaving.

Alice was to travel with the sumpter mules and baggage waggons, which would convey Cressida's dowry in plate and linen, besides her chests of clothing and personal belongings, to the Strand. Her old nurse, at least, was to remain with her, a confidante and friend. Cressida could not have borne to be parted from everyone from her former life.

The Queen had given her leave to be absent from

117

her duties at Court for two weeks or longer if the Earl should request that.

'My dear,' she had said fondly, 'you will take quite all of that time to make yourself acquainted with the house and its appointments, besides getting to know the staff. Enjoy the time Martyn can spare to be with you. I know he is particularly busied about the King's affairs, but this time is important for both of you. Use it well.'

Cressida was by no means sure that she wanted any time free to spend in her husband's company, nor did she think that he was too anxious to spend time with her. They had breakfasted together almost in silence this first morning of their new life together.

Cressida had been unwilling to meet Alice's enquiring eyes when her maid had come to wake her. She had spent a wakeful night, lying still and straight beside her husband's muscular form, afraid to disturb him. Finally she had drifted off into an emotionally drained doze after the dawn had thrust spears of grey light through the gaps in the shuttered windows.

When she had roused at Alice's gentle but imperative shaking, it was to find her husband already risen and gone to dress in an adjoining chamber. Alice had brought warmed water for her toilet and helped her dress after sweeping up the used sheets and thrusting them into a wicker basket to be collected by one of the palace's laundry maids.

She had made no comment, nor had she questioned Cressida, to her profound relief, but when Cressida had turned and impulsively hugged her Alice had stroked her hair gently as her mother had done the previous night and the embrace had been sufficient to comfort the stricken girl.

She turned now to look at the Earl's averted face as he gazed abstractedly over the water. He did not appear angry, but she saw that his brows were drawn together as if in deep thought and she wondered what problem was troubling him. Not, she thought, concern for his young wife's injured feelings.

She told herself, irritatedly, that she was fortunate that he would not prove importunate as she had feared, but she would have liked some evidence of his attention to her at this moment, when everything in her world was fast becoming so frighteningly strange.

The barge ground against the private landing stage and the oarsmen lifted their oars in unison. A liveried servant, waiting ready for their arrival, made haste to make fast the barge and the Earl stepped out, then leant down, hand outstretched, to help Cressida from the barge. He hastened her through the dank garden to the rear of the house and into the hall.

The undercroft was of red brick, the upper storey of timber and lath, but she saw in one hasty glance from the outside that all the windows were glazed and the plasterwork was newly maintained and bright with lime-wash. A stately steward came to greet them, bowing low. He was so impressive that Cressida almost felt inclined to answer his greeting with a deep curtsey of her own. He had drawn up the senior members of the household for her perusal, but the Earl waved away his steward's anxiety to present them, murmuring hastily that the Countess was cold and wished only to have mulled ale and cakes served in her solar.

'Send up the Countess's maid, Mistress Croft, when she arrives, and see to the disposal of the Countess's baggage. There will be time in plenty for her ladyship to come to know the other members of the household. I wish a cold dinner served in my chamber. I am needed at a council meeting later this afternoon and shall need the barge ready at the steps prompt for two of the clock.'

Cressida smiled at the steward, who bowed again and preceded them to the foot of the stair. The Earl himself divested her of her cloak and hood and handed them to Peter, attentive as ever, behind him.

The house seemed immense, even to her eyes, used to the comforts of Gretton. Through the screen door she had glimpsed a sight of the dining hall and, opposite the stair, another half-opened door which she presumed led to the winter parlour. Above stairs the Earl established her into the comfort of the solar, bright with firelight and luxurious, with finely painted plastered walls and carpets from the East upon polished floorboards. She gave a little gasp of wonder at the court cupboards laden with silver and the jewel-like colours of the wall tapestries.

Two cushioned chairs stood at either side of the hearth and the Earl smilingly indicated that she should seat herself.

'This will be your domain. I have a small study and office where I deal with household accounts and interview the servants. I will see to it that you are soon shown to your sleeping chamber. There is a smaller room adjoining for Alice.

'The house is well run. You will find Master Rawlings most efficient. He needs to be. I am rarely at home these days. The King has need of my services and affairs in France keep me constantly occupied.

'I have given instructions that you are to be instantly obeyed and all your wishes granted. Eventually you will want to make some changes in household arrangements and you will find Master Rawlings amenable, but, for the present, allow yourself time to discover what is needful. Your mother has prepared you well, I know, for the management of a household, but do not be alarmed; I shall not expect too much of you too soon.'

Cressida managed a half-smile. There it was again, this tacit reminder that he considered her too young and immature to cope with the usual tasks expected of a wife. Elinor Maudsley would have known immediately what was required of her.

A serving girl came in with a tray and a youthful page who had opened the door for the girl came forward hurriedly to pour ale for his master and lady. Cressida gave the boy a nervous glance. Was she expected to school him in music and song? She played the lute well enough and was told she possessed a pleasing enough voice, but she had never given those accomplishments a great deal of attention, preferring to be out of doors frequently when at Gretton.

The Earl was clearly in a great hurry to leave her and be about his own affairs. She felt a total stranger and at a loss in her own house. Tears were very near the surface again and she angrily controlled the pricking of her lashes. She had never been one to use such wiles to gain her attention. With or without her husband by her side she would take control of this grand house and, most likely, she would be better able to achieve that in his absence, which she believed would be frequent.

After noon when he had departed Cressida sat disconsolately staring into the fire. She was unused to inactivity. Always at Gretton she had been busied about the house or out riding.

She had examined her sleeping chamber with Alice and overseen the unpacking of her baggage. The room was as splendid as she had expected and newly prepared for her. Obviously the brocaded curtains round the bed and matching coverlet had been only recently purchased, though she had wondered fleetingly if indeed Lord Martyn had readied the chamber for his former love. She had cast that thought aside with the dour knowledge that Elinor would undoubtedly have shared her husband's chamber.

No, all this, including the beautiful wall hanging depicting an Attic hunting scene—French, and wickedly expensive—beside the finely carved and upholstered prie-dieu which matched her bed-covering, had clearly been bought for her.

Wearily she had acknowledged that since everything was in such pristine order there was nothing she could set her hand to. She had never been an accomplished needlewoman, had often complained about the necessity to learn the art, which her mother had patiently taught her, but repairs to worn arras would have provided some occupation and here none was needed.

Alice had gone off to stitch the hem of Cressida's bridal gown which had been torn, caught on her chair during the banquet, and Cressida had been somewhat relieved that that had necessitated a search for suitable thread. She was lonely, certainly, but did not wish to sit opposite her maid and try to conceal her sinking spirits from her. Alice was very shrewd. Already she must have divined that all was not well between her master and mistress.

Cressida tapped an impatient foot. This would not do. She refused to be confined to her room like a refractory child. She summoned attendance by ringing a small silver hand-bell laid ready for her use upon the table. In seconds the same page who had waited on them earlier tapped and entered. She was sure he must have been waiting outside.

He bowed low. She smiled at him reassuringly for she thought she detected an anxious look on his youthful features. Was the Earl so fierce a taskmaster that his attendants feared physical punishment if they did not appear promptly at his command?

'What is your name, boy?'

'Philip, my lady. Philip Kenton.'

She judged him to be about ten years old. He was small and almost skinny, a brown-haired, elfish child. He stood, moving his weight nervously from one foot to another.

'Come here, near to me. There is nothing to be frightened of. Have you been appointed to wait on me?'

'Yes, my lady. The Earl said I was not to leave your side for a moment.'

'So you wait outside my door?'

'Yes, my lady. You only have to ring the bell.'

'Yes, well, I do not think it will be necessary for you to dog my every footstep, not when I am used to the house. Take me on a tour of inspection, Philip. I have yet to see the winter parlour and the downstairs chambers.'

He bowed again and waited until she rose, and then went to open the door for her.

'You resemble Peter Fairley,' she said as she signalled for him to walk beside her. 'Are you related?'

'Yes, my lady. Peter is my cousin. Our mothers are sisters. My father died last year and my lord Earl immediately took me into his service. My mother is most grateful.'

Cressida nodded. Poor child, to lose both father and home at one fell swoop and to be catapulted into the service of a demanding master who clearly terrified him.

She nodded her satisfaction at the condition of the winter parlour, acknowledging the hurried curtsies of two waiting maids who scurried by her in the corridor, then paused with her hand on the opposite door.

Philip said quickly, 'That is my lord's study, my lady. He allows no one to enter without being specially commanded to do so.'

She smiled thinly. 'So you think he would not wish me to do so. Does he conceal Bluebeard's secret?'

The boy flushed darkly but looked blank. He was unacquainted with the tale, she thought, and did not understand her grim pleasantry. She did not insist upon her right to enter. Philip believed that he would be in dire trouble if she persisted and she had no desire to worry him further. She had seen her husband's study at Westminster. If this room was similarly dismal she had no wish to be further acquainted with it.

'Now take me to the kitchen—the most important room of the house, don't you agree, Philip? Perhaps we can coax the cook into providing us with honey cakes. You could do with some feeding up.'

'I should request Master Rawlings. . .'

'Nonsense. Why should we trouble him? Surely I have right of entry into my own kitchens?'

'Master Wainwright is very fussy. . .'

'No doubt he is. So am I, Philip.'

The boy's face fell, but obediently he led her to the back of the house.

Even before she reached the cavernous domain of the cook she could hear his voice lifted in furious admonition.

'You thieving, lying little toad. Do I take you into my kitchen to laze away the hours? I set you to watch the spit and ye cannot even do that to my satisfaction.'

The booming tone was accompanied by the sounds of blows falling on hapless shoulders and squeals of protest. Cressida lifted her skirts and forgot her dignity in her race into the overheated, frenzied activity of the principal kitchen.

The victim of abuse and summary punishment was cowering away from the biggest man Cressida had ever seen. He was a positive giant, barrel-chested, powerfully built, looming over his captive, whom he held down with one great paw on the thin shoulder, while with his other hand he rained down blow after blow on the boy's back with the long, flat wooden paddle he used to draw fresh-baked bread from the oven.

The recipient of his fury had slipped to his knees and, since the breath had been knocked from his body by the onslaught, had ceased to protest or cry out, but remained almost prone on the stone floor, making no further resistance.

The page tried to call out a warning, but Cressida ignored him as she did the startled glances of cooking maids and scullions as she erupted into the kitchen and called an imperative command for the cook to cease punishment.

'Stop it; stop it at once. You will kill the boy. Can't you see how frightened he is?'

'Aye, and will be more so when I've done with him,' the cook boomed, and dealt yet another blow.

The boy collapsed on the floor, attempting to shield his head with his hands.

Cressida marched up to the pair, her blue eyes smouldering with rage. She could not bear to see cruelty to any creature. No one at Gretton, not even the youngest scullion or stable-boy, was treated so.

'I said stop it.' Her voice was raised to a screech in an effort to make herself heard over the loud accents of the giant. 'How dare you, sir, treat a child so, and so small a one, and you so great a bully?'

The cook, desisting from further punishment, straightened to face her, hand on hip. He had a big round face, perspiring from the heat of the huge fire in the hearth, from which spiky, dark, short hair was thrust back from his bulging forehead. 'And who in the devil's name be you to give me orders in me own kitchen?'

'I am the Countess of Wroxeter,' Cressida snapped, 'and your mistress. You will obey me and refrain from bullying the boy.'

'Boy, is it?' The giant put back his huge head and laughed until tears came to his eyes. 'Aye, he's a boy in years and the devil incarnate in wickedness. Leave him to me, my lady, as his lordship would do. He'd tell you not to interfere and that's the truth of it.'

'That's as may be,' Cressida returned haughtily, 'but

now the kitchen and the well-being of the servants are my responsibility, and I tell you now I'll have no deliberate cruelty meted out to anyone in my service. Do you hear me?'

The cook lowered the paddle and stared back at her unblinking. He showed no deference but continued to stand, legs straddled, regarding her defiantly.

'Aye, my lady, I hear you right enough and I tell ye to ye're face, you're wrong to challenge me rule here. The lad deserves what he got.'

Cressida was breathing hard. Her gaze went beyond him to the round-eyed onlookers. The kitchen showed signs of the usual frantic activity before supper was prepared, but was in good order like everything else in the house. She could not doubt that this hectoring fellow was well served. She turned back to him slowly and deliberately.

'My lord informs me that I am to be instantly and implicitly obeyed by all in this house,' she said icily. 'I repeat, I will have no cruelty, whatever the cause. Send the boy to his sleeping quarters. He'll need treatment for his bruises before he resumes his duties. Disobey me again and I will see to it that you are dismissed, Master Cook. I am mistress here and will brook no challenge to my authority.'

There was a concerted gasp from the assembled wenches, who stood open-mouthed, paring-knives stilled in their chapped work-worn hands behind the chopping blocks. The cook expelled his breath in a little hiss and looked over her head towards the door.

The quiet, authoritative tones of the steward broke across the embarrassed silence.

'Is there trouble here, my lady? Please return to the solar and I will deal with this matter for you.'

She said between gritted teeth, 'I do not wish to have matters dealt with for me. I am capable of asserting my own authority. This boy is injured. See to it that he is

tended.' She swung on her heel. 'I will take up this
matter with his lordship on his return to the house.
Philip, escort me back to the solar.'

When Alice joined her later she had stopped shaking
with anger and was poring over a printed book from
Master Caxton's press at Westminster, reading a tale
she had not encountered before about the knights of
the legendary King Arthur. She recalled the night she
had seen enacted the sinister story of the Green Knight
and shivered again at the thought of that terrible
beheading. She did not acquaint Alice with what had
happened in the kitchens.

She ate alone in the hall. Lord Martyn had apparently been kept late at Westminster. Cressida picked
idly at her food, while Philip Kenton served her attentively. The fare was excellently cooked and served and
she gave a little sniff as she thought of that odious
man's reign in the kitchen. She must find out more
about him, how long he had been in Lord Wroxeter's
service.

At the close of the lonely meal she returned to the
solar and, again, picked up the book. Alice, opposite,
was busily engaged in sewing seed-pearls on a frontal.
Cressida gave a little sigh. She would be relieved when
she could return to attendance upon the Queen. She
was bored and restless. She wondered what business in
the city continued to occupy her father and how long it
would be before Howell Prosser returned home to the
Marches.

There came a tap at the door and Cressida called
permission to enter. Peter Fairley came in and bowed.

'My lady, my lord Earl requests your presence in his
study. He will not keep you long, since he is sure you
will soon wish to retire.'

Cressida glanced up at the squire sharply. Was she
to be summoned to her husband's study like a naughty
child? Why could he not have waited upon her in

person here in the solar? She was about to snap out a
refusal when she met Alice's warning glance and the
hard words froze on her lips. Such a response could
only bring down wrath upon poor Peter's head and she
was becoming aware that retribution fell fast upon any
recalcitrant servant in this house. She nodded and rose.

'Alice, will you go and prepare my bedchamber? I
shall not be long.'

It was no longer necessary for Alice to accompany
her when alone in her husband's presence, yet she
could not brush off the notion that she was not yet
truly a wife.

Peter opened the study door for her respectfully then
withdrew. Her husband was seated at an oaken table
strewn with unrolled parchment and held a quill. He
wrote his own letters, then, and did not employ a
secretary as many nobles did.

She advanced and he looked up and leaned back
lazily in his chair. She was somewhat relieved. She had
had the feeling he was angry with her and yet she could
think of no reason—unless— She frowned. Surely he
could not object to her exercising authority in her own
household? She tilted her chin and tapped an impatient
foot.

'Peter tells me you wish to speak to me. Why you
could not have—'

'Please sit down.' He had risen now courteously and
was pointing to the chair opposite the table.

'Peter said the matter was urgent, but I was about
to—'

'Please, Cressida, sit down. I asked you to come here
since this study is absolutely private. No one will dare
to approach, let alone enter, without specific instructions to do so, and I do not wish to be overheard.'

She subsided sulkily into the chair. Again she had
the helpless, lost feeling that a prisoner must have felt
when facing an interrogator—or jailor. Now she was

his possession, chattel; she considered herself a prisoner in this house, luxurious as the prison was.

'Rawlings has informed me about the contretemps in the kitchen. I thought we should talk about it quietly.'

She stared back at him, her eyes sparking blue fire. 'Do you take me to task for coming to the assistance of a badly used boy. . .?'

'I take no one to task. I said I wished to talk to you about it.'

She was irritated by his easy, pleasant mien and the way those hooded eyes of his hid his true reaction from her. There was steel behind that slow, leisurely manner and perversely she wished he would come straight out with it and express anger if that was what he felt.

He was leaning back in the chair again. 'I simply wish to put you in the picture. That "badly used boy", as you term him, is a lazy, idle good-for-nothing I have brought with me from my Welsh manor because, for the third time, I have had to rescue him from being hanged for poaching and theft. I could wish to leave him to the fate he so richly deserves, but that his mother has wept and pleaded with me to save him. She was my wet nurse and I love her dearly.

'Wat Forrester is the last of her brood and she dotes on the rogue. Unfortunately he does not take after her or his brothers, my foster brothers, and constantly gets into trouble. I decided that the only thing I could do was to remove him from temptation and bring him here to the city and put him under Jack Wainwright's control. If anyone can discipline the lad, Jack's the fellow to do it.'

'By harsh physical punishment?'

The lazy eyelids swept back and he regarded her steadily.

'You would prefer that I had left the boy to his fate?'

'I do not like cruelty to underlings. The man is a bully. . .'

'Jack Wainwright is a soldier and a very fine cook to boot. I'm sure you have no complaint to make about supper.'

'Of course not, but it does not excuse the man from beating the scullions.'

He smiled infuriatingly. 'Cressida, I'm sure your father found it necessary now and then to discipline men on his own manor.' His brown eyes twinkled. 'Possibly his own daughter.'

'My father has never once laid a hand upon me in anger.'

He smiled and she thought angrily that he was considering that perhaps she would not have been so impetuous or difficult if he had. Again she would rather he had said it openly than play this tantalising game of reasoning with her.

'Jack has been on campaign with me over the last six years. He is a valued servant—and friend. I trust him with the boy. He could get service in any household he chose. If left to his own devices I suspect he would rather leave me to return to active service, but he knows I depend on him. I would be grateful, Cressida, if you do not impel him to do so.'

She drew a hard breath. 'In other words, I am not to interfere, not to be mistress in my own house?'

'I did not say that. I asked you to take time to become acquainted with the method of service here. No one will countermand your orders. Rawlings would not have told me of this affair, and Jack has not complained, but the boy has gone missing and Rawlings knows I am anxious to prevent his being taken by the Watch on some foolish expedition into the city.

'We can only hope he will return when his belly is empty and that he does not find other ways of filling it by more nefarious means. I simply wanted you to know the circumstances of this particular incident so that you can avoid open conflict over the lad in the future.'

She felt considerably deflated and childish. Of course she should not have rushed into the situation without acquainting herself with the details. The steward would have settled the matter for her if she had consulted him. Her mother would have castigated her for undue haste in judgement. She swallowed hard to keep back a sudden rush of tears. She had acted childishly, giving the household a picture of her as a spoilt, impetuous mistress too anxious to have her own way.

'You wish me to speak with this man, Wainwright, apologise for...?'

'Certainly not. You are mistress here. That would give quite the wrong impression. Jack understands that perfectly well. I shall not refer to the matter with him, now or at any time. I can only hope damage has not been done to young Wat's chance of survival. Frankly I do not give him the possibility of a long life if he doesn't mend his ways, and I see little hope of that at present.'

She rose and curtsied. 'I will consult with Master Rawlings before taking any further action or reproving any of the servants. Now, with your permission, I will retire. I am very tired.'

It was the last thing she wished to do, but she had to get out of his presence before he reduced her to useless tears.

Smilingly, he rose to accompany her politely to the door where Peter Fairley waited patiently to escort her to her chamber.

Alice had prepared her bed and was waiting to help her undress. Though she looked at Cressida curiously she asked no questions. As she was preparing to go to her own adjoining chamber Cressida said, 'Alice, will you find that young page, Philip Kenton, the one who attended me in the hall this evening, and ask him to come to me?'

Alice gave a puzzled shrug and went about her

errand. She stood stoutly in the doorway when she brought the boy back with her. As usual his expression was anxious and Cressida quickly reassured him that he was in no trouble.

'Philip, I want you to find out if anything more has been heard of that young scullion who was being beaten today. I understand he ran away.'

The boy's expression cleared. 'Oh, he's back, my lady. Master Wainwright—that's the cook—went out with two of my lord's men-at-arms to look for him. They found him in a tavern on the South Wark and it's said Master Wainwright cuffed him about the ear and dragged him back to Wroxeter House.'

'Oh.' Cressida smiled thinly. 'I'm glad to know he's safe. Master Wainwright will not thrash him, do you think?'

The boy grinned. 'His bark is worse than his bite, my lady. He caught me stealing some tarts one day and I feared for my life, but he cuffed me and sent me off. He didn't tell my lord Earl, either. He's harsh, but he's fair, they say.'

'Good. Thank you, Philip. I thought the boy might have come to harm in one of the thieves' sanctuaries. You can go now, and goodnight.'

Alice said dourly, 'And what was that all about, if I dare ask?' as the page scurried off.

Cressida said, a little breathlessly, 'Oh, I interfered in his punishment and I've discovered he's a decided rogue. My lord Earl is constantly trying to keep him from trouble.'

'Ah.' Alice's single syllable summed up her opinion of Cressida's incursion into discipline at Wroxeter House.

Some twenty minutes later Cressida lay in her lonely bed, wondering wryly why she was finding it so. Most of her life she had slept alone and been glad of it. Now, strangely, she felt that she had been cheated. She had been as good as instructed to keep silent about house-hold affairs and her husband kept from her bed; not a state of affairs her mother would have approved of.

Next morning, again in the solar, working with Alice upon the embroidering of another velvet frontal for her court headdress, Philip admitted master Rawlings.

The steward bowed low. 'A Master Prosser has arrived, my lady, and asks if you will receive him.'

She started up from her chair eagerly. 'Oh, yes, at once, Master Rawlings. Master Howell Prosser is a family friend newly come to London. I shall be very glad to see him.'

The steward nodded gravely. 'And is there any matter on which I can render you assistance today, my lady?'

She flushed, recalling the man's presence at the undignified scene in the kitchen.

'No, no, thank you. The house appears to be run excellently in your hands, Master Rawlings.'

Again he nodded gravely and withdrew, to return only moments later to admit Howell Prosser to the solar.

Cressida advanced to meet him, all smiles, her hands outstretched in welcome. 'Howell, how good it is of you to call.'

Alice withdrew to the window embasure and Cressida could not miss the slight tightening of her maid's lips as she bent her head industriously over her needlework.

Howell's lips brushed Cressida's cheek as he mur-mured that he hoped he was allowed the privilege of kissing kin. For a moment the lips lingered longer than ever before when he had greeted her in company, and, blushing even more now, she led him to a chair near to the hearth and sat opposite.

'I hope this does not mean that you have come to

say goodbye, Howell. You do not intend to leave the capital yet awhile?'

'I came to say farewell, but only for a short time. I must travel to Dover on an errand for my father.' He grimaced. 'Something to do with wool sales to Calais. You would not wish to know the boring details.'

He thought how very beautiful she looked, flushed and rosy with her delight at seeing him. She wore a velvet gown in green, which brought out a hitherto unknown greenish tint in her irises, making those glorious eyes almost aquamarine in the light from the oriel window. The particular soft tint of green, the colour of elf land, made his heart race, adding as it did to her exquisite fairy beauty.

'I was afraid my lord Earl might refuse me permission to see you.'

'He is not in the house. He is at Westminster or the Tower. There seem to be so many hastily convened council meetings held there these days.'

'He leaves you alone so soon after marriage?'

She looked down at the priceless Eastern carpet, veiling her embarrassment from him. 'He is very busied about the King's affairs. News from France is not good, I hear.'

'No,' he said grimly. 'Not for the King, at all events. You have heard, I imagine, that Henry Tudor has made it plain that he wishes to wed the Lady Elizabeth?'

'I do not think that likely,' Cressida laughed. 'Not unless he usurps King Richard's throne.'

'You would call that usurpation? He is King Henry of Lancaster's only surviving heir.'

She looked round hurriedly, placing a warning finger upon her lip. 'You speak treason, Howell. Henry Tudor has no strong claim, and that only from the illegitimate line of the Beauforts. In any case, the King's throne is firmly occupied.'

'Not all are satisfied,' he said softly. 'Your father

being one of them as mine is. I suppose you have heard about Sir Roger Clifford's execution?'

Cressida looked startled. 'Sir Roger Clifford? I do not think I have heard of him.'

'Aye, he was taken near Southampton, arraigned and tried.' Howell shrugged. 'He could not hope for mercy. The Yorkist Princes have never forgiven the Cliffords for their support of the Lancastrian cause.

'When he was being drawn on the hurdle to Tower Hill, the escort had to pass through the sanctuary of St Martin le Grand. The common people were so incensed at his sentence, they tried to pull him from the hurdle and help him escape. His confessor was urging those about him to save him and the attempt almost succeeded—would have done so had not the sheriff's officers summoned assistance. They managed to hold him down till other men-at-arms arrived and dragged him off to his execution.'

Cressida shuddered. 'Did he—did he die the terrible traitor's death?'

'He was beheaded but it's said that afterwards his body was cloven in two.'

Cressida was appalled by such senseless brutality.

'Sweet Virgin, I would not have thought such malice to be in the King's nature.'

Howell nodded. 'He fears insurrection is in the very air. There is trouble in Hammes Castle, near Calais. The Earl of Oxford has been imprisoned there since soon after poor King Henry's death. He managed to suborn the governer, James Blount, to release him, and, to cap all, Blount has fled with his former prisoner to Henry Tudor and the castle is ready to withhold a siege by the King's forces.'

'But King Richard is powerful enough to break the siege and hold the castle?'

'Oh, I am sure of it, but these happenings show that

even his own people are turning from him. Your father will welcome this news, I'm sure of it.'

'Hush.' Cressida was really alarmed. 'My father speaks well of the King. He has honoured him lately, arranged my marriage.'

'Aye,' Howell said bitterly. 'I know that right enough. How did I manage to contain myself during the wedding feast? I cannot bear to think of you in that fellow's arms.'

Taken off her guard, she said quickly, 'You need not distress yourself over thoughts of that, Howell.'

He stared at her dumbfounded, and she realised, too late, that she had betrayed her neglected state.

Hoarsely, he said, 'He has not—does not—?' He was leaning very close to her and Cressida, frightened now that she had revealed so much, heard Alice stir restlessly on the window seat.

She lowered her head, flustered, and whispered, 'He considers me a child still.'

'By all the saints, the man is an arrant fool,' Howell said fiercely. 'Then I am to believe you are not yet a wife?'

She shook her head slowly, feeling the warmth well up from her breasts to her throat.

'Does your father know?'

'No, of course not—and is not to be told. Howell, you must not shame me. I should not have let you know. . .'

He was staring at her intently and she avoided his eyes. 'There is no shame in your virgin state, Cressida. I, for one, thank God for it. Who knows? It may well be fortunate in the time to come that you are so.'

'Howell,' she stammered, thoroughly frightened now by the gritty determination of his tone, 'these are early days of my marriage. The King would never consent to an annulment, whatever the circumstances.'

'No, he would not,' Howell agreed, 'but affairs might not always stand as they do now.'

She put out a hand and touched his fiercely beating heart. 'Howell, watch yourself. There is danger in uttering such words, even to think such thoughts. My husband, the Earl, is a far more ruthless man than you suppose. Do not be fooled by his pliant manner.'

He took her hand and turned the palm to kiss it. 'Do not fear for me or your father, Cressida. Look to yourself and do not despair. When I return from Dover I'll visit you again if allowed. Do you wait attendance again on the Queen?'

'Yes, in a few days I shall return to my duties. I shall be glad to. Time hangs heavily upon my hands here. Everything is so well run I have nothing to do.'

He nodded, smiling, and they rose together as he made his excuses to leave her.

'I need to be well on my way before dark.'

She watched wistfully as he left her. He was a link with the old happy days at Gretton and she hated to see him go.

CHAPTER SIX

CRESSIDA had heard mass and was about to eat breakfast in her own chamber when her husband came
unexpectedly into the room. He dismissed Alice curtly
and flung himself down into a chair near the table.

Cressida asked quietly, 'Have you breakfasted, my
lord?'

'I have. Please make a start if you have not yet done
so.'

Cressida shook her head and sat back, waiting for
him to speak.

He stirred restlessly. 'I understand that fellow
Prosser called on you yesterday in my absence.'

'So Master Rawlings made his report.'

'No, I was informed by—other means.' He avoided
her gaze. 'Rawlings merely confirmed that report when
I questioned him.'

Cressida waited but since he remained silent for a
moment she said mildly, 'Am I to undertand that I
must have your permission to receive visitors, my lord?'

He said testily, 'I wish you would not continue to
address me in that fashion. When we are alone, please
call me Martyn.'

'It is strange to me.'

'That can easily be remedied and will be soon
enough.'

'Yes, but that does not answer my question. You
appear to be angered that I received Howell Prosser
without consulting you. Would I have received
permission?'

'No.'

He was rarely so ill-tempered and Cressida found

herself trembling inwardly, though she made a brave effort not to reveal her doubts.

'I think I explained that Master Prosser is a friend of long standing. He merely called on me to wish me well in my new life and to inform me that he was soon leaving London.'

Wroxeter chewed his nether lip. 'Yes, I am informed that he took the Canterbury road.'

Cressida was astonished. 'So your spy informed you of that too?'

He turned and regarded her deliberately. 'I know you find my retrictions on your acquaintances hard to bear, Cressida, but I have good reason for making them. These are difficult times, as you know very well. It would be better for you not to associate with this man.'

His eyes were hooded again and she knew she would get nowhere, if she protested or tried to question him further. She gave a little sigh.

He sat back in the chair, crossing one long leg over the other. 'I trust everyone in the household has been attentive?'

'Yes, my—Martyn,' she corrected herself tonelessly.

'I regret that events have forced me to be absent from your side so much during these early days of our marriage.'

She had reached for manchet bread and was beginning to spread clear honey on it. 'I imagine dealing with condemned men has taken a great deal of your time,' she said coldly. 'I hear Sir Roger Clifford has suffered a barbaric traitor's death. Were you present, my lord, and did it please you to witness the agony of one of the King's enemies?'

He shot up in the chair and she saw his eyes flash dangerously. 'No, I was not, but I am glad to hear you admit the man was a traitor. I imagine you heard of this from Prosser?'

'And if I did? He was merely informing me of the feelings of the common people. I understand there was a vain attempt to free Clifford?'

'Made by his own supporters, yes.' One finger tapped an imperative tattoo upon the tabletop. 'I'm sorry that such information distresses you, but the man was fairly judged and condemned. He was taken in Southampton in possession of treasonable correspondence.'

'Fairly condemned to die, possibly, but was it necessary for the King's spite to extend to treating the man so barbarously?'

Wroxeter's brows drew together in a frown. 'Not so barbarously. Clifford was beheaded as befitted his rank. The King is not a cruel antagonist.'

'But his body was badly mistreated.'

Again he frowned. 'It is not unusual for the bodies of traitors to be quartered and displayed as a measure of deterring others, as you know well enough. Spite does not enter into the matter.'

'But the Cliffords have always opposed the House of York, or so I—was told,' she finished uneasily, aware of the source of that information.

'Did your informant also tell you that it was a Clifford who cut down the King's brother, young Edmund of Rutland, on Wakefield Bridge?' His tone was scathing. 'The battle was well over, the Duke scarcely more than a boy and fighting his first battle. It would have cost nothing to spare him, but he was butchered for all that.'

Cressida was appalled. In her mind's eye she saw that terrible moment, the young Duke at bay, surrounded by his enemies, possibly pleading for his life.

She swallowed hard. Only too well she realised that family fueds grew from such battle-hardened occurrences. So the King could be understood to hold a grudge against such a family and, if Martyn was to be believed, had held his hand from condemning his enemy, caught in an act of dire treason, to suffer the agonies of the traitors' death of disembowelling.

'I—I feel for all men—so slain,' she said uncomfortably.

'Indeed,' he said tartly, 'and for that reason I spared you all talk of it.' He rose to his feet and leaned both hands on the table to look down at her. 'Prosser has no business to discuss matters of policy with you and you would be wise not to repeat the fellow's opinions—to anyone,' he asserted harshly. 'Do you understand what I say?'

'I am not a fool, sir.'

'No, you are not a fool,' he said slowly. 'No one would excuse you for incautious talk on that premise. Particularly, you are not to talk of these matters within the Queen's hearing when you return to your duties. She is not well and is not to be distressed by talk of any antagonism to the King's will.'

He was holding her gaze with his brown eyes and she looked away at last and nodded in acceptance of his command. He sighed. She was determined to oppose him and it was essential that he keep her from all harmful influences. Later he would attempt to win her heart so that they could dwell more comfortably together during the long years ahead of them.

He was about to leave her when Peter Fairley knocked urgently upon the door of the chamber. Martyn bade him enter.

'Yes, Peter, what is it? I shall be down and ready to leave soon.'

Peter's eyes went anxiously from his master to his mistress. It was obvious to him that matters were tense between them.

'My lord, a messenger has just arrived in haste from Westminster, sent from the Lady Elizabeth Plantagenet. She begs my lady Countess to come quickly to attend on the Queen whose condition has worsened.' He lowered his eyes, concerned at the ill news he brought. 'The messenger said he understood the Queen, poor lady, to have suffered a severe haemorrhage, and that the King's physicians have been summoned urgently to her bedside.'

Cressida gave a little cry of pity. 'Of course; I will come at once. She will need all her ladies near her.' She challenged her husband to refuse his permission, but his stern gaze had already softened and he nodded.

'Aye, Peter. My lady will be at the landing steps within half an hour. Fortunately the barge is all ready for my departure. Send a page to alert Mistress Alice and ask her to prepare a single saddle-bag of belongings and linen to accommodate both herself and her mistress for the next few days.' He turned hastily to Cressida. 'Alice had best accompany you.'

'Yes, of course.' Cressida had already left the table and was turning to her clothing chest to look for a warm cloak and more sensible outdoor footwear.

She heard Martyn say, 'Has the King been informed?'

'I do not know, my lord, or even if he is present at Westminster or already at the Tower in Council.'

Martyn dismissed Peter on his errand and turned to watch Cressida find her more serviceable garments, suitable for the river journey. He muttered uneasily, 'God help Richard now, when he has most need of comfort.'

Cressida sat huddled for warmth against Alice as the barge pulled out from the landing stage and stared miserably over the pewter-grey waters of the river. The Lady Elizabeth had sent for her directly, so, despite all efforts to part her from the Queen, she was still in attendance. If the Queen was spitting blood she was, indeed, very ill. All their forebodings were coming to fulfilment.

Cressida's eyes filled with sudden tears. Poor, gentle lady, who had had sorrows enough over these last months. She would do all in her power to serve and comfort Anne in her need, and Cressida tightened her lips and looked mutinously towards her husband, seated opposite her. The Lady Elizabeth had need of her friendship and services. Nothing was going to prevent her from working alongside the Queen's niece.

The palace seemed unaccountably silent when they arrived. It was thronged to bursting point as usual with officials, courtiers, men-at-arms and clerics and clerks, and they were all talking to each other, but very quietly, each turning to look over his or her shoulder as if what was said might be overheard and give offence.

Cressida shivered and Lord Martyn's grave expression deepened. If the Queen should die, there would be constant speculation about the King's future. The recent death of his only son had left him without heir and he would soon be advised to remarry. Cressida blanched at the very thought. How could these folk think of anyone but the Queen at this moment? She shied from the thought that Lord Martyn had also been badgered to marry soon after the loss of his betrothed—and by the King himself.

At the entrance to the Queen's apartments Lord Martyn took his leave. He drew her close and kissed her full on the lips in full view of several ladies passing in the corridor. She drew away as quickly as she decently might, conscious that many of them envied her. If only they knew, she thought bitterly.

'I shall stay close in my own office. There is a settle there which I can call into service as a bed if need be. Send Alice if you have need of me.'

She curtsied dutifully and waited while Alice went in search of the Lady Elizabeth, unsure whether she should immediately enter the Queen's bedchamber without being summoned.

The King's physician, Dr Hobbes, emerged from the
double doors of the royal apartment, followed by his
young apprentice carrying a bowl covered by a fair
linen cloth. The physican's mouth was held in a tight
line and he gathered his gaberdine robe close to his
thin body as he acknowledged Cressida's presence with
a jerky little nod of his head.

Behind him came Elizabeth of York. The physician
paused for a moment, holding her in talk, then he
bowed low, nodded to his apprentice, and turned and
walked majestically off along the corridor.

Lady Elizabeth came at once to Cressida, her hand
outstretched. 'Thank you for coming. Things are difficult—and delicate. Her Grace's women try to be help-
ful but they gossip.' Her lips tightened. 'You are my
friend, Cressida; I can be easy with you.'

'How is the Queen?'

Elizabeth shook her head. 'There has been no further
bleeding, but she coughs constantly and exhausts herself. As you saw, Dr Hobbes is concerned and—' she
shrugged helplessly '—over-careful not to alarm the
King too much, but. . .'

'Does he realise how gravely ill she is?'

'Richard?' Elizabeth's blue eyes grew dark with pity.
'Oh, yes; how can he fail to? And Richard was never
one to refuse to face up to reality. He has seen too
much horror to deceive himself.'

'And the Queen?' Cressida whispered pitifully.
'Does she know truly—how serious her condition is?'

Elizabeth's eyes were wet with tears. 'She knows
well enough she is dying. She—she tries so hard to—
keep from breaking down—lest—lest she distresses the
King further. He is the light of her life.'

Cressida's lips parted soundlessly. 'Sweet Virgin help
them both,' she murmured softly.

'Come now. I told her I had sent for you and she is
anxious to see you.'

The Queen was propped high up on the embroidered pillows. As the Lady Elizabeth advanced to the bed with Cressida in tow her attendants withdrew. Anne was deadly pale but for a hectic flush which darkened her cheeks and her lips were bloodless, but she was breathing more easily for the moment. She greeted Cressida with a roguish smile.

'Ah, our lovely child bride. How does married life suit you, little Cressida?'

Cressida curtsied low. She smiled bravely, determined that the Queen should not glimpse the alarm she felt at the drastic change she perceived in Anne's appearance, and after only a few short days.

'I am very well, Your Grace, and glad to see you resting. They tell me your cough has been giving you trouble.'

Anne's smile broadened. 'It will give me less trouble soon. No,' she said, putting out a gentle hand to Cressida's shoulder, 'do not turn from me to hide your pity. Though you are very young, I realise you are practical and brave and honest—too honest to try to deceive me with useless comfort. I am glad to have you with me, though I would rather not have spoilt these early days of marriage for you.'

'Your Grace knows that my lord Martyn loves you well and is ever willing to spare me for your need.'

'He is a loyal friend,' Anne said softly. 'Richard will need more like him when—when the time comes. Thank the Sweet Virgin he has them—Frank Lovell, Dick Ratcliffe, Rob Percy—so many true companions. I shall not fear for him—whatever transpires. I know he is brave and stalwart. He will suffer, but—later—he will do what is best for the realm.'

Cressida was accommodated in her old chamber and for the next few days worked alongside the Lady Elizabeth. Their duties were light since the Queen was too ill now to leave her bed. All they could do for her was to keep her comfortable and amuse her as best they might. The cough came and went, sometimes tearing the frail body almost apart.

At those times when she was seated beside the bed, Cressida felt a chill of fear. She had never nursed someone so close to death, had never felt that angel's icy breath on her cheek before. Her parents had remained healthy throughout her childhood and her only griefs had been for pet dogs. Certainly she had suffered then, deeply, for she had a sensitive and affectionate nature, but this long-drawn-out agony touched her to her very soul.

The King spent as much time with his dying Queen as possible. He was gentle with her, tending her intimately when there was need. His eyes were deep-shadowed and his mouth close-held. It was impossible to gauge the depth of his suffering. He would draw apart with Dr Hobbes, nodding gravely at the physician's instructions, and his gratitude to the Lady Elizabeth was marked.

Once Cressida saw him, just outside the chamber, stoop and take Elizabeth's hands within his grasp and kiss them fiercely, then he strode off to his own apartments as if he could no longer linger in the vicinity of the chamber where his wife lay stricken.

Lord Martyn presented himself often at the sick room. Always the Queen would greet him cheerfully and he would remain by her side, joking with her, chatting about the old days at Middleham Castle.

On one occasion he drew Cressida outside when the Queen began to cough harshly and Dr Hobbes was summoned.

'You are very young to have this charge,' he said, his voice harsh with emotion. 'We shall all understand if you feel this is too much for you to bear, if you are afraid. . .'

She stared back at him, blue eyes wide and blazing. 'Of course I am afraid. We all fear for her, the Lady Elizabeth most of all. That does not mean that we wish to run away.'

He was looking intently into her eyes and bent to tilt up her chin with one gentle finger.

'You are having to grow up very fast, little Cressida. I am sorry for it, but I applaud your spirit. Do what you can for Anne. She deserves all our prayers and good service.'

'She is not neglected for a moment; the Lady Elizabeth sees to that,' Cressida said fiercely.

He turned from her for a moment and when he again looked full at her she saw that his eyes were troubled.

She was both disturbed and angry when he left her to return to his duties. Why did he continue to consider her a child? Why could he not acknowledge the fact that events had forced maturity and it was a true woman who attended the Queen and waited, though with inner trembling, for the foreshadowing of death which must come soon?

She was taking a hasty break from attendance in the sick chamber later that morning, sitting on a window seat within an oriel of the hall, when a page approached.

'My lady Countess, there is a man asking to speak with you on the river terrace. He says he is a family friend and has news...'

Cressida stared at the boy sharply. 'He gave no name?'

'No, my lady; he is a young man, finely but plainly dressed, brown-haired...'

'Yes, I know the man.' She rose at once, her heart beating fast. 'If I am needed in the Queen's chamber come to the terrace and summon me immediately. Do not wait.'

'Yes, my lady.'

She had snatched up a cloak earlier, knowing she might need to slip from the overheated apartment for a while, and the rooms outside the Queen's chamber were still chilly. March had come, but there was little sign of approaching spring yet. Cressida sighed as she made her way through the courtyards towards the terrace. A cold wind was blowing hard from the river and the brown earth of the palace pleasance was still barren of shoots. The Queen would be unlikely to see the earth burgeon.

So Howell had returned from Dover. She hoped fervently that Lord Martyn was closeted with the King. He had forbidden her to see Howell Prosser without his permission, and Howell must have had some suspicion of this for he had begged word with her privately.

She had no need of news from her parents. They had called at the palace only two days ago. They had not been able to see the Queen—she had been sleeping—but Cressida had spent a hasty hour with them and received reassurance that all was well with them and matters were as usual at Gretton.

She had been almost relieved that her time with them was so short and there was no opportunity for them to question her about her relationship with Martyn. Her father had said little, but Cressida believed her mother had been more perceptive, though she had tightened her lips and had not pressed matters. Cressida hoped that her reserve with them had been put down to her concern for the Queen.

Howell was waiting in an angle of the river wall, his brown-hooded cloak pulled well up, hiding his features from passers-by who came and went between the landing steps and the palace. Cressida had pulled her own fur-lined cloak around her against the dank chill of the morning and her hood was drawn carefully over the intricate folds of the wired butterfly veiling of her court hennin.

'I needed to see you. The boy was not averse to taking coin and promised to approach you when you were alone.'

She was somewhat breathless for she had hurried, but was aware that some of her fast breathing was due to the illicit nature of this meeting.

'I am glad to see you, Howell, naturally, but I do not think you should have risked coming here.'

'Your lordly husband has forbidden all contact with me, eh?'

'Not exactly, but he insists on being present or at least that he gives his permission.'

Howell was stooping to kiss her fingers, and so passionately that she began to move nervously away.

'We must be careful. We must not be seen.

He shrugged lightly. 'There is so much coming and going in and out of the palace, no one will have time or interest in our doings.'

Cressida looked up as two officials hurried by talking earnestly.

Howell said quietly, 'How is the Queen? All this commotion and speculation is because of her illness. The citizens are anxious. The future of the dynasty is in doubt.'

Cressida shook her head sadly. 'My news would be hardly likely to reassure them. She is very poorly, my sweet lady.'

His eyes narrowed. 'You are in constant attendance? You do not eat anything within the royal chambers, do you? There is talk of poison.'

Cressida's lips parted in soundless amazement. 'Poison? Nonsense; the Queen is sick with lung rot, the wasting sickness. All know her own sister, Isabel, also died of it.'

'Aye, that is well known, but she could take some

time to die and it is thought the King might be impatient.'

Cressida expelled her breath in a decided hiss. 'What idle gossip abounds in the city? The Queen is tended lovingly, and particularly by her own husband. All who witness him with her would know that. Her own niece is constantly watchful. . .'

'The Lady Elizabeth?' His eyelids flickered oddly.

She stared back at him wonderingly. 'What are you suggesting? The Lady Elizabeth loves her aunt dearly. . .'

'And her royal uncle?'

This time Cressida gave a decided gasp. 'Howell, how dare you. . .? The Lady Elizabeth—wish to see her aunt die—because. . . That is scandalous—and utterly preposterous.'

'Then there is nothing in the rumours that should the Queen die he might wish to ally himself with the people's darling, Elizabeth; that he had already consulted the Queen Dowager, her mother, on the matter?'

Cressida's eyes were wide with shock. 'Wed his niece? It is forbidden by Holy church—incestuous. . .'

'In the case of kings' desires, we all know dispensations can be obtained.'

'She would never countenance it and. . .' Cressida stared past him, shocked beyond measure, yet—she saw vividly once again the scene within the corridor—the King stooping to kiss Elizabeth's hand, his eyes filled with tears of emotional gratitude. Were they in truth tears of gratitude? She pushed away the unworthy thought and turned back to Howell.

'Is this really what the people are saying? But, Howell, that is terrible. You said yourself that Henry Tudor has declared himself willing to ask for the hand of the Princess.'

'And you said, "Not unless he usurps King Richard's

throne."' His expression was bland. 'She is her father's heiress and the beloved of the Londoners. A marriage with her could foil, once and for all, the Tudor's hopes.'

'But her brothers, the Princes?'

He gave a short, hollow laugh. 'Who really believes the Princes still live?'

She sucked in her breath. 'I cannot believe that the King would contemplate such a possibility. Nor would Elizabeth. . .'

'Yet all London talks of her appearance at the Twelfth Night feast in a gown resembling that of the Queen.'

Cressida bit her lip uncertainly as she recalled Wroxeter's undoubted fury on that occasion. Had he heard rumours? No, she dismissed the thought. He could not consider. . .

As if he read her very thoughts, Howell bent close and whispered, 'It is also said she has written to the Duke of Norfolk, speaking of her love for the King and desire to do him service and begging the Duke to speak well of her to His Grace.'

'A sentiment any good subject would express, and especially now that the King needs all our love and goodwill,' Cressida said hotly. 'Howell, you must not repeat these ugly rumours. Such talk could cost you your head.'

'Only if it were proved to be untrue.'

Howell gave a sudden muttered oath as a man, walking hurriedly down the path towards them, head down against the wind blowing from the river, stumbled awkwardly against him. The man stopped, lifted his head and made a fulsome apology.

'Sir, forgive me. I am clumsy this morning, have just stepped ashore. The river barges toss uncertainly on the rough waves today.' He backed away as Howell acknowledged him with a stiff little nod.

Cressida stared after the man, her brows creased in doubt.

'I have seen him somewhere about the palace.' She gnawed at her nether lip uncertainly. 'I hope he did not overhear...'

'No, no.' Howell forced a laugh. 'You heard him. He said he had only just stepped ashore.'

'Yes, he did.' Cressida drew her gaze from the retreating figure back to Howell. 'How long will you be in London now?'

'Several days. I wait for a business reply—concerning the wool clip.' He made a little grimace. 'After that I must return to the Marches—far too great a distance from you, Cressida.'

She forced a smile. 'I shall miss you all, Mother and Father too, when you leave me. Howell, I should not stay here with you longer. I shall be missed and—and the Queen might call for me.'

He nodded. 'Be careful. Promise me you will be watchful of all about the Queen, but give no open sign of suspicion. That could bring you into further danger.'

She inclined her head. Despite her brave words of repudiation of his ugly fears, he had disturbed her. He bowed. This time he did not seek to take her hand for she had withdrawn some distance from him, as if she could put space between his horrifying words and her own beliefs. She forced a smile.

'Give my good wishes to all at home. God keep you, Howell, and—and keep yourself from all treasonable dealings, especially this foolish rumourmongering...'

'I swear I will, but I fear for you.'

'I am sure there is no need to do so,' she assured him, yet her eyes were dark with concern as she turned and left him, her thoughts in turmoil.

Alice met her at the entrance to the Queen's apartments.

'The Lady Elizabeth has been asking for you.' Alice

eyed her doubtfully. 'I went to your chamber and into the hall. One of the pages said he had seen you heading for the river quay.'

'Did he?' Cressida's tone was brittle-hard. 'And why should my movements interest him, I wonder? Was he set to spy upon me?'

Alice sniffed. She knew well enough that her mistress would not have adopted such an attitude had there been nothing to hide.

'I doubt that,' she said mildly. 'Pages are notorious gossips. They gain favours by entertaining the ladies with any titbit of information they think might be scurrilous, a reason, perhaps, why it is best not to give them arrows for their suspicious bows. It is very cold by the river.'

Cressida gave a little laugh. That last remark had been made so lightly yet had achieved its purpose. Very little could be hidden from Alice, but she could be trusted implicitly.

Cressida said anxiously, 'Is the Queen worse? Have you heard?'

'I do not think so. Nothing has been said and there has been no racing about after physicians. His Grace has been sitting with her.'

Cressida suppressed the terrible doubts that Howell had aroused in her mind. So the King was still attentive to his sick wife, but—would he not wish to appear so— outwardly at least. Once sowed, that horrible suspicion would grow, however assiduously she attempted to dismiss it.

'Thank you, Alice. Where is the Lady Elizabeth now?'

'With the King and Queen, I believe.'

Cressida nodded and moved into the outer chamber. Some of the Queen's other attendants were seated here, some chatting, some working at embroidery or reading from illuminated Books of Hours. One or two

looked up at Cressida curiously, but few smiled in
welcome. Still she felt an outsider though no barbed
taunts were thrown at her now that she was my lady,
Countess of Wroxeter.

She undid the neckties of her cloak and seated
herself some distance from the rest on a window seat.
She could not enter the Queen's bedchamber now
without invitation, since the King was present there.
She must wait to discover if the Lady Elizabeth had
particular need of her services.

The King emerged at last and stood close to his
niece, once more in grave consultation with her. The
attendant ladies rose and curtsied low. He acknowledged them courteously and took his leave. Cressida
bit her lip doubtfully as she observed how wistfully
Elizabeth followed the King's retreating back with her
eyes. Then she caught sight of Cressida and nodded for
her to approach.

'You wanted me, my lady?'

'The Queen asked for you earlier but she is asleep
now. She tires so easily. This rest will be good for her.
Lady Allard is watching by her. We should leave her to
rest.' She looked thoughtfully at Cressida's cloak. 'You
have been out?'

'Only to the river terrace for a breath of air. I felt
suffocated.'

Elizabeth nodded. 'It is stifling within the chamber.
Mind you, I am thankful to be warm. You cannot
imagine how cold it was when we were all immured
within the Sanctuary of Westminster; even on the
warmest days of summer the chill seemed to come from
the grey walls of the place.'

It was the first time she had referred to the time
when her mother, the Dowager Queen, had hastened
them all into sanctuary, so quickly that a wall had had
to be demolished to accommodate the royal baggage,

soon after the death of King Edward and during the uncertain days of her elder son's brief reign.

Months later she had allowed herself to be convinced that she and her daughters would be safe under the protection offered by King Richard and—now—Elizabeth had been established at Court to wait upon her aunt—and her royal uncle. Had some sort of bargain been struck then? Howell had intimated that the Dowager Queen was willing to countenance a marriage between her eldest daughter and the King—should the Queen die...

Cressida shivered nervously. It was totally unthinkable. For the first time in their acquaintanceship she felt uncomfortable in the company of her friend.

The Earl did not call at her chamber that evening to ask after her well-being and the Queen's health as he usually did.

Cressida was thankful. She was aware that she would have found it difficult to hide her guilt from him. Not only had she disobeyed him in meeting Howell Prosser in private, but she was conscious that what had passed between them was of a treasonable nature, and she sensed that it would not only have displeased Lord Martyn, but possibly prompted him to take some action against Howell.

Over the next few days the Queen kept to her bed, sleeping exhaustedly most of the time, only rousing or showing interest when the King arrived at her bedside, which he did frequently.

Cressida found herself watching him covertly whenever the Lady Elizabeth was present, but saw that his attention was fixed only upon his sick wife. He was very gentle with her and though he continued to smile bravely in her presence Cressida saw how haggard he appeared when he emerged from the chamber. Deep lines of suffering etched his nose and mouth and his eyes were deep-shadowed.

When Cressida *did* see her husband, she realised that he too showed signs of strain. His brows were drawn together as if in deep concentration and his usually sleepy expression had been replaced by one of alarmed watchfulness. He spent long hours in his small office and Cressida wondered if news from abroad and the realm at large was worrying him unduly and, naturally, he would not wish to bother his sovereign with such disturbing matters at so sad a time.

Cressida was with the Lady Elizabeth in attendance in the sick chamber when the curious darkening of the sun occurred in the afternoon of March sixteenth. Cressida had gone to the window to gaze curiously at the crowd of servants, grooms and officials thronging the courtyard, gaping up into the lowering sky. She knew it was said to be an eclipse of the sun, but had never experienced such a phenonemon. Though it was still early the room darkened unnaturally and she knew a sudden frisson of fear, as if the world itself were about to come to an end.

The Queen had been sleeping and the Lady Elizabeth was seated by the bed. Anne's breathing had been laboured earlier and her cough had given her a sleepless night. Now Cressida and Elizabeth were relieved that it had eased for the moment and she had managed to rest for a while. Dr Hobbes had come and gone in the morning, had examined her, nodded sagely and taken his departure now that the troublesome cough had stopped.

Cressida leaned down from the casement, frowning, then began to relax as the sky started to lighten again and there was a concerted gasp of relief from the watchers below.

'It seems to be passing,' she called to the Lady Elizabeth. 'I confess it is quite frightening. No wonder superstitious people in the past have regarded these occurrences as dire warnings of some disaster.'

Elizabeth gave no reply and Cressida turned abruptly as there came a strangled gasp from tbe bed. The Queen was struggling up onto her pillows. Elizabeth had risen and was trying to help her when the Queen coughed harshly and gouts of bright blood spurted from her pallid lips over the coverlet and pillows, staining both the fine linen of the Queen's night-shift and Elizabeth's hands and gown.

Elizabeth gave one sudden shrill cry of terror and Cressida, for the breath of one heartbeat, stood stock-still by the bed, too horrified to move.

The Queen's blue eyes were distended in terror and she was striving to speak, her fingers clawing at the bed coverlet as she struggled for breath. Still the frothy blood poured from her mouth and Elizabeth put a hand to her own to stifle her sobs.

One of the Queen's senior ladies burst into the chamber, alerted by Elizabeth's first cry. She took in the situation quickly and took charge.

'My Lady of Wroxeter, go at once; find a page to summon Dr Hobbes and the King must be informed.' She turned to the Princess.

'We must try to lift her higher. We'll need men to put some supports beneath the bedstead and servants must go for water.' She called to Cressida as she reached the door, her voice deadly calm now. 'Summon the Queen's confessor. He should be here—just in case.'

Cressida could hear her uttering soothing words to the frightened Queen. 'There, there, my dear. This has happened before. It will be momentary. The doctor will come. All will be well.' Lady Allard had attended upon the Queen for many years, even before she and the then Duke of Gloucester had wed. Her husband, Sir Dominick, was one of the Royal household knights and, like Lord Martyn, he had served the King with

Lord Francis Lovell, Sir Richard Ratcliffe and the other
known companions of Middleham.

Cressida's limbs were threatening to let her down,
but she found a page and sent him off on his errand.
Most of the household were out watching the eclipse
and the boy seemed half-bemused, whether at her
frightened expression or the fearful happening in the
sky she could not tell.

She exhorted him to find his companions and send
them off about the palace to find the King, the Queen's
confessor and serving wenches to bring water and
towels to the chamber. Though she was thoroughly
alarmed, she returned to the bedside to help Lady
Allard.

The older woman looked her up and down briefly,
then nodded briskly. She addressed the Princess. 'My
lady, you should return to your chamber to change
your gown. Lady Wroxeter will help me strip and
change the Queen until the other attendants arrive.'

Cressida concentrated grimly on the task in hand,
gently removing the sheets and coverings slimed with
blood and hastening the white-faced maids, who
entered with water and towels and fresh linen. The
coughing had stopped now and with it the bleeding,
but the Queen had ceased to struggle to speak and lay
back, doll-like in their hands, as they carefully tended
her.

Later, Cressida was thankful when the physician and
his apprentice arrived and Lady Allard quietly dismissed her from the chamber.

'Thank you, my lady. We can manage now. Go and
take some rest. We may need you later.'

In the corridor Cressida passed the King. He was
biting down so savagely upon his nether lip that bright
drops of blood showed. His face was as white as the
linen sheets Cressida had replaced upon the Queen's
bed and his grey eyes looked tortured in his haggard

face. Behind him his attendants drew back apace as if they could not bear to witness his grief.

Two hours later she was summoned with the other attendants and senior members of the royal household to the anteroom of the Queen's chamber while the King's chaplain said mass. She knelt beside her husband, hearing the solemn words through the open doorway, and smelt the acrid yet over-sweet smell of incense.

At last Dr Hobbes ordered them all from the chamber so that the King could be alone with his wife. Lady Allard was crying quietly and the King's friends were unashamedly wiping their eyes. Cressida could feel her own hot tears falling onto her cheeks as Martyn led her down the corridor towards her own chamber. The Lady Elizabeth stood, white-faced and tearless, near the door as Cressida looked back. The Princess's eyes were fixed wistfully on the King's back as he remained kneeling by the bedside.

Alice, as ever, was quietly efficient yet mercifully silent. Cressida had been in attendance for hours and Alice helped her from her gown and encouraged her to lie upon her bed. It seemed that hardly any time had passed before they heard the tolling of the bell that told them Anne, Queen of England, was dead.

Cressida sat up, her hands clasped around her drawn-up knees, and cried soft tears which relieved her overwhelmed heart. She had known the Queen for only four months and had learned to love her unreservedly. She wondered, half-afraid, if she would be expected to help lay out her mistress, but no one came to summon her to the death chamber and Alice said that she thought the Queen's oldest and dearest friends would do that final service for her. Would her niece be amongst them?

Cressida bit her lip uncertainly as she sat and thought about the outcome. The King must mourn his wife a

little time and then—then he must remarry—and
soon—but to the Lady Elizabeth? Would the scandal-
mongering tongues in the packed streets of the capital
accept such a marriage? Would those courtiers who
had loved the Queen ever forgive him?

Lord Martyn had left Cressida alone, gone about the
very necessary business which the King's Council must
put in hand, plans for the royal obsequies, proclama-
tions which must be issued, instructions concerning
royal mourning. Cressida thought dully that those
superstitious folk who had warned of calamity after the
darkening of the sun would consider themselves proved
right. What greater disaster could afflict the realm at
this time of uncertainty than the death of its Queen?

Alice came to her side as she stirred. She was
carrying a silk gown in mourning black. She shook her
head as Cressida stared at it and flinched.

'We all knew it must come soon,' she said flatly. 'I
knew it was necessary to prepare. Let me help you to
change.'

'Lord Martyn will grieve. He loved the Queen well.'

'Aye, for all I hear there was no one here who did
not.'

Cressida looked at her sharply. 'There is no talk
amongst the servants of. . .?' She bit back the dreadful
doubts she could not frame into words.

Alice sighed heavily. 'There will always be those who
cast doubts on the probity of others.'

'They are saying the King—wanted her to die?'
Cressida whispered the question fearfully.

'All knew it must be soon and while there was
uncertainty—' Alice shrugged. 'She could not give him
an heir. It will be said he wanted it over and who could
blame him, poor man? The physicians have forbidden
him to share her bed for the last few months.'

'The Lady Elizabeth must be especially stricken. I

should go to her.' Cressida waited while Alice adjusted the black veiling over her truncated hennin.

'Aye, she will be glad of your comfort. I doubt she'll get much understanding from that mother of hers,' Alice retorted laconically.

Cressida could not entirely repress an almost hysterical laugh as she considered what Howell had said—that the Dowager Queen had been most anxious to conclude a marriage contract between her daughter and the King.

'And what shall I tell my lord Earl if he asks where you are?' Alice was clearly not unaware that Lord Martyn was not entirely pleased about the friendship between his wife and the Princess.

Cressida bit her lip. 'Tell him—tell him the truth. Surely he must realise that I am in duty bound to try and offer solace to the Lady Elizabeth at this time of her suffering.'

She was informed that the Lady Elizabeth was not within her chamber. The young maid who told Cressida looked uncertain as to what she was to say concerning the whereabouts of her mistress. Cressida stood still for a moment outside the closed door of Elizabeth's chamber. Could she, even now, be with the King?

She dismissed that thought as unworthy. Even if it were so, it would be natural enough for a niece to be with her uncle to offer comfort. Cressida decided to seek her friend within the antechamber to the Queen's apartment where other of the Queen's ladies might be expected to gather.

She found the place deserted and was about to leave when a sudden sound from inside the death chamber alerted her attention. She drew near to the slightly open door and peered inside.

Richard of England knelt upon the floor by the bed. Terrible sobs racked his body as he leaned forward over the bed, his two hands outstretched imploringly over the coverlet. In all her young life Cressida had never heard a man cry. It was a dreadful, anguished flood of overwhelming emotional agony. She knew she should go. She should not witness this, yet she could not move.

Realisation struck her with full force. Howell had slandered the King. No man could suffer like that and dissemble. She was hearing the true expression of the man's despair. Richard had loved Anne truly. She could no longer be under any misapprehension and she stood transfixed, one hand to her mouth to keep back her own sobs. All this time he had watched her slowly draw away from him, had dreaded this moment, and now she was gone — and he could no longer hold back his grief.

A powerful hand caught Cressida, drawing her back, while another pressed hard against her lips lest she cry out in sudden fear. Inexorably she felt herself pulled to the outer door and into the corridor. The door was closed and she was dragged round to stare into her husband's furious face.

'What in the Sweet Virgin's name are you doing? Can you not see he needs to be alone? Dear God, can he have no privacy?'

She gave a terrible choking sob and collapsed against Martyn's shoulder.

'I'm sorry. I did not mean to spy upon his grief. I — I did not know — did not know he was there. I — I thought — people said he — he — Oh, Martyn, I did not understand how — how he loved her. If — if my father had lost my mother he —' she choked '— he could not grieve more —'

Lord Martyn's expression softened and he drew her back, his hands upon her shoulders, and smiled into her blue eyes, which were wet with tears. He shook his head gently.

'We who have known them all these years, we know

how deeply he loved her and how he has suffered over these months and will suffer yet more. Little Cressida, you have been under great stress over these last hours. I told you, you must rest.'

He cupped her chin in his hands and bent to kiss her gently upon the mouth. As he straightened his lips curved into an understanding smile.

'You have been very brave. Lady Allard told me how you helped to tend her when the bleeding came. That must have been very frightening. I am very proud of my wife. You will not be needed now until the burial ceremonies. We must go home to the Strand house for a while. I'll call for our barge and send word to Alice to come on later with your clothing and necessities.'

As if in a daze she allowed herself to be drawn along to his office, where he stopped briefly to give instructions to his assistant and collect his fur-lined cloak, which he wrapped around Cressida.

She sat in the stern of the barge, her head pressed againt his shoulder, numb with grief and reaction and intense relief that he had so quickly changed from his fury against her to an attitude of loving sympathy. There was a great aching within her, as if she was wanting to cry inside herself.

She stole one look at his strained features as he looked out beyond her over the river. He too grieved for the loss of a dear friend. She gave a little sigh and pressed yet nearer to his strong body, at this moment needing only to feel the comforting warmth of him.

She was glad of the welcoming heat from the fire in the solar hearth. It seemed that already the servants in the house had heard of the Queen's death and they went soft-footed about their tasks, watching carefully their lord's grim demeanour.

Lord Martyn requested that a light supper be served to himself and his lady in the solar. Cressida was overwhelmingly glad that he had decided to join her.

She could not have borne to be alone at this time. Philip Kenton served them at table and took his leave at the close of the meal, respectfully drawing the door to after him.

Cressida found herself crying softly again, unable to stop herself. Martyn turned and, seeing her, came to her chair and drew her upwards into his arms.

'I'm sorry,' she gulped. 'This is so foolish—I. . .'

'Not foolish at all. The death of the Queen is cause enough for you to weep, but the strain of court life, which is new to you, bring its own problems.'

He sat down in the opposite chair, drawing her down onto his knee, cradling her against his heart. She could feel his own beating steadily against hers and felt suddenly, totally safe and protected. Her father had always been demonstratively affectionate, and she had known herself fortunate in this, but her feeling now, for her husband, was completely different. He was kissing her gently, wiping away her tears with a gentle thumb.

'I have been considering you a child still, my wife, and I am realising that is no longer true.'

She felt a sudden surge of longing and, as if in answer to her unspoken thought, he bent and kissed her passionately upon the lips. She responded eagerly, pressing her body against him, willing him to caress her as she knew, instinctively, a man caressed his lover. She needed him now; they were alive, together, and she wanted to feel that release of emotion that proved to herself that she was needed as urgently as she needed him, so that as he drew away she looked up sharply into his face.

'You felt the King's grief so deeply because you had suffered so yourself—for—for the Lady Elinor,' she whispered. 'Do—do you still love her?'

His brows were drawn together in thought and he peered down at her lovely face, tear-stained yet unmarred. She was like that faery queen of legend, who had welcomed the dying Arthur into the barge to convey him to Avalon. Mourning black served only to intensify her beauty. She had the rare ability to weep without the swelling and reddening of lids which other women suffered.

His heart missed a beat. He needed her as he had never needed a woman before, to convince himself that he was truly alive—yet this was not the time. She would respond, she desperately wanted comfort as he did, but it would be unfair to take her now when she had no real understanding of what she was doing.

He said gently, 'Yes, I loved Elinor, will always hold a place for her in my heart, but she is gone, my darling. No one can live with the dead. She was sweet and gentle and dear to me, but you are my wife. When the time is right I will show you that my heart is not closed to love.

'For now you need a quiet time to recover. Let me take you to your chamber. I think your maid, Alice, should be here by now. You must try to sleep and in the morning we shall still be sad, for we have lost a dear friend to both of us, but we shall also accept God's will and rejoice that the Queen's suffering is over.'

At her chamber door he stooped and kissed her again. She experienced a sudden, violent resentment, so strong that she almost pushed him away vehemently. He was her husband. He should be here tonight, within her chamber, offering her the solace of his body.

Despite his assurance, she was by no means convinced that he had put his love for Elinor aside. She came between them still, a lovely ghost—and one more worthy to share his bed than Cressida. Instantly she regretted her revulsion. He was grieving. There was nothing in his thoughts at this time but the need to support his sovereign. She made him a curtsey and turned to enter the chamber.

CHAPTER SEVEN

LORD WROXETER stared incredulously at the Lord
Chamberlain, Lord Lovell, seated opposite him in the
chair near the roaring hearth fire of the winter parlour.

'My lord, what you say is totally impossible. I cannot
believe my wife capable of what you suggest.'

Lord Lovell shifted uncomfortably in his chair.

'Martyn, I was loath to come to you with this story
but, after due consideration, taking into account your
duties in the Council, I thought it imperative that you
should know of it immediately. There can be little
doubt about the matter. Dick Ratcliffe told me he had
it from one of his grooms that the man heard Lady
Wroxeter actually talk of the King's plans to marry his
niece. He passed her on the river quay and could not
fail to recognise her.'

'God in heaven, does the King know of this?'

Lord Lovell looked away into the fire. 'Dick went to
the King and challenged him.'

'What?'

'Well, you know Dick, the bluff Yorkshire knight
personified. He loves Richard well but, as we all did,
well-nigh worshipped the Queen. He told Richard
bluntly that were he to proceed with this his loyal
northerners would desert his cause.'

Martyn took a harsh breath. 'Were you present?'

'Fortunately or unfortunately, whichever way you
look at it, yes.'

'What—what was his reaction?'

'Like you, he was at first dumbfounded. Dear God,
Martyn, he's still raw from his loss. He simply sat there
and stared at Dick Ratcliffe. I thought he might enter

into a right royal rage. I hadn't the courage to move. All I could do was stand stock-still and stare at both of them. His hands were gripping his chair arms and white to the bone, then he said quietly—dangerously quietly—"I would like to know, Dick, just where you obtained this slanderous story."

'I think Dick had recovered from his first shock by then and realised just what he'd done. He went first red, then white, and opened his mouth like a fish gasping for air, then it was he related the story his groom had told him. In the end he blustered, "Do you tell me, my lord, it isn't true?" Richard just looked at him and Dick went down then on one knee and sobbed out a plea for pardon.'

Martyn was looking full at his visitor, not moving a muscle. It was clear to Lord Lovell that his host was taking some moments to digest the truth of his news. He said at last, evenly, 'Please, my lord, tell me exactly what Sir Richard Ratcliffe said concerning my wife.'

Lovell cleared his throat nervously. 'It's as I said earlier. Ratcliffe's groom had landed at the King's steps. He said he was walking up the quay when he saw Lady Wroxeter in talk with a man. . .'

'Did he describe this man?'

Lovell hesitated, then resumed his story. 'Naturally I demanded that this fellow be brought before me. The King insisted on being present, though I counselled him to withdraw from all knowledge of the affair until we had probed the source of the rumour completely. The groom was a new man. Dick says he had recently been taken into his household in London, not one of the known men from Yorkshire. I questioned him closely and warned him of the consequences of lying and, of course, he was in awe of the King.

'His story bore out what Dick had said. Apparently he had recognised Lady Wroxeter because he had seen her at her wedding feast, though both she and the man were well muffled against the cold. They were speaking quite loudly, he said, and he pricked up his ears when they spoke of the King's love for his niece and—and of the gossip that the King was in haste for the Queen to die—and the man cautioned her to beware of poison used in the sick chamber. . .'

Martyn rose and paced the room with long, impatient strides. Lovell was aware that his friend's hands were clenched into fists and winced at Martyn's harsh questioning.

'But the man? What did this groom say about the man?'

Lovell shrugged slightly. 'As I said, he was wrapped up so he was not glimpsed too clearly; he was young, well set up; there was no chance to see his hair colouring.'

'Prosser,' Martyn gritted between his teeth. 'Yes, I think I know the fellow.'

Lovell said gently, 'She was merely repeating what she had heard elsewhere, Martyn. Lady Cressida is very young, new to Court. She could not be entirely aware what damage has been done to the King's reputation. You must not be too harsh with her.'

Martyn had come to halt before the Lord Chamberlain's chair. 'What have you counselled the King to do?'

'Since the rumour is abroad, it will be necessary for him to make a public denial.'

Martyn's jaw worked and his eyes bore the suspicion of moisture. 'How did he take it?'

'I think he is still numb with shock. He listened very carefully. I don't think he could believe it—that anyone could think— You know him, Martyn; he never stoops to explain or deny any slur on his character.

'You'll recall the slanders which connected him with the death of young Edward of Lancaster and the murder of poor King Henry, when he was not even in

London at the time, even the malicious talk that he wished his brother, George, dead. None of these he deigned to comment on, but this—this has to be answered. There must be no hint of scandal which could harm Anne's memory. He has charged me to arrange a place and time when he can make a public statement of intent.'

Martyn sighed and nodded. 'God knows how he will find the courage to do this, but he will, thank God. And—and did he speak of the Lady Elizabeth?'

'He saw the wisdom of removing her from Court immediately. She is to go to Sheriff Hutton.'

'Good,' Martyn breathed. 'That should have been done months ago. I never dared broach the matter to him.'

'You saw some grain of truth in this vile slander?' Lord Lovell half started up in his chair.

Martyn held up a hand to indicate that he needed to explain. 'My lord, you know it is my duty to collate rumour and intelligence concerning any danger or threat of danger both to the King's personal safety and to his reputation. Those vile accusations concerning the death of his nephews, the Princes, emmanated from the Tudor faction, as we know well. All this will aid Henry Tudor's cause. Any mud he can sling at Richard will be well received by his enemies and those petty lords who envy his position and gain nothing from his elevation to the throne.

'I have watched the Lady Elizabeth closely. It is clear she has a deep affection for her uncle, possibly innocent enough. She means well and she loved the Queen, I am sure, but her closeness to the King encourages gossip.'

He frowned. 'That unfortunate happening on Twelfth Night when she came dressed like the Queen was due to careless talk between herself and Cressida. It was Cressida who, unknowingly, she says, told the Princess what the Queen was to wear. She brushed it

aside as merely women's talk of current fashion and I
believed her...'

He passed a weary hand over his brow. 'The King
was anxious to restore his brother's daughters to their
rightful place at Court, to counteract evil rumours
concerning their brothers. He danced with her, paid
her avuncular interest in all innocence, but the Queen
was ill and—and he cannot afford such insinuations as
lewd folk will draw from the friendship.

'I forbade Cressida to associate with the Princess,
but could not avoid their being thrown together during
the last days of the Queen's illness—yet I still cannot
believe that she would knowingly spread such filth.'

Lord Lovell rose. 'I should return to Richard. He
may need me.'

'And my wife? She could find herself charged with
treason for this.'

'Martyn, there could be no question of that. What
happened was done in naïve innocence. Perhaps it
might be wiser if she were to stay from Court for a
while. Perhaps you could arrange for her to leave
Westminster, return to the Marches.'

'I could not be absent from my duties at this critical
time.'

'I was not about to suggest that. I know you are
newly married, but—' again Lovell shrugged '—the
King might be happier if he were not to see Lady
Cressida for a while. Could she travel with her parents?
Gretton came to court today to offer his condolences
and to beg to be excused so that he might return to his
manor and attend to urgent business there.'

Martyn nodded grimly. 'I would prefer her not to
return to Gretton at this time, but, as you say, I will
think of it. Certainly I will keep her from the King's
sight.'

Lovell leaned forward and placed a hand on his
friend's shoulder. 'I counsel you not to be too hard on

her, Martyn. She can have no conception of the harm that has been caused.'

As Martyn escorted the Lord Chamberlain to the door and called for his steward to attend him and see him well served in the stables, he said through his teeth, 'I must see that I make her well and truly aware of the facts.'

Cressida addressed Alice from the comfort of the great bed as her maid prepared to curtsey and leave her for the night.

'Alice, what is it like to be—to be in love?' The last words came out in a little embarrassed rush.

Alice returned to the bedside and looked down at her former nursling.

'I suppose it differs from person to person but—well, the one in love almost always knows without being told.' She was frowning a little.

It was not lost on Alice that all was not well between her master and mistress, and this probing question had her really and truly worried. She suspected that Cressida had met with someone while absent from the Queen's apartments. She had searched for her in vain in the usual haunts of the Queen's ladies.

Cressida had not been forthcoming about her absence and she rarely kept secrets from her maid. If Lord Wroxeter had failed to express his feelings adequately to his wife, had she, perhaps, turned to someone else more anxious to flatter her interest? That could spell disaster indeed.

Cressida sighed. She said wistfully, 'I suppose I shall never know the ecstasy they talk of in the romances the troubadours sing. They say your heart beats madly and you feel strangely excited in the presence of the loved one and—'

'My lady,' Alice said sternly, 'you have not done

something which would anger your husband or—even worse, shame your parents?'

Cressida's blue eyes widened in astonishment. 'No, of course not, but—' her voice faltered uncertainly '—well, not exactly.'

Alice sat down on the side of the bed. 'I think you should tell me.'

'Well. . .' Cressida eyed her guiltily '. . .when you were looking for me the other day—well, I was with Howell—on the river quay.'

Alice took in a hasty breath. 'You mean you met him by assignation?'

Cressida tilted her chin defiantly. 'A page came to tell me he wanted to see me. I would never have done so there—like that—had not my lord ordered me not to receive him. We did nothing to be ashamed of. Howell is leaving London and merely wished to say goodbye, but—my lord would be angry if he discovered we had met clandestinely.'

Alice was silent for a moment while she digested this information, then she said slowly, 'Were you talking about Howell just now?'

Again Cressida's eyes widened and darkened in shocked surprise. 'Howell? That I might—love Howell? No, of course not. He is a friend, has always been so, and—'

'Praise the Virgin,' Alice muttered fervently. 'I feared—but no matter. What is all this, my lady? Why this talk of love and feelings?'

Cressida flushed darkly and clasped her hands round her bent knees.

'My lord, he—he treats me as if—as if I were a child still. Last night he was very kind. He knew I was very upset over—over the death of the Queen and he brought me home, as you know, and we supped together and. . .' Her voice trailed off awkwardly. 'Then he brought me to my chamber door and—and he left me.' She said flatly in a frightened whisper, 'Alice, I want to be a true wife to him.'

'So that is it?' Alice gave a heavy sigh. 'Child, this marriage was one of arrangement and entered into hastily. You must be patient.'

'I know.' One of Cressida's hands stole out and seized that of her nurse. 'I cannot confide in my mother. My father would be angered if he thought—'

She swallowed. 'I do not know how to deal with my feelings, Alice. When he is near—my lord Martyn, I mean—I feel frightened and anxious and almost sick with excitement. I do not know why, for he has never flattered me as other men at Court have done, and he rarely touches me, except to give me a pat or kiss of comfort when I am distressed as you would to a pet dog. But—but he looks at me sometimes— Only I know that he cannot forget his former love who died.

'I want to love him, Alice, and—and for him to love me, as Father loves Mother. Is that too much to ask?' Her lip trembled. 'I often seem to anger him without knowing why. The first time we met I was doing something foolish and—and I think he despises me for a simpleton.'

Then she said, passionately, 'I am no longer a child, Alice. I know how I feel when he is near—that is not the response of a child. How can I make him see. . .?'

Alice gently stroked back the lovely fair hair. 'I say again, sweeting, you must be patient. If I am any judge of men, Lord Martyn is a true and honourable husband who waits lest he destroy too soon what he wishes to create between the two of you. Despite your protests you are still very young and new to this life. He is busied about the King's affairs and this is no time for him to be distracted.

'For all that, it was very foolish and disobedient of you to meet like that with Master Prosser. Promise me you will do nothing stupid like that again.'

Cressida nodded solemnly. 'I promise. To tell truth, I dare not, for all that I—I want my lord Martyn to—love me, he frightens me too. I dread him finding out about this last meeting.'

'Aye.' Alice tightened her lips as she rose. 'Best keep all this to yourself. Your father would not be pleased with me if he thought you had behaved so thoughtlessly. Now try to sleep, child, and pray to St Catherine to give you your heart's desire.'

Cressida began to snuggle down beneath the coverlets. Already she was beginning to feel better. All day her thoughts had been confused and confession to Alice always helped her.

Alice had almost reached the door when it was flung open and Lord Martyn strode in. His face was black with fury.

'Leave us,' he commanded harshly.

Alice shot one anxious glance at her mistress, then, stealing another hasty look at her master, curtsied and hastened from the chamber.

Martyn strode to the side of the bed. He reached down and tore back the coverlet. 'Get up.'

Cressida struggled up against the pillows and, seeing his furious expression, cowered back. She was not easily frightened, though had been vaguely excited in the past by Lord Martyn's anger, as she had told Alice, but the look in his eyes now terrified her.

'I said, get up.'

She reached for her bedgown, laid across the fur covering, and he snatched it up and threw it towards her.

She stood up hastily, though her limbs were trembling, and fumbled to pull the furred bedgown around her to cover her nakedness. She dared not look at him, but was uneasily aware of his smouldering anger.

Impatiently he pulled her to face him as she struggled to tie the cord. 'Look at me. Look at me, I say.'

She obeyed unwillingly. He was standing, feet
astride, his back to the hearth, fully dressed still, so
something had kept him from retiring. A late visitor?

Suddenly she realised that he had discovered the
truth about her secret meeting with Howell and her
lips compressed in anger to match his own. How dared
he berate her so, when, had he been fair, she could
have met with Howell openly and there would have
been no need for disobedience on her part? He had no
right to forbid her to take farewell of her friends.

Taking the initiative, she said, 'Well, what is all this
pother, that you drag me so unceremoniously from my
bed and alarm my maid? Whatever the matter is, could
it not wait for the morning?'

His eyes flashed ominously and, despite her resolve,
she drew back apace.

'Do you know what you have done?'

His tone was so venomous that she was becoming
even more alarmed, but was determined to put a brave
face on it.

'I don't know what you are talking about. If you
would explain. . .?'

'Explain?' He gave a single harsh laugh. 'Explain,
when I discover my wife has committed an act of
outright treason? Why in the name of all the saints
should I *have* to explain? Surely that is your business,
madam?'

Cressida was totally bewildered by the accusation.
Was he mad? How could her innocent meeting with
Howell be deemed treason?

She echoed the word. 'Treason? I don't understand.
Has the King commanded his attendants not to speak
to people outside the Court. . .?'

'How dare you make light of it, madam? Not only
have you endangered yourself but you could destroy
His Grace's trust in me, one of his most loyal councillors.' He came close again and took hold of her, shaking

her so roughly that her hair fell about her shoulders in wild disorder and she scarce had ability to draw breath.

'Do you know what the penalty is for treason should a woman be found guilty? For a man it's disembowellment at Tyburn, but for a woman, madam, it is burning at the stake.'

She went deadly cold, limp in his grasp. Whatever he was talking of, he was in deadly earnest. What had she done? Had Howell been arrested and had he, under torture, involved her in some nefarious scheme? But in what?

Her eyes implored Martyn for an explanation and, again, he gave that short bark of a laugh. 'You don't realise the harm you've done, do you?'

She shook her head, too afraid now to attempt to defend herself.

'You accuse the King of wishing to poison his wife and, God help us, commit incest by intending to marry his niece, and this before his sweet Queen has breathed her last; and, to cap it all, you do it in front of the world and his wife passing along the busy river quay! And you ask me for an explanation?'

Her eyes had darkened and grown huge in a face gone completely white, devoid of even the flush of previous anger.

'But,' she whispered piteously 'you don't understand. It was not like you say. The gossip was merely repeated, what had been said by others. . .'

He released her abruptly and began prowling the room, his hand gripping the ornamental dagger he wore at his belt. It seemed he was not even listening to her attempt at explaining herself.

'Sir Richard Ratcliffe has been forced to demand an explanation from the King. His northern men-at-arms are loyal to the Queen's memory. She was great Warwick's daughter, I remind you. Any implied insult to her could lose the King the support of his followers.'

She gave a terrible gasp of understanding and clutched at the carved bedpost to keep from falling. Slowly, inexorably, the deadly truth of this matter was seeping into her bewildered brain.

'The King, the supreme sovereign, must now stoop to explain himself to his people, and at such a time when he needs to know the deepest sympathy and support from all of us. He must go to Clerkenwell, to the hall of the knights of St John, and publicly, humiliatingly declare that he has no intention whatever of marrying his niece.

'God knows how anyone could ever have believed such a possibility in the first place. The King marry a bastard, niece or no, when his own claim to the throne depended on that very bastardy of his brother's children? Did you consider that, or were you so besotted with your friendship with the Lady Elizabeth that you would accept anything she chose to say?'

Cressida now felt that she must exert all her strength to refrain from a cowardly faint. She forced her spine to remain rigid and stiffened her trembling limbs.

'My lord,' she managed to whisper, 'you cannot believe that I meant to harm the King's cause. If we were overheard. . .'

'"If we were overheard",' he mimicked cruelly. 'I take it by that you mean you and Master Prosser?'

Unable to find her voice, she managed a tremulous nod.

He was very close to her again now, bending down, his wine-scented breath fanning her cheek. After Lord Lovell had left he had taken solace from a carafe of brandy wine.

'So you deliberately disobeyed my orders.'

'I did not mean to. It was just that. . .'

'Your desires outran your fears?'

She stared at him incredulously. He could not believe

that she had deep feelings for Howell Prosser—that she would cuckold her own husband?

He caught her by the shoulder again and she could hear the harshness of his rasping breath. 'Well, you wanted to see Master Prosser again in spite of my strictures. Tell me what was so urgent that you risked discovery.'

'He—he was going away and. . .'

'Ah, so you could not bear the thought of that. He didn't suggest you should go with him, I take it? Did his gallantry not extend so far, or was he afraid of the consequences?'

Her own breathing had quickened now and fear had turned to anger that he had so deeply misjudged her.

'What you suggest is obscene,' she snapped. 'There has never been anything but friendship between us. My father would never have countenanced it. Howell knew that and respected me.'

'And, like a dutiful daughter, you were forced to a loveless marriage,' he sneered. 'That did not stop your feelings running riot, though, did it? You see him again and cannot resist—'

She struck out at him then, catching him a glancing blow upon the cheek pressed so close to her own with her wedding band. He gave a slight hiss of pain, but did not loosen his grasp on her. She could feel the bite of his fingers through the brocade of her bedgown.

'How dare you?' she stormed. 'Yes, I married you at my father's command as you wed me at the King's. It pleased neither of us, but I do not break my vows whatever the provocation and, in all events, I am not a true wife. . .'

He released her momentarily in his fury, then reached out and seized her by two flowing tresses of her hair which fell on either side of her face onto her shoulders. He tightened his grip so that she needed to control herself from giving a sudden cry of pain. His usual lazy, good-natured expression had left his features. She could see a pulse beating fast at his temple. His neck muscles bulged with strain and there was a frightening glitter to his eyes.

'So,' he muttered thickly. 'That is what disturbs you, is it—that you are not a true wife? That I, thinking you a child still, spared you what I feared might be an ordeal? But I misjudged the situation, didn't I? You are not a child. Your behaviour proves that.

'In that case I need no longer consider your feelings. I can treat you like a wife, beat you as is my right, and, by God, you deserve it. Only by the good offices of the Lord Chamberlain and the magnanimity of the King will you escape the full consequences of your treasonable actions. They, thank God, still think of you as a child bride.'

His grip on her hair, which he twisted tightly, was cruel and she gasped, but she found the courage to cry, 'All right, then, beat me; whip me to within an inch of my life. It is your right, as you maintain, but do not dare to believe ill of me. I merely said farewell to Howell Prosser. I will swear it before the altar.'

'What you did with Master Prosser or any other man can be discovered,' he said thickly as he released her hair with one hand, cast the free hand around her shoulder then snatched her up into his arms. She gave a little scream as he dumped her unceremoniously down on her bed and began to tear at the fastening of her robe.

She was thoroughly alarmed now. He was drunk and so lost to reason that in his unthinking madness he might well strangle her where she lay.

She had wanted to lie in his arms, become a true woman, but not like this, taken in anger. Wife though she was, this would be more a rape than a bedding.

Her own temper had dissipated now in her terror of what he intended. He could not do this. If he did, they

would never be able to live together in amity. She
would never forgive him. Tears were streaming freely
down her cheeks and she clawed frantically at his
impatient hands, still occupied in the remorseless task
of attempting to untie her girdle, trying to beat him off.

'No, please, my lord, you must not—not like this. I
beg of you. . .'

Something of her desperation reached his clouded
brain and he checked. Her bedgown had fallen open
and he stared down, bemused, at the ivory young body
fully revealed to his view, touched with the gold of the
fire-glow. Her proud young breasts stood taut as her
body arched in terror.

It was as if someone had drenched him in icy cold
water. He was kneeling above her, and he straightened
on his two arms as she said softly, pleadingly, 'Please,
you must listen. Punish me if you must, but—not like
this. If you do, you will regret it for ever.'

He let out one terrible great sob and she reached up
and wonderingly touched a sweat-dampened tendril of
his hair.

'You must understand. I was foolish. You are right—
I have had my own way too long and—and I do have
feelings for Howell, but not as you suppose. He is a
friend. As a friend, I went to meet him and bid him
goodbye and—and as a friend I listened to the tale he
told me as—as I had listened before to what he said of
Clifford.

'I—I think now—he—he meant us to be overheard—
to create a scandal. He—he used me. I would not have
him come to harm for his part in this, for old times'
sake, but there is nothing between us.'

'Dear God,' he murmured throatily. 'What was I
about?'

'You are not yourself, my lord, and you have every
right to be angry. I have harmed your chances of
preferment, come between you and your lord, but I

swear to you I had no intention of doing so. Last night—when I saw the King in his access of grief—I knew—knew how he loved his wife. I do not know how—how I can ever be forgiven for—'

'So it was Prosser who spoke of the King's marital intentions?'

'Yes, but the listener must have misunderstood. . .'

'No,' he said curtly. 'There was no misunderstanding. The man deliberately spun the poisoned web and you were caught in it.' His lips curled in a little cynical smile. 'You, my wife. The plotters were very aware of my role in the King's household. To involve you was very clever indeed.'

'And Howell was part of it?' The extent of the bitter hurt she felt was revealed in the wistfulness of her shocked tone.

'The King has many enemies,' he said. 'They are totally ruthless. You were to be used and discarded. Do not feel besmirched by this. It was not your fault.'

How lovely she looked, with those great violet-blue eyes of hers staring at him appealingly, the tears glistening wetly on the sculptured smoothness of her cheeks.

'What will you do?' It was so soft a whisper that he was forced to bend yet closer to catch the words.

His lips curved into a smile of ineffable sweetness. 'Well, I shall not ravish you, if that is your fear.'

A rosy flush crept from her breasts to her throat, staining the curve of her cheek. 'I—I do not fear that now, my lord.'

He blinked incredulously and stared down at her in wonder.

'By all the saints, I was right. You *are* no child, are you?'

'No, my lord.'

He gave a soft chuckle and bent to kiss her full on her mouth. 'Then it is time I did make you truly mine.'

She felt a rising sense of panic as she heard him
moving softly near the bed, divesting himself of his
clothing, then he was bending over her again, leaning
down on extended arms.

'You aren't afraid?'

She shook her head. 'Not now.'

He bent to fondle her hair, twisting a tress of it
gently, this time, round his finger.

'You are the most exquisitely beautiful creature I
have ever seen. No, don't say anything.' He silenced
her objection with a loving kiss. 'Lovely and lively
and—disobedient, and I love that in you—when you
don't threaten to bring down the whole of the
Establishment on our heads.'

'My lord, you will not be punished for. . .?'

'No, no, my sweet, and, if I were, it would be worth
it.'

His kisses were sweet on her mouth—honey-sweet—
and butterfly-soft on her throat, breasts and the curve
of her belly. She gave soft little murmurs of acute
pleasure. She was completely ready when he took her
at last, the momentary pain swiftly retreating and giving
way to total ecstasy.

He found her more responsive than he had dared to
hope. Since their marriage he had schooled himself to
wait; now he knew she was as eager for the delights of
love as he was to teach her.

He had remained celibate since Elinor's death, feeling that the taking of some wanton would be an insult
to her memory. His desires had been quenched, only
to be rekindled at the first sight of this fairy child. His
anger had drained from him at the first realisation that
he might have taken her in anger, destroyed for ever
any hope of abiding love between them. Now he lay
spent at her side, bathed in the health-giving sweat of
contentment.

She stirred and he gathered her close to his heart.

Her arms stole upwards, around his neck, to draw his head down so that he might kiss her again. She gave a faint sigh and he tilted her chin with one finger, stroking back the bright cloud of her hair that he might see her face more clearly.

'That was a sigh indeed. You have no regrets?'

She shook her head fiercely. 'No, no. I wanted—' She turned from him, avoiding his gaze, and he gently turned her back to look fully at him.

'Tell me. What did you want that I have not given you?'

'No, you don't understand. I have what I want—now. My mother and father have always been in love. Even as a small child I was fully aware of that. I thought— feared that I would never know it. You always seemed so remote, sometimes kind and indulgent, but not— loving. I think had I been a favourite hound you would have given me the same kindly, affectionate care—and the same admonishments for wrongdoing.

'And I always seemed to be found to be in disgrace, always guilty of some childish prank, until—' her voice broke a little '—until tonight, when I knew I had made you really angry and I thought—feared—that in that anger you would hurt me beyond recompense. I could not have borne that for—' she felt shy now, and sought to avoid his gaze again '—for I think I am beginning to love you, my lord.'

He chuckled, low in his throat. 'I should hope so, sweet madam, else your conduct tonight would be deemed wanton indeed.'

They lay silent for moments, then she said with a little catch to her voice, 'Will they—force you to send me away?'

He considered. 'I think it might be politic. You should be away from the King's sight for a while.'

She struggled free of his encircling arm and half sat up.

'Martyn, you cannot send me from you, not now.'

'Sweetheart, you know how things are at Court. I cannot leave the Council at this critical time. I have work to do—important work.' His tone was grim and she closed her eyes as she thought what that deadly work would be.

'You will seek out those who wish to harm the King's cause.'

'That is my duty. The King's need is great. I thought you should go to the Marches for a while.'

'To your manor at Wroxeter?'

He frowned in the half-darkness of the firelit room. 'I had considered that, but I would have wished to take you there personally. Unfortunately that is not possible at this time. I must think this out carefully and—and I must wait for the King's command in this matter.'

She said softly, 'What is to happen about—about the Lady Elizabeth?'

'She is to leave London for the north—Sheriff Hutton, one of the King's Yorkshire castles. She will join other members of the royal household there.'

'I—I have done her great harm, for I do not think she was fully aware—of all this and the consequences. I should contact her, beg her to forgive me.'

His voice, when he answered, was decidedly chilly. 'Cressida, you must swear to me that you will not communicate with the Lady Elizabeth—that is a direct order. I should be truly angry with you if you were to disobey me in this grave matter.'

He turned to look up at her and she inclined her chin in answer.

'Do you think I will be allowed to attend Her Grace's funeral? Oh, Martyn, I want to so much, to do her honour with the rest of her ladies.'

He sighed heavily. 'For that I must obtain the permission of His Grace.'

She nodded sorrowfully. With this she must be

content, for she knew that Martyn would need supreme care to so much as approach the King with such a request, considering the magnitude of the harm she had done him.

Whatever pleas Martyn made to the King Cressida was never to know, but she was granted permission to follow the Queen's body with her other attendants when she was laid to rest within Westminster Abbey. Later, as the coffin was lowered into the cavity prepared for it near the choir stalls, Cressida saw that the King was openly weeping.

She did not attempt to hold back her own tears, for the Queen had been so very kind to her, considering the short time she had remained in her service, and she found she was not alone, for the other ladies were declaring that there was none quite like the dead Queen and they would never find another mistress so forbearing, for all that she had been no fool and could hold her own in dispute with any like the great Earl, her father.

The funeral feast that followed afterwards in the palace hall was a subdued affair, no one of the guests taking opportunity from the abundance of good food and wine provided to overindulge.

The King sat apart beneath the cloth of estate and Cressida saw that he ate little and drank even more sparingly than usual. He was flanked by his two oldest friends, Lord Lovell and Sir Richard Ratcliffe, and Cressida was relieved that there appeared to be no coldness between the bluff Yorkshire knight and his sovereign.

Apparently no great harm had been done by the gossip engendered by Howell Prosser. She glanced uneasily at Martyn, who sat by her side, only too aware that the King must yet face the ordeal of open declaration of intent within the hall of the knights of St John at Clerkenwell, which occasion, Martyn had informed her, had already been arranged.

'His Grace has also written to the mayor and aldermen of York, informing them of their duty to scotch this baseless and ugly rumour, with orders to apprehend any person speaking dishonourably of the King in this matter,' he had told her.

'But surely this cannot affect people outside the capital?' Cressida had said unhappily.

Martyn had shrugged. 'This rumour was put about to blotch the King's reputation by those rebels who mean him harm,' he'd replied, 'and is as likely to have reached all parts of the realm as here in London and Westminster.'

The King left the hall very early but issued a command to his courtiers to remain and continue to feast in honour of the Queen, but even after his departure the mood within the hall remained sombre.

Martyn leaned towards Cressida. 'I must go to my office and attend to some pressing business but will only be gone for a short time. Will you remain in the hall until I return to you?'

'No,' she said hastily. 'I will come with you. I—I do not feel comfortable here in the hall—considering what has happened.'

'It is unlikely that the other attendants are aware of your involvement,' he assured her. 'Lord Lovell has promised to keep your name out of this affair.'

She swallowed hard and cast the Lord Chamberlain a glance of profound gratitude as she left the hall with Martyn.

'I will wait in the Queen's antechamber,' she said, 'until you have completed your business.'

Martyn nodded and turned to Peter Fairley, who was in attendance and had followed them from the hall.

'Peter, find young Philip Kenton and tell him to attend his mistress in the Queen's antechamber.'

Peter bowed and hastened off on his errand.

Cressida found the room deserted and desolate. She seated herself in a window seat and looked round sadly at the evidence of happier times she had spent there: a discarded beribboned lute, several pieces of uncompleted embroidery, a tapestry frame. Would she be summoned again to attend a new queen when the King remarried, as she knew he must?

She blinked back bitter tears of grief and regret for the part she had unwittingly paid in deepening his anguish.

The place seemed so forlorn and cheerless, despite the fire burning in the hearth, that she could not bear to wait there until her young page joined her and rose to seek out Martyn's office.

The corridors seemed cheerless and almost deserted, reflecting the saddened mood of the palace inhabitants, and, without concentration, she took a wrong turn and found herself very close to the presence chamber where she had first been presented to the King and Queen and seen Martyn clearly and recognised him as a possible bridegroom.

The door had been left ajar and the pikeman who normally guarded it was not in position outside. Had the King dismissed him or sent him on some errand or was he in his own private chamber? But, even so, this door should not have been left unguarded. Cressida found that strange and alarming. Knowing what she now knew, she feared that some ill-wisher might have lured the guards away, though she could in no way account for such negligence.

She peered anxiously round the door as she had done that night when she had found the King in an access of grief at his dead Queen's bedside.

Gazing round somewhat apprehensively, she encountered the King's cool grey-green eyes as he sat

slumped in the armchair near the hearth. He was totally
alone and her eyes widened at the lack of attendance.

His lips curved into a slightly bitter smile. 'Come in,
Lady Cressida.'

'Your Grace,' she stammered uncertainly. 'I would
not dream of trespassing upon your privacy. It is just
that I thought—feared that—'

'I might be lying slain upon the floor?' The smile
deepened now, though she could see the ravages grief
had made only too clearly graved upon his features.
'No, I sent the guard to the outer corridor. I had no
desire to be spied on, which is why I left the hall, and
though he protested I needed to be rid of the fellow for
an hour.

'Kings rarely have the luxury of being alone, Lady
Cressida, and, to be honest, I have no need of a guard.
If necessary, I can take care of myself, even should I be
attacked by an intruder as beautiful and charming as
yourself.'

'Then I must take myself off immediately, Your
Grace.'

'Now that you are here, come in.'

'Your Grace, I am sure that my husband would not
approve of my intrusion, nor do I think he would—'

'Approve of my lack of care for my own life? No,'
he acknowledged. 'It is his business, amongst others',
to guard my back and I agree with you—he would
censure me—oh, in the most respectful of terms, but
roundly, and for my own good, for all that.'

She curtsied low and approached as his signal bade
her. There was so much she needed to say, but could
not, and to her great shame she burst into tears. He
waited until the storm subsided then gestured her to
seat herself on a stool near him.

At last she whispered brokenly, 'Your Grace, how
can you ever forgive me?'

He sighed deeply. 'I understand you were ill informed, Cressida, and cannot be blamed.'

'But the harm I have done. . .'

'That others have done. Oh, Cressida, you must put all this from you, as I must do. The Queen loved you and you served her well.'

'We would all have given our lives for her.'

'Yes, I believe that,' he said quietly. 'You know, I understand what it is to be held to account for something I had not done.'

He was musing, gazing into the distance, and she waited courteously for him to explain himself.

'I loved Anne so deeply and when she was widowed I thought all would be well with us, for I knew she did not love Edward of Lancaster, so I had hopes she would turn willingly to me.'

'And she did not?' Cressida said, unwilling to believe that there could ever have been ill feeling between the sovereigns. Anne had shown only too plainly how much she adored her husband.

He made a little rueful gesture with one ringed hand. 'Someone anxious to make mischief between us informed her I had murdered the Prince.' He tapped one finger meditatively upon the arm of his chair. 'He was killed in the pursuit at Tewkesbury.'

'If—if you were not responsible, Your Grace, why did you not explain?'

He smiled down at her sadly. 'He was badly disfigured, trampled by horsemen and men-at-arms. I did not wish her to know the hard facts. It took some time for me to convince her of my love, but, despite interference from others, she came to me at last, and I have never regretted a moment of the precious time we have had together.

'Never forget that, Cressida. When you love, make the most of what you have. Swear to me you will do

that, for in this uncertain world it might not be as long
as you hope for.'

'I will, Your Grace.'

Fleetingly, he touched her mourning veil. 'I trust
Martyn was not too hard on you. Frank Lovell tells me
he was furious when he was first told.'

She bowed her head in shame. 'He was, my lord, and
I thought—feared—that—but all is well now, my lord.'

He nodded, satisfied, as she raised her chin and
looked steadily at him through a blurring of tears.

'I hoped he would find contentment in this marriage.
I still have faith in my own judgement.'

She blushed hotly. 'I think I—we—I think I will learn
to love him, my lord.'

The tight line of his mouth relaxed momentarily.
'Good. I need to believe that those I love can trust
those about them as I need to do.'

She knew she should leave now and waited for his
dismissal, which he gave with a smiling nod, but at the
door she said hesitatingly, 'Your Grace, I—I am afraid
for the Lady Elizabeth. She befriended me and I fear I
have done her grave harm.'

She waited in dread lest he would become angry with
her for her temerity, but he sighed again and said
gently, 'The Lady Elizabeth knows I have deep affection for her and will always have her best interests at
heart. You need not fear for her.'

'My husband has forbidden me to try to contact her,
Your Grace. If only I could express my regret that. . .'

'Can you write, Lady Cressida?'

'Oh, yes, Your Grace, I was well tutored.'

'Then write to her telling her from your heart what
you truly feel and I promise you it will be delivered
into her hands and none other.'

She ran back to him and stooped to kiss his fingers,
resting still now on the chair arm. She was sobbing

again. 'Dear my lord, I do not know how to thank you. I feel so guilty. . .'

'Guilt is a useless and harmful emotion,' he said ruefully. 'I have learned many times to put it from me. Do not be too hard on yourself. Go now into the adjoining chamber and write your letter. I'll see to it that Lord Martyn does not know of it.'

She rose, gathered up her skirts, and began to back from his presence, then a harsh voice behind her froze her in her tracks.

'My lord, why do I find you unattended and unguarded? I shall see to it that these tardy fellows pay for their negligence with their lives.'

Lord Martyn stopped in his stride as he approached the King and caught sight of Cressida. His face darkened with fury.

'Your Grace, I cannot find words to apologise for this intrusion. What my wife is doing, daring to approach you, I cannot think.'

'In truth, Martyn, I believe she was as concerned for my safety as you are yourself,' the King said mildly. 'She too was alarmed at the absence of my guard and came in to discover if anything untoward had occurred. I explained I had myself dismissed the fellow and kept her to talk further—of her love for the Queen.'

The last words were spoken very softly and slightly hoarsely as if tears thickened his throat.

'You must not take her to task for this and must allow my erring guard to keep his neck intact. Actually, I asked her to write out for me some words she herself has found comforting. Will you do that, Lady Cressida, and give them to me personally before you leave Westminster?'

Martyn blinked, bewildered, and Cressida gave her husband a frightened glance as she fled past him into the adjoining chamber.

When she returned the King was in earnest talk with

Martyn and he held out his hand smilingly for the
sealed missive.

'Thank you, Cressida. This will be a salve to both
our hearts.'

She curtsied low again, knowing she owed him a
great debt of gratitude. Martyn was bowing and led her
outside.

'By all the saints,' he fumed, 'cannot I leave you
alone for moments without you getting into some
dangerous venture? I think yours is the face the King
must least wish to view at this time.'

Cressida flushed hotly, her fingers clutching tightly at
the black silk folds of her skirt. They were wet with the
sweat of guilt.

'My lord, I am sorry. I had no wish to embarrass you
but it was as the King said. I mistook my way, saw the
door unguarded and feared—feared the worst. After
all, I above all others have seen evidence of malice
directed towards the King. He was, as always, very
gracious to me.'

Martyn drew a hard breath. 'As you say, he has been
more forbearing than we could hope for or deserve. I
trust now you will think more kindly of your sovereign
than I believe you did formerly.'

She lifted her face to his. 'Martyn, I know now how
deeply I have wronged the King in my thoughts and
will pray continually to the Virgin to grant him comfort
in his great grief.'

'Amen,' he murmured fervently as he led her back
towards the great hall where his squire and other
attendants waited to escort the Earl and his Countess
home to the Strand house.

CHAPTER EIGHT

THOUGH her heart was still heavy, Cressida returned to the Strand house with her burden of guilt lightened by the King's understanding. She was grateful that he had not revealed to Martyn her plea to contact the Lady Elizabeth for she still feared his anger over their association.

That night he did not come to her chamber. She told herself that the King's business kept him working late, but could not quite convince herself of the fact. She had waited so long to become Martyn's true wife that it was a distinct blow to her pride that he did not also long for their time of privacy within the curtained bed.

She remembered, blushing darkly, the expression on Alice's face when she had hastily collected up the blood-smeared sheets that morning. She had flashed Cressida a glance of pure triumph. Now Cressida lay in the bed alone, praying that Martyn would come, however late—but he did not.

He did breakfast with her, however, and after the page had been dismissed she ventured to question him.

'My lord, you were working into the small hours last night?'

He nodded abstractedly, spreading honey on fine white manchet bread.

'There is still much to be done to prepare for the King's presence at Clerkenwell. The Lord Chamberlain has placed the responsibility for the King's personal safety in my hands.'

Her lips trembled slightly. However much the King had declared his forgiveness, she was aware that those in the know would always consider her partly to blame

and her guilt would rub off upon her husband's
reputation.

'He will be well guarded?'

'I shall see to it. Be very sure of that.'

Her hand shook as she moved her ale cup nervously.
'I was afraid you were still angry with me last night
since—since you did not come to me.'

He was avoiding her eyes, frowning slightly. 'It was,
indeed, very late. The day had been a difficult one for
you. I wanted you to sleep undisturbed.'

She did not reply and he turned to face her, his dark
eyes unhooded, looking directly into hers.

He hesitated, then reached across the table and took
her hand within his. 'Cressida, dark days lie ahead. I
do not wish you to be burdened. . .'

Her own blue eyes widened. 'You mean I might bear
a child? But I want to bear you an heir, Martyn. That
is my duty.'

He sighed. 'In time, when life is more settled.' He
looked away again. 'Over the next months I think it
might be better if you were away from the capital.'

She had to hold back a cry of protest. It was what
she feared—separation from Martyn now, when they
should be getting to know each other—beginning to
love each other—and because she had been foolishly
naïve she must be exiled from Court, from her husband's side. It was a harsh punishment.

'I am an embarrassment to you.' She swallowed back
the tears. 'I understand.'

'No, you do not.' His voice was almost harsh with
pent-up emotion. 'If it were simply that, we could live
this down—together—but hard days lie ahead, dangerous days, and I want you safe out of harm's way.'

She was alarmed now. 'Is your life in danger? If so I
should be at your side.'

'Cressida, *all* our lives may well be endangered. The
Tudor spies are everywhere. The King's reputation is

at its lowest. The people are distraught over baseless rumours concerning the Queen's death. It is time for Henry Tudor to strike. He will not wish to wait another year.'

'You mean he will invade?' She was incredulous.

'I think it will come—this summer. The King knows it too—and, I fear, at this time of anguish, is not so dismayed by the prospect as he should be. You should be well away from London and so should your father.'

It was a bald statement of opinion that made her catch her breath again. Sir Daniel was a Marcher baron and many of the Welsh lords could well be under suspicion of supporting the Tudor.

A cold frisson of fear touched her heart and she nodded, but she would bide her time. Yes, her parents should leave the capital, but she had every intention of trying to persuade Martyn to allow her to remain with him. Now was not the time; she must wait for a better opportunity.

She watched him leave the house later and knew he would be beside his sovereign at this humiliating occasion within the hall of the knights of St John and was forced to hold back the sharp bile in her throat, knowing she was partly to blame for the necessity.

The following days were long and tedious. The Court was in mourning, there would be no place for her there, and the hours stretched before her endlessly. She was determined to get to know the household and one morning Master Rawlings escorted her on a tour of inspection. In the kitchen her encounter with Jack Wainwright passed without too much embarrassment on either side, though a quick glance towards the spit revealed that Wat Forrester was back at his duties.

Throughout this difficult time when Martyn was absent for long hours Cressida was thankful for the friendship of Alice and the assiduous attentions of young Philip Kenton, whom Martyn had assigned to wait on her.

She was delighted when Master Rawlings informed her that her father had called, three days after the Queen's funeral. She rose to greet him, hands out-stretched, when the steward ushered him into the winter parlour.

'Father, it is good to see you. I had thought you might soon be travelling home and feared that I might be at Westminster when you came to bid me goodbye.'

He embraced her warmly and she led him towards the hearth.

'It is still very cold, even for March, but we have promise of spring at last. There are shoots pushing through in the pleasance. If the weather continues to improve you should have a pleasant journey home.' She was chattering away in her happiness at seeing him and did not, at first, notice his strained expression.

He looked deliberately at young Philip Kenton, who was preparing to replace his lute on its nail on the wall, for the boy had been strumming to Cressida while she sat at her embroidery.

'Can your page fetch me some ale from the buttery, daughter?'

Cressida had been about to offer him malmsey from the wine jug on the table and she followed his gaze towards Philip's back, a little bewildered, but instantly understanding that her father had need to talk to her without any other present.

'Of course. Wine can be cloying at this hour of the morning, and you will want the ale mulled. Go at once, Philip, and wait while one of the kitchen wenches gets it good and hot and well spiced.'

Philip withdrew at once, ever anxious to be useful, and after the door closed behind him Cressida turned quickly towards her father.

'There is nothing wrong with Mother, is there?'

'No, no, child. As you say, we shall be off about our travels in a couple of days. Your mother believes I am here to tell you of our impending departure. I did not want her involved in this business.'

Cressida was becoming alarmed. It was unlike her father to keep any matter from her mother and she now saw that he was very pale indeed and frowning.

'You are not ill. . .?'

'No, no. Child, is your husband in the house?'

'No, he left early for the Tower. He is often there these days and—'

'Has he a place of business here?'

'He has an office, yes, where he reads all his correspondence concerning the Council.'

'Is there a secretary at work there?'

'No. Master Standish is with him at the Tower. I saw them go down to the river quay together.'

'Can you gain admittance?'

Cressida paled. 'To the office? Without Martyn's consent? I would not like to do that. He—'

'But if the matter was of paramount importance?'

She hesitated. 'Well, probably. It may well be locked, but the servants here give me complete obedience.'

She was growing pale now. It was obvious that her father was in some trouble and had come to her for help.

'What is it, Father?'

'Howell Prosser is in grave danger of arrest.'

She started visibly. 'I thought he had left the city.'

'I wish to God he had.' Her father paced the room, his hands locked behind his back. 'Your husband has control of the ports. The situation is grave and the Council fears possibility of invasion. Any man wishing to leave the country is suspected of being a spy for the Tudor and is required to answer to strict questioning or to have licence to travel.'

'I know,' she said soberly. 'Martyn thinks the invasion will come soon.'

Sir Daniel nodded. 'That fool Prosser has been in communication with the Tudor faction. He needs to be got clear of England. He could be arrested at any moment. He is convinced he is under suspicion and is in hiding at present—where, you had best not know.

'I need you to obtain a licence for him to travel. My Lord Wroxeter issues men with such documents. It is likely there are some forms within his office. If you could obtain one I could smuggle Howell, under an assumed name, of course, out of the capital and he could be well on his way to Dover or Lynn within the next few days.'

Cressida drew a hard breath. 'You ask me to commit treason, Father. The King has been good to me—and to you. I would not wish to take part in any action which might bring him to harm, however much I think of Howell Prosser as my friend.'

'Aye.' Sir Daniel sighed heavily. 'The King has been good to me and I swear to you I am his loyal subject— at least, I am now.'

Cressida's heart turned to ice and she came very close to him. 'Father, what have you done?'

'Before we were summoned to Court I—' He licked dry lips. 'Long ago, I was true to the Lancastrian cause, Cressida. I was disturbed when King Richard took the throne and concerned for the fate of the boy Princes.'

He turned away, avoiding her eyes, his voice a little hoarse with shame. 'I toyed with the thought of offering allegiance to Henry—only thought of it. I wrote letters, encouraged by the Prossers—and received replies from some exiled Lancastrian lords.'

'Sweet Virgin,' Cressida said fervently. 'Don't you realise that it is my lord's special responsibility to ensure the safety of the King's Grace and to prosecute anyone suspected of treason or harbouring any man so accused?'

'I know that, or rather I suspected it. The truth is, if Howell Prosser is caught and interrogated, I could be in direct danger of arrest, and at this critical time, when every man's motives are questioned, there is little doubt I would be charged with treason— yes, and more than likely found guilty.'

Cressida went white to the lips. She recalled Martyn's account of what had happened to Sir Roger Clifford only weeks ago. Her heart was racing.

'And you think such blank documents are kept by Martyn and handled by his secretary?'

Sir Daniel nodded. 'These licences to travel are issued and unchallenged at the ports. Armed with one, Howell could reach Henry's court in safety. We have to help him, Cressida. If he is caught he will talk of his fellow conspirators.'

He swallowed nervously.

'However brave he thinks he is, he will be made to talk and I would be doomed by any such disclosure.'

She nodded. 'The document would need to be signed?'

'Probably not. Your husband's secretary may well issue them under Wroxeter's seal. There must be many of the King's officers who need to go to Calais on business frequently and in a hurry without need to consult the Earl personally. It is a chance, daughter. Will you go and search for any such blank licences— for Howell—and for me?'

She compressed her lips. 'I will go for you, Father, but only on your sworn word that you will enter into no more conspiracies with the Tudor. I will not betray my husband's honour in this underhand fashion— except for your most pressing need.'

He caught her to him and kissed her fiercely. 'I would not ask you if the need were not desperate,

Cressida. If I go down it could harm your husband's reputation and bring him down with me.'

Her eyes widened in horror but, as Philip knocked at the door requesting permission to enter with the mulled ale, she nodded, and turned immediately to call to the boy.

Philip served the ale and Cressida dismissed him once more.

'Philip, will you go to the stables and make sure my mare has been exercised? I shall not be able to ride today but she should be taken out.'

As the boy moved to go Sir Daniel said softly, 'Could he not go first to the office and fetch the document for you?'

Cressida shook her head vehemently. 'No, I prefer to go myself. Go and do what I ask, Philip.'

The page looked at her curiously but she waved him off and he hastened out.

'Surely the boy could not be blamed if he were seen and it might be better so.'

'No, Father,' she said quietly but firmly. 'I would not have young Philip blamed for what we must do.' She gave a faint shudder as she thought how the boy might well be punished.

She rose at once and gestured to her father to remain seated. 'Wait here for me. I should not be long.'

He nodded, though his expression was still anxious.

As she suspected, Cressida found the door to her husband's office locked. Fortunately Master Rawlings was approaching down the corridor and she summoned him to provide the key.

'Lord Martyn promised to show me a letter which had arrived from the Wroxeter manor. He must have left in a hurry and forgotten it. It will be on his desk, I dare say. Give me the key, Master Rawlings.'

The steward hesitated, but his mistress was clearly

showing signs of impatience, and he produced the key from a bunch at his belt and opened the door.

Cressida explained as she entered. 'My father is here, as you know, and would like to see the report.'

Master Rawlings appeared to be waiting for her to re-emerge with her letter so that he might lock up once more, but firmly she sent him off to the kitchens.

'Tell Master Wainwright that supper should be delayed tonight as my lord might be kept late at the Tower.'

He went reluctantly, looking backwards towards the office door, and she waited in the doorway, obviously determined to see him go on the errand. She smiled to herself inwardly. Master Rawlings's dignity must have been ruffled. He was unused to being sent off to give instructions to underlings as if he were a page or serving wench, but she had no wish to see him blamed either, if anything should go wrong and the loss of the travel licence were discovered. She alone, should it come to it, must shoulder the responsibility.

There were several rolls of parchment upon the desk, together with quills, penknives for sharpening and bottles of ink. One parchment lay open, a knife discarded by it as if either the Earl himself or Master Standish had been employed in scraping it clear for further correspondence. Cressida examined the rolled ones feverishly, but they appeared to be household accounts and a letter awaiting Lord Martyn's attention giving orders for the setting to rights of the Wroxeter manor for the possible arrival of the lord and his bride later in the year.

Cressida bit her lip and straightened. She had been optimistic indeed to expect travel licences to be left in full view of anyone who entered.

There were two small chests and she pulled at the lid of the left one impatiently. It was locked and she could see no small key in evidence. Obviously the Earl or his secretary carried those pertaining to private correspondence upon his person, and it would be useless to recall Master Rawlings and demand such keys from him. He would be unlikely to have access to such an item. Was she to be frustrated? If so, she would find it almost a relief—yet her father would remain in danger.

She pulled experimentally at the lid of the other chest and, to her astonishment, it came open. Either there was nothing of importance inside or Master Standish had been summoned to attend the Earl so precipitately that he had forgotten to secure it. Careful not to disturb the contents unduly and reveal the search, she sifted cautiously through them. To her joy, she discovered four small pieces of parchment sealed but unsigned, granting the bearer—and here there was space for the insertion of a name—permission to travel outside the realm.

She caught up one, returned the rest hastily to the chest and slammed it shut. Her heart was pounding erratically as she stood upright and listened to hear if Master Rawlings was about to return. He had not left the key with her, so undoubtedly he would do so very soon.

Her brows drew together as she realised he would report her presence there to his master. She would have to make some excuse for entering. That she must consider later but first she must get this to her father immediately.

It was then that she heard voices in the corridor and froze where she stood. She could not mistake her husband's peremptory tone. Why had he unexpectedly returned from the Tower? She stood irresolute as she heard Master Rawlings explaining himself.

'I was just checking that my lady the Countess had left your office, my lord. I know well your orders that the room is to be kept locked at all times when you or Master Standish are absent.'

The door was jerked open abruptly and Martyn stood on the threshold staring across at her. She looked beyond him to the anxious countenance of the steward and tried to smile reassuringly.

'That is quite all right, Master Rawlings. I would have sent a page to tell you when I had finished in the room and you could lock the door again.'

'You can go.' Martyn dismissed his steward curtly.

He advanced further into the room, firmly shutting the door and enclosing them together, apart from prying eyes. Cressida waited, dry-mouthed, for him to demand an explanation. At last it came, coldly uttered and without any attempt at courteous preamble.

'Suppose you give me what you took from the desk.'

She still remained silent, her eyes imploring, one hand behind her, resting on the desktop as if for support.

He said harshly, 'Come, Cressida, obey me. I know that nonsense you talked to Rawlings about wishing to examine the Wroxeter manor accounts to be totally false. Obviously you came here to read my private correspondence, not out of curiosity but for some more dangerous purpose. Give me what you took or copied—now.'

She gave a little apprehensive shudder then took the small scrap of parchment from the modesty vest of her gown where she had placed it and handed it to him without a word.

He scrutinised it quickly then sighed.

'I imagine you are not willing to tell me for whom you obtained this but I can make a calculated guess. Prosser.'

She had gone very pale and her eyes shone like bruised velvet violet flowers after rain as she looked back at him, but there were no tears or hysterics as he might have expected.

'Well?' he demanded, his patience wearing thin. 'Am I correct?'

'Yes,' she said quietly.

'You know the man to be a traitor?'

'Yes,' she admitted again.

'This declaration of friendship only is wearing a trifle thin, my dear. I am sure you are quite unwilling to tell me where the fellow is hiding or, incidentally, how you came to receive a message from him.'

She shook her head mutely.

He sighed again and moved a fraction nearer to her. She flinched away from him and his level brows rose in annoyance.

'Do you believe I would beat the truth out of you?'

'I do not know,' she said flatly, 'but you would be within your rights, I know that. Please do not ask me to betray Howell.' She hesitated. 'Please, Martyn, I beg of you. I have my reasons and they are not what you suppose. I tell you again, there is nothing between Howell Prosser and I that could constitute a threat to our marriage.'

He sighed again then moved away from her to the window and stood staring out, his back to her.

She said softly, 'For my sake, my lord, will you let Howell Prosser go? If you do not it could harm others—others I love. I am assured the man can do no more harm to the King's cause. I swear I would not help him if I did not believe that.'

He turned, shrugging, then, abruptly, he thrust the travel permit to her across the desk which now was between them.

'Then I suggest you get this to your messenger as quickly as you can before I change my mind.'

She moved to the door and turned to speak to him again, but he had once more turned his back on her.

She swallowed back tears and left the room.

Her father looked up anxiously as she returned to the winter parlour. She handed him the permit and he gazed up into her taut, pale little face.

'Were there difficulties? You were not discovered?'

There was little point in alarming him further. Unexpectedly Lord Martyn had capitulated and given in to her desperate plea. She drew a hard breath as she thought it possible that her father might be observed leaving the house and be followed. It was a risk they all must take.

Somehow she believed that Martyn had understood her fear and would allow her messenger to pass unchallenged. Her alarm mounted as she thought that he might be well aware of the messenger's identity. If he intended to arrest her father, he surely would have done so already? She would pray to the Virgin that her family remained safe.

She said hastily, 'No, all is well, but I think you should leave London very soon now. It will be safer—for all of us.'

He took her into his arms in a bear-hug embrace.

'Don't think I am unaware of what you have done for us and what it has cost you. You are growing up fast, my daughter—too fast. Know that I love you very dearly. I will not endanger you again. I promise.'

She forced a smile. 'Go with God. Kiss my mother for me. I pray I shall soon see you both again.'

He paused in the doorway. 'Have you any message you wish me to give to Howell?'

Two bright spots of anger burned in her cheeks as she recalled how he had used her in that final talk they had had together on the Westminster quay.

'No,' she said in a tight, hard voice. 'Only that I wish him safely out of the country as soon as possible.'

Sir Daniel bowed his head slightly as if he read the hidden message to her former friend in her contempuous tone, then he left the room and she heard him speaking to a page outside with instructions to call for his horse to be saddled.

* * *

That night Martyn came to her chamber. Without waiting to be told, Alice made a discreet exit. Cressida waited apprehensively for her husband to approach the bed. She well understood that he was furiously angry with her but, as yet, he had made no move to reproach her or punish her.

He looked down at her impassively and she controlled the urge not to flinch from him again as she had done in the office.

'I have sent a messenger to your father requesting that he escort you to his own manor for the next few months until I am able to come and take you to Wroxeter.'

She blinked uncertainly. 'Tomorrow? That is very soon. I shall scarce have time to pack...'

'I have already given instructions for your maid and the other servants to see that that is completed very early in the morning.'

She said appealingly, 'I know you said you thought it best for me to be out of the capital during the coming summer, but could I not wait until you can take me to Wroxeter yourself?'

He said coldly, 'I have told you what I have decided. For once you will obey me without question.'

'How—how long do you think it will be before...?'

'I have no idea, but I will convey my later orders to you by courier.'

His manner was so cold that he might have been dismissing some importunate mistress he wished to discard. She swallowed back salt tears. She had cost him dear too many times for him to forgive her. Was this to be the sum of their lives together, this polite endurance of a bond which had been forced upon them?

It wasn't enough for Cressida. She had tasted of the fruits of love and found them sweet. She ached to pull him down to her, compel him to love her as he once had, but knew she dared not. She could only hope and pray that in some future time he would find it in his heart to forgive this foolish child bride who had both embarrassed him and today forced him to acquiesce in an act of treason.

She wanted to weep, plead with him not to forsake her, but it would be useless, and she could not wound him further with pointless childish behaviour.

She shook back her hair and forced a smile to her stiffened lips.

'As you wish, my lord. My parents will be glad to have me spend some time with them.'

He held her gaze deliberately with his own. 'Your presence may suffice to prevent your father from taking part in any indiscreet actions.'

Her eyes opened wide and he nodded coolly, then turned towards the door again. 'I shall send Philip Kenton with you. I shall have need of Peter Fairley's services over the next months.'

Her mouth went dry again. Peter Fairley was his squire. Did he expect to need the boy's services in battle?

As he raised the door-latch she resisted the urge to call him back. This might well be the last time she saw him. As if to reinforce that thought he said, chillingly, 'I shall have left the house before you embark, having ensured everything for your comfort. Your father will doubtless dispatch a courier to assure me that you reached home safely and that all is well with you.'

He was offering her no farewell kiss, no assurances of his devotion. This cold little exchange was to be their parting words and he had spoken of months, so he fully expected their separation to be lengthy. She waited until he had withdrawn, then buried her head in her pillows and sobbed out the agony of her grief.

The journey back to the Marches was as uneventful as their previous journey to London and Cressida's spirits were as low. She forced herself to be cheerful and excused her frequent laspses into despondency by references to the death of the Queen to whom she had been deeply attached, as her parents knew.

Not even the sight of her beloved manor could completely lift her heart, though the servants received her joyfully and she felt herself once more enclosed in the loving cocoon which throughout her childhood had always meant so much to her.

Sir Thomas Prosser came frequently to visit Sir Daniel and they seemed as much on good terms as previously, but no mention was ever made to Howell's absence and Cressida was not informed as to whether he had safely left the realm.

Despite her inner anger towards him for the way he had shamefully used her, she missed him. When she rode out towards Ludlow as before she found herself expecting to see him riding towards her. At least no word reached them that he had been arrested and they could only hope that all was well with him.

Her father dispatched a courier to London soon after their arrival home to inform Lord Wroxeter his wife was safe and well, as he had requested. He sent back formal messages thanking Sir Daniel for his care of Cressida and a brief, equally formal letter to Cressida, assuring her of his constant devotion and desire to see her soon on their Wroxeter manor. He passed no comments on events at Court and it seemed that he had deliberately determined to cut her off from any further disclosures which could possibly harm the King's cause if related to any of those barons thought to be secretly in league with Henry Tudor.

Cressida had hoped passionately that she had conceived but as the weeks passed that hope was dashed and, though her mother never referred to the subject, delicately avoiding the issue, Cressida was aware that her parents believed the marriage had remained unconsummated.

It seemed that they had obtained this information from Howell, though Cressida had regretted her hasty unhappy disclosure and had begged him to keep it to himself. In some strange way it was communicated to her that they were relieved that this was so and she refrained from informing them otherwise. Alice, she knew, could be relied upon to keep her own counsel.

News came to them through passing chapmen, Welsh minstrels and herdsmen who had driven their flocks westward towards the border towns of Hereford and Gloucester.

The King had declared John of Lincoln, his sister's son, his heir. The claim of his late brother's son, the youthful Earl of Warwick, had not even been considered. Clarence's lands and hereditary claims lay still under attainder and his boy heir was said to be simple-witted.

Cressida knew the boy was living at Sheriff Hutton along with his cousin, the Lady Elizabeth. She wondered how her friend was faring and would have given much to hear from her. Would the King consolidate his hold on the throne by announcing new wedding plans? She knew that that was politically necessary and, remembering the man she had seen overcome with anguish, understood how that would cost him dear.

Days and weeks passed slowly, or so it seemed to Cressida, who was impatient now to be joined by her husband and visit her own lands near Wroxeter as he had promised. She had always loved the coming of spring and the warm summer days on the Marches—the splendours of sun on grass, hawks hovering overhead in bright blue skies, the profusion of wild flowers—but now the procession of days seemed irksome.

She fretted against the necessity of sitting in the solar with her mother on those days when it was too wet for her to ride out, working on new altar cloths for the church and the repair of tapestries, in preparation for the draughty autumn and winter days to come.

She rode out one fine May day with young Philip Kenton in attendance and returned to find considerable activity within the stables. Grooms were busy rubbing down newly arrived mounts and judging by their appearance the beasts had been ridden hard. Cressida felt a sudden constriction round her heart. It had been such a day, though in winter, when she had come back from a ride to find that a courier had arrived to summon her family to Court.

She had been afraid then that her father might have been in some danger. Now she was even more alarmed. They had received only snippets of news lately, though all their neighbours were openly discussing an imminent invasion by the Tudor. Had it come at last, the danger which Martyn had known was threatening and which would cast its deadly shadow over her father's household?

She asked no questions of the grooms, but handed over their mounts and hurried Philip inside the manor house. Her mother stood near the oriel window in the solar, gazing down over the herb plot, one hand pressed against her heart. It was clear from her expression that she was disturbed. She forced a smile at sight of Cressida.

'It is such a fine day I thought you might stay out longer.'

'You wanted me away from the house?' The question was posed brusquely and Lady Gretton glanced pointedly at Philip, who stood uncertainly in the doorway.

Cressida said sharply, 'I shall not want you for a while now, Philip. Go and practise that new ballad you promised to sing to us tonight after supper.'

The boy bowed and withdrew.

'Is there news from my lord?'

Lady Gretton shook her head. She sighed wearily. 'No, a messenger has arrived from Rhys Ap Thomas.' She sank down on the padded window seat and stared bleakly back at her daughter. 'There are two of them, sounding out your father's allegiance. I wish devoutly it were otherwise.'

'You are afraid for him?'

'Of course. Ap Thomas is a devious man and, in my opinion, not to be trusted. He hasn't decided on his own loyalty yet, I imagine, but could draw in his neighbours further than any of them would be wise to venture.'

Cressida gave a sharp intake of breath. 'Has there— been any news of Howell?'

'Not that I have heard. He was in deep. I doubt he will risk himself just yet in England.'

'Father would not ally himself with the King's enemies?'

'No. He toyed with the idea once, I think, but not since your betrothal has he been in any doubt concerning the King's honour. But even the presence of these men here at this house could smell of treason. I wish we could openly refuse to receive them.'

'Why does not Father make his allegiance plain to them?'

Lady Gretton turned slowly to face Cressida. 'I think he considers it politic to show no hostility to either side at this stage.'

Cressida was shocked. 'He would not fight for the Tudor?'

'No, he would never go that far, but he is a border baron. He is considering carefully our safety should there be a change of ruler.'

'But the King could never lose, not in an outright

battle for the crown. He is an experienced warrior *and*,' she finished indignantly, 'he is our anointed sovereign.'

Lady Gretton smiled a little wanly. 'I see you have changed your tune since you met him. Less than a year ago you were all for joining his enemies.'

Cressida's reply sounded rueful. 'Now I am a married woman and my husband is deep in the King's confidences. Where would he be if I were to show any counter-interest?'

'Just so, and was not this entirely in the King's mind when he pressed for this marriage?'

Cressida flushed hotly. 'It was in his mind at the beginning, but I believe he saw advantage in this match for me too—when it came to it.'

'Do you love Martyn, child?' It was a very direct question and Cressida drew another hard breath.

At last she said, 'I—I think I do. I must. He is my husband.'

Cressida's mother placed a hand gently on her daughter's arm. 'It is well you are dutiful, but—but I wish he had not neglected you so blatantly for these months. It was not so between your father and I.'

The two messengers rode out soon after and Sir Daniel strode into the solar, red-faced and grim of expression. Cressida guessed there had been hard words and argument between him and his visitors. He did not enlighten his wife and daughter as to what had occurred and neither Cressida nor her mother thought it wise to ask.

Sir Daniel stretched his legs out before him as he seated himself in his padded armchair.

'I hear the King has fitted out a squadron under Sir George Nevill to watch the coast and intercept any possible invaders. Lovell has been appointed to command the fleet at Southampton.'

Cressida was deeply shocked. The situation must be serious indeed for the King to send his closest friend from his side at this critical time. She assumed that Martyn would still be at his sovereign's disposal and too occupied to write to her.

A pedlar called just after Whitsuntide and informed them that the King had left the capital for the north.

'It's being said, my lady,' he said in his falsely bright, gossipy manner, 'he will head for Nottingham to spend his time hunting and hawking, but we all know my lord the King 'as never bin one for such sports. Nottingham being the middle of the realm, like, he'll doubtless think it a fine spot to wait for news—'

He broke off as it dawned on him that he was about to speak what might be termed treason and Lady Gretton bestowed her most wintry smile on the man.

'Those ribbons will be all.' She dismissed him coldly. 'I imagine you'll want permission to sell to the serving girls. You may go to the kitchens.'

He bowed himself out backwards, almost as if he were leaving the presence of royalty.

Cressida sat with a tangle of bright ribbons in her lap, her thoughts occupied with the fellow's news.

Martyn would doubtless be at Nottingham with the King, ready for any threatened action. She would not remain here waiting idly for news. Whether Martyn liked it or not, she would have no more of this enforced separation. Her place was at his side and she would not be gainsaid.

She stood up abruptly, spilling the bright ribbons to the polished oaken floor. They had stood out starkly against her mourning gown, which she continued to wear for the dead Queen. Now she knew that her drab gowns must soon be set aside again; court mourning would be over after these long weeks of her absence.

'I have decided,' she said firmly as her mother looked up at her askance. 'I shall send Philip to Wroxeter for an escort. I am going to Nottingham.'

Recognising finality in her daughter's tone, Lady Gretton closed her lips on her intended protest and forced a confident expression.

'Since he has not sent for you, I take it Lord Martyn has been over-busied with state affairs. Doubtless he will be glad to have you with him.' Privately she considered that unlikely to be the case, but there was no arguing with Cressida in this present mood, as she would inform her husband. Warningly, she glanced across at him as his head jerked up in sudden alarm.

He frowned, considering. 'Well,' he conceded after a moment's thought, 'you should be safe enough with an escort from your husband's manor, but without sufficient men-at-arms to form a safe escort I cannot allow you to go. Times are too unsettled.'

Cressida was determined to go whatever happened but she did not argue with him now. Instead she cast him an approving smile.

Protected by an escort of ten of her husband's men-at-arms, Cressida rode out of Gretton on a fine hot day in early July. Philip rode happily at her side and it was obvious that he was as anxious to rejoin his master as she was. The burly sergeant in command of the escort was by no means so pleased. He had been summoned to Gretton by his new Countess and, despite all his argument to the contrary and his protestations that he had no orders from the Earl to leave the manor, he had been constrained to do his new mistress's bidding.

It had been very clear to him from the beginning of the interview that this authoritative young woman was by no means the docile and biddable child bride he and the rest of the Wroxeter household had been expecting, but a very formidable lady indeed. Cressida had made it very plain that, with or without his support, she would journey to the Midlands, and reluctantly he had given way and had agreed to provide the necessary company of armed men. Blame would undoubtedly fall upon his hapless shoulders if any harm was to come to the Countess on such a rash undertaking, but he had bowed to the force of her determination.

Now he rode sourly at the head of the escort, his eyes peeled for any possible danger lurking behind forest land and hedges bordering their road and the glint of sun on metal which would apprise him of the presence of mounted men in the vicinity.

He cursed under his breath. Anything could happen on this ill-advised venture and, whichever way events came, he would be blamed. Already he was hearing in his imagination the blistering rebuke he would receive from the Earl on his arrival in Nottingham. He had been put in charge of the defence of Wroxeter in the light of possible alarms within the volatile Border country and had been hard put to it to find a suitable man to leave in charge there.

Undoubtedly his principal duty was the defence of his Countess, but he was no happy man and constantly cast Cressida dark glances whenever he thought himself unobserved.

Cressida was far too busy with her own thoughts to give heed to the man's brooding disapproval. She was hearing again in her mind her mother's question—'Do you love Martyn, child?' If she did not, why was she in such haste to reach his side? He would not be pleased. She bit her lip uncertainly as it occurred to her that he might well have found some other, more accommodating mistress to warm his bed.

She had been a constant thorn in his flesh since her arrival in Westminster. She had been pressed upon him, willy-nilly, by his sovereign, and the doubtful loyalties of her father made association with her family dangerous in the extreme. He had shown irritation, downright exasperation with her, but—her cheeks flushed red as she recalled the ecstasy of their lovemaking—he must have had some deep affection for her to give her such joy.

What did she feel for him? From the beginning he had aroused her interest. She had been piqued by his determination to treat her as a child, while the excited arousal she experienced whenever he was near told her the contrary was true. She had never felt such stirrings during her long association with Howell. She had longed for Martyn to consummate their marriage and now that he had done so she was not disappointed.

She pictured him in her mind's eye: that tall, rangy body, hard-muscled, the deceptive sleepy gaze, which gave the appearance of slow-witted joviality. She knew his mind was razor-sharp and feared his ability to strike mercilessly at those he considered his King's enemies. He would be a gallant and loyal friend and a dangerous and ruthless antagonist. In this coming struggle for the crown Richard would need him, as he would need all those loyal northern gentlemen who had been his companions since childhood.

In combat Martyn could be killed. An icy chill swept through her at the thought. She *must* reach him, beg his forgiveness for her final betrayal of his trust. Her mother's question was answered by the terrible fear she had for his safety. She loved him, desired him, ached for his nearness. All these days of separation had been a torment. Now, despite the anger she would see in his expression on her arrival, she had to be near him.

CHAPTER NINE

LORD MARTYN handed his latest report to the King as he sat sprawled in his favourite armchair in the hunting lodge near Bestwood. Richard had left Nottingham Castle some days ago, intent on filling his restless hours in the hectic pursuit of the chase. He watched Richard now as he sat forward in the chair to catch the light the better to peruse the report.

These waiting days were trying for all of them around the King. He could see that these last months since Anne's death had aged Richard more than he could have believed possible. There were purple shadows below his eye sockets, deep lines of suffering from nostrils to mouth, and that mouth, which had always been held in a tense line of concentration and anxiety, showed signs now of rigidity, revealing a harshness of purpose which Martyn had never seen there before.

He told himself, with a sigh, that that was just as well. Richard had ever been too trusting and willing to forgive those who betrayed him. Now it was necessary for the good of the realm that he should face squarely the guilt of those who would destroy him and eliminate them without mercy.

The King looked up and sighed. 'So you distrust the motives of Lord Stanley in failing to come to join our force here, insisting on remaining on his Cheshire estates? You think his excuse of poor health suspect?'

'Your Grace, one must always keep in mind that the Lady Margaret, Lord Stanley's wife, is Henry Tudor's mother. Despite his protestations of loyalty Lord Thomas would have much to gain if the Earl of Richmond were to ascend the throne. You were wise to request that Lord Strange remain at Court during his father's absence.'

'As a hostage?' The King's lips twisted sardonically. 'It is not a course I find to my taste, Martyn.'

'But Your Grace must see the necessity.'

'Yes, yes,' he replied a trifle testily. 'Your report informs us that the Marquis of Dorset appears to regret his offer of support to Henry Tudor and apparently attempted to leave him and return home.'

'My spy is sure that that move was prompted by a letter from the Dowager Queen advising him to return to his allegiance. Unfortunately—' Lord Martyn shrugged regretfully '—he left Paris heading for Flanders to take ship for home, but was taken into protective custody at Compiègne by Humphrey Cheney and was forced to return with him to Paris.'

The King's lips parted in a smile. 'Poor Thom; he appears to be able to do nothing right. At least I am reassured that the Dowager Queen now seems to trust me to do what is best for her children.'

Martyn nodded. 'I think it behoves us to keep a very close watch upon Lord Stanley's heir, Lord Strange.'

The King was about to reply when a knock came on the door and Martyn turned angrily.

'Your Grace, I gave strict instructions that we were not to be disturbed and left Peter Fairley outside to see that my orders were obeyed implicitly.'

'It would seem that either Peter has been removed forcibly—since nothing else would cause him to desert his post—or he has something of great importance to tell us. I think we should admit whoever it is.'

Lord Martyn's squire looked anxiously at his master's grim countenance as he entered and bowed at the Earl's barked invitation.

'Your Grace, my lord, forgive me for intruding, but I thought you should know, sir—' here he gave another alarmed glance towards his master '—that—that my lady, the Countess, has arrived.'

Lord Martyn looked thunderstruck. 'Countess? Countess of what?'

'I think Peter is endeavouring to explain that my lady your wife is here at Bestwood.' The King was smiling hugely now.

'Cressida, here?' Martyn was about to explode into a furious oath, but the King gently shook his head, indicating the presence of Peter.

The boy nodded mutely in answer to his master's questioning glance.

The King signalled to the squire. 'Admit your lady, Peter. It would be discourteous to keep her waiting.'

'How dare she disobey me and leave Gretton without my leave?' Martyn fumed.

'She is indeed a lady of spirit.'

'But, Your Grace, now is not the time for—'

'I know that, Martyn, and so does she. I imagine her presence here is not the result of a whim, but of a genuine concern to be near you in time of crisis.' He turned away and Martyn was aware that his unspoken thought was that the Queen, had it been possible, would have moved heaven and earth to be by her husband's side at this time.

There was a flurry of movement by the door and Martyn turned to see Cressida curtseying low, flanked by the stolid form of Alice Croft.

The King gestured for her to come forward. 'It is good to receive you at Bestwood, Lady Cressida.'

Cressida avoided eye contact with Martyn as she bent to kiss the King's extended hand.

'Your Grace, I should not have dared to come to the lodge without direct invitation, but I discovered in Nottingham that my husband was here and felt I could not ask the castle castellan for lodging without his permission and I—'

He waved aside her apology. 'Of course you will be welcome at the castle. I suggest you escort your lady there, Martyn, and remain there yourself for a while. You can report to me here whenever it is necessary.'

Martyn began to protest, but the King was insistent. 'I would like you to go at once and dictate that letter to my secretary—the business concerning Lord Strange.' He rose and, placing an arm on Martyn's shoulder, moved with him to the door. 'Then return here. I insist that Lady Cressida dine with us before you withdraw her from our company.'

He smiled genially. 'Meanwhile I shall spend one or two private moments with her. I trust you will grant me that pleasure, though I know you must now be anxious to have her to yourself.'

As they reached the door he bent and said very softly, 'I know you are angry, Martyn, but go easy. Take my advice, my friend; spend time with your lady. This opportunity may not come again. If I read you rightly, these moments will be very precious and who knows when or if they will ever come again?'

Martyn stared at him wordlessly. The warning communication passed between them and Martyn gave a great sigh.

'My lord. . .'

'I know you love her.'

'More than my life. . .'

'Do not waste these hours, Martyn. You and I both know there is a world of time for regrets.'

Martyn bowed his head, unwilling for his sovereign to see the tears sparkling on his lashes. He had been too close to Richard over these last months not to realise how the man was suffering the terrible pain of loss. Not even his constant occupation with the threatened invasion and perusal of the many reports from scurriers, nor the recent issuing of commissions of array, could take away the hours of loneliness when he was withdrawn from his companions.

He had, himself, felt the separation from Cressida. In the lonely hours of the night he had ached for the sight of her, but had considered it best for her welfare if she could be kept clear of this. Now she was here and he could not prevent his whole being from crying out a paeon of joy. He could not play the tyrant now and send her home, not without some time for them to enjoy each other's company for what might very well be the final time.

He said a trifle hoarsely, 'I take your meaning, Your Grace. For these next days I shall cherish her, but I must soon dispatch her to safety again.'

'You will know the time.'

The King waited while Martyn turned down an angle of the corridor and was lost to sight. His lips twisted at the sight of Peter Fairley's puzzled countenance. 'Stay at your post, lad. Never fear; I doubt that the full force of your master's fury will fall on you. More likely to descend on the sergeant-at-escort's head.'

Cressida was staring at the King wide-eyed as he returned to her side then crossed to a small travelling chest which stood on a stool near the window.

'I needed to get rid of Martyn for moments.'

She started and he laughed at her concern. 'I have something for you which I think you would rather he did not see.'

He lifted the lid of the chest and withdrew a small book which he placed in Cressida's hands. 'There is a letter inside from the Lady Elizabeth. I have been puzzling for some days over how I might get it to you without undue notice.' His eyes were twinkling as she gazed down at the rubbed leather cover, then up into the King's shrewd grey gaze.

'The Book of Hours belonged to my brother.

Elizabeth thought I would wish to have it. She put the
message to you inside.'

Cressida fumbled to extricate the message but his
hand closed on hers. 'I would like you to have the
book. I know how you value her friendship. I have
other gifts from my brother, the late King. It would
please me to know you treasure it. Anne would have
liked you to have it, I know.'

She stooped to kiss his hands, her eyes brimming
with tears, but there was no time for further words of
gratitude for at that moment Martyn arrived back in
the chamber and the King dismissed them, jovially
ordering them to withdraw and to prepare to eat dinner
in an hour's time.

The return to Nottingham Castle was made almost in
silence. Cressida had hardly exchanged more than a
word or two with her husband during dinner, the King
having dominated the conversation, chatting pleasantly
about the environs of the hunting lodge, their successes
and failures in the hunts, and also enquiring politely
after the health of her parents. All the time Cressida
had been conscious that Martyn was sitting beside her,
simmering with rage.

Partly thankful that the meal was over and with it
the need for court protocol, and half-alarmed at the
explosion of temper which she feared would descend
upon her hapless head when they were at last alone
together, Cressida dismounted her jennet in a confused
mood, only glancing up briefly at their sergeant-at-
arms, whose expression told her that he was as alarmed
as she was at the prospect of facing his lord's wrath any
moment now.

Lord Martyn ordered Cressida's baggage to be
brought up to the apartments in the castle set aside for
him and strode through the hall, Cressida and Alice
striving hard to keep pace with him.

The Earl's chambers were surprisingly commodious. Cressida had been used to cramped quarters at Westminster, but then, few courtiers were now in attendance on the sovereign and those who were were hardened campaigners in advising the monarch as to future combat strategy.

Cressida found that, though the bedchamber was luxuriously furnished, Martyn had apparently unpacked few of his clothes or possessions—or perhaps, she mused, he had brought little with him, wishing to travel light in case of need.

Alice glanced round briefly and immediately set about unpacking for Cressida. Shortly afterwards Lord Martyn strode grimly into the chamber and dismissed the maid.

'Go and see about arrangements for your accommodation. Send one of my men to obtain a truckle-bed for you and see it set up in a room near your mistress. I'll send when I want you.'

Philip had been sent off to the great hall with Peter Fairley. The boy would soon make friends amongst the other assembled pages. Cressida would see to it that no blame would be laid at his door for her disobedient conduct.

Once alone with her husband, she decided to take the initiative. 'There is not the slightest use in raging at poor Philip or at Sergeant Chubb either. I and I alone am responsible for the decision to leave the Marches.'

She faced him squarely and he caught his breath at the splendour of her lovely young body held rigid with steely determination, spine erect, head high, chin jutting obstinately.

'I am sure of it,' he returned mildly, 'and had no intention of punishing either.'

She was put off course by his agreeable tone and stared back at him in amazement.

'I insisted—said I would travel alone if Chubb would

not provide an escort. He had to agree, but I understand he has made adequate arrangements for the defence of Wroxeter in case of need...' Her voice trailed off as she recognised the reason for his decision to isolate her from Court in the first place.

He remained silent, seated in the window seat, staring out over the castle pleasance, which had been sadly neglected over the last year, although a climbing white rose had bloomed in spite of lack of careful pruning and its scent was heady in their chamber. He turned and looked full at her.

'Come here.'

She hesitated, then moved from the bed to come doubtfully towards him.

'I'm sorry, my lord, but I had to come. We heard news. Events were following each other so rapidly that I—I—'

'Yes?' he prompted softly.

'I—I wanted to be with you in case—in case—' She rushed on almost incoherently, 'I know you cannot really want to be bothered with the need to watch over me at this time, but I swear I will not prove to be difficult and—'

'Cressida, you have always been difficult.'

She swallowed hard, feeling tears threatening. How could she explain how she felt? 'I am your wife,' she declared defiantly, shaking back her hair. She had removed her hennin and veil, thinking that she and Alice would be alone in the chamber until he had entered unexpectedly. Her glorious golden locks streamed unrestrained down her back and her luminous eyes were lambent with unshed tears.

He had never seen her so lovely and his loins had ached for her over these long months. The light from the window limned the rounded beauty of her upthrust breasts, the thin stuff of her blue summer riding gown moulding them tight by the fashionable high waistline, for she had put off mourning for the journey.

Here was no child bride, but a mature and passionate young woman. He made a little inarticulate sound deep in his throat, stood up abruptly and pulled her fiercely into his arms.

Startled into instant acquiescence, her mouth opened sweetly under his and her body responded, pressing itself close to his, without the need for restraint. His kiss scorched her, sending waves of heat through her whole being. She had wanted this for so long. She returned his kisses passionately, accepting his absolute need for her. For moments they clung together, wordlessly, her arms stealing up around his neck while he pressed her even closer.

At last he drew away, holding her gently by the shoulders at arm's length.

'Let me look at you.'

She stared back at him proudly, the ivory of her cheeks flushed with the warm glow of love.

'Sweet Virgin, how I've longed for sight of you all these months, and now here you are, a fairy queen, rather than the fairy child I was remembering.'

She said softly, 'I do not think I was ever the child you imagined, my lord, not even when you first mistook me for one in the tilt-yard at Westminster.'

He gave a little laugh. 'Perhaps you're right. You are so tiny, so exquisite, it seemed a sacrilege to touch you then.'

'And you were full of guilt because you thought you'd not completed the full mourning for the Lady Elinor.'

'That may be so. Who knows what guilt can do? I only know that the first time I saw you properly, in the King's presence chamber, desire gnawed at my loins.'

She was content now to tantalise him a little. 'You are glad to see me, then?'

'Sweet wounds of Christ, how can you ask me that? How in the name of all the Saints am I to send you back? Anywhere now you could be at risk, with armed men at large. I sent you to the Marches for your own safety. I cannot escort you myself. I—'

'Then you must keep me near you,' she said confidently, 'which is what I intended. Where can I feel more secure than near my husband?'

'Cressida, I must soon fight for the King.'

'Will it come soon?' she asked softly, and he nodded.

'We already know Henry has borrowed considerable sums of gold from the French king. We hear he has gone to Normandy. At any moment I expect my spies to inform me he has embarked.'

Her lips parted in wonder. 'The kingdom cannot be in danger, surely? The King has all his forces at his disposal, Henry just a few disgruntled rebels.'

'More rebels than you think.' He had released her and was about to pace the room as he often did in times of doubt. He saw her face change and put an imperative hand upon her arm.

'Your father has not foolishly involved himself in this?'

She shook her head. 'Messengers have been riding in, two from Rhys Ap Thomas, but my father has sworn he will take no part in open insurrection; rather he will put what few men he has at His Grace's disposal.'

Martyn frowned. 'He would do better to hold himself ready to defend his own land. Were it possible I would send you back forthwith to him.'

'But suppose the invasion were to come from Wales?'

Those heavy lids of his swept upwards and she saw a strange gleam in his eyes. 'You have some suspicion of this?'

'No, none at all. It is just that—Ap Thomas is in league with Sir John Savage, they say, and Jasper

Tudor was Earl of Pembroke. If the Welsh see Henry as their natural leader. . .'

'He is no more truly Welsh than the King,' Martyn snapped. 'I would wager Richard speaks more Welsh than the Tudor. The man is French in outlook, has spent his youth there and relies totally on French gold and support.'

She reached up and gently touched his cheek. 'You are fearful, Martyn? I think this is unlike you.'

He gave a rueful grin. 'Like His Grace, I shall be confident enough when we are on the march and know what to expect, but it has been my work to sift through these varying reports and I do not altogether like what I read.'

'You fear betrayal?'

'Aye.' The single word was grimly uttered. 'We have had a quiet time in England after Tewkesbury, with only minor alarms and skirmishes, but men will risk much for offers of land and preferment and the Lancastrians have never been content. To add to this, the people have been disturbed by scurrilous tales of the King's perfidy, as you know well, and the doubtful fate of the Princes weighs hard against him.'

Cressida's lips tightened. 'You do not believe the King capable of. . .?'

'No, no. I am one of the few knowledgeable about that matter, but, for obvious reasons, Richard will not divulge the truth of this business, especially at this time, even to secure the trust of doubting subjects. He fears for the boys' safety.'

Cressida gave a little shudder. Only too clearly did she see how vulnerable the Princes would be should Henry Tudor wed their sister and claim right of sovereignty through her.

Martyn drew her close again. 'It seems I have only one course now—to protect you myself. While I am alarmed for what might come, I will not deny it will comfort me greatly to have you near me at this time. Well, wench, since you are here, I shall set you to work to refurbish my shabby banners and take charge of my domestic household.'

She shook her head regretfully. 'I fear I am no hand with the needle, as Alice will testify, and your household has always seemed perfectly disciplined, if I am any judge. I am at a loss to know what help I can be to you.'

He laughed then, unproariously. 'Do you not, my lady? Then I shall very soon tutor you in the skills I require.'

He laughed again as her answering flush spread from her glowing cheeks to her throat and breast.

'I shall strive to be a responsive scholar, my lord.'

It was after she had retired with Alice and was waiting for Martyn to join her that Cressida remembered that she had not yet looked at the letter from the Lady Elizabeth.

It was quite short, but affectionate enough in tone to relieve Cressida's mind.

My very dear Cressida,

It was a great comfort to me to receive your message, which His Grace was magnanimous enough to forward to me. Please absolve yourself of all blame for my dismissal from Court. Unfortunately, we are all unwilling pawns of those about us. I have only regret that, unwittingly, I may have harmed the King's cause by my wish to serve him. It is necessary always to be guarded in all matters. From your affectionate and dutiful friend, Elizabeth Plantagenet.

The letter was addressed to 'The Lady Cressida, Countess of Wroxeter, from the hand of the Lady

Elizabeth Plantagenet, written at Sheriff Hutton on the fourteenth day of June in the year of our Lord 1485.'

Hastily Cressida returned the missive to its hiding place within the Book of Hours which was the King's gift. The seal on the letter had not been broken, or so it seemed, but the tone was indeed guarded and Cressida could not be sure that it had not been read by eyes other than her own.

Had the King seen his niece's letter? She thought not, doubting that he would betray her trust in his discretion. At all events, Cressida was unwilling for Martyn to know that she was still in contact with the Lady Elizabeth. Their friendship had always been a bone of contention between herself and her husband, and at this moment, when he gave every sign of wanting her love, she had no wish to allow this difference to come between them.

When Martyn came at last she saw that he was still troubled.

'Has there been further news, my lord?'

He shook his head. 'No—or, at least, nothing of importance. One of my couriers came in an hour ago. He gives me information about the movements of one or two lords whose loyalty I doubt, but nothing to give us cause for concern.'

He looked down at her and his expression cleared. Her bedgown of pink brocade had fallen open and he had a tantalising glimpse of rosy-tipped breasts as round and firm as apples just ripe to be picked. Her belly was flat and taut, yet her hips were already rounding deliciously with advancing womanhood. He discarded his clothing hurriedly and drew her hungrily towards the bed.

His lovemaking was tender, yet Cressida guessed at the desperation held in check by his determination to treat her considerately. Again, as at the first time, he wooed her body with gentle, teasing kisses until he sensed she was ready to respond. She did so with equal hunger, delighting in the ecstasy of fulfilment, and, afterwards, lying beside him content, her body glowing with the sweat of love.

Once, in the night, when she wakened suddenly, it was to find him sitting up in the bed staring down at her so intently that she wondered if the force of his desire had caused her to waken. She gave a shaky little laugh and reached up to wind her arms round his neck and pull him down to her again, revelling in the feel of his hard-muscled body against her own.

He took her passionately this time, satisfying his own need quickly, and she thought that perhaps he had not taken his pleasure with other women over these last months as she had believed. Certainly she would never question him about it. She was content to know that he wanted her now, and desired only to give him happiness.

Over the next weeks Cressida was to know nights of intense delight, tempered by the unspoken knowledge that they could end very suddenly. By day Martyn was often from her side, his duties on the King's war council keeping him fully occupied at Bestwood where the King continued, outwardly, to give the impression to his people that he was enjoying the hunt.

At the beginning of August the royal household returned to Nottingham Castle and Cressida rejoiced, for it was no longer necessary for Martyn to leave her so early each day.

During the heat-laden nights when the heady scents of lavender and rose seeped into their chamber from the opened casement—for Martyn, unlike her parents, rejoiced in the cooler air, refusing to believe that it carried contagion—she would lie in his arms replete with love, hardly daring to sleep while he rested secure beside her.

She would wake often to gaze down at him where he had pushed the sheets impatiently aside, marvelling in the ever familiar knowledge of his body, the soft brown hairs, intermingled with the lighter golden ones of his chest, the slim waist and strong, muscular thighs which would hold her fast in the act of love, even the one or two whitening scars which spoke of the battles in which he had taken wounds.

One evening she ran her fingers lightly along a deeper grove extending from his neck to his shoulder. Here the skin was still puckered and the scar itself still purplish.

'Where did you get this?'

He guided her fingertips, feather-light, down to his waist.

'On the border. We encountered a thieving reiver band and they struck us from ambush. I fear I was ill prepared that day. One stinking borderer's sword pierced between my gorget and breastplate and our surgeon was forced to cauterise the wound.'

She winced inwardly at the ugly mind picture of him being held down while a heated sword was laid flat, smoking, on his agonised flesh.

'Did you kill the man?'

He gave a grim splutter of laughter. 'No; thanks to the Virgin, my lord Richard saw all and rode the fellow down, felling him with his battleaxe.'

She compressed her lips. Martyn's love for his sovereign was all-encompassing and would lead him to risk himself rashly in the cause he served so loyally. She suppressed a frisson of fear and bent to press her lips to the puckered flesh.

She prayed continually that she would conceive Martyn's child. Once or twice he had looked at her quizzically, as if he feared that she might do so, and she remembered how he had spoken of his wish that her family might continue to believe that the marriage was unconsummated.

Had he such fears concerning the outcome of this coming campaign that he would wish to leave her utterly free if the worst happened? At such time, fear would freeze her very marrow until she saw the air of calm confidence on the King's face and the cheerful exuberance of his principal officers. If the King was so sure of success, why should she fear?

Very early on the morning of August the eleventh Cressida was startled upright in the bed by urgent knocking upon their chamber door. Struggling up from deep sleep, Martyn sat up blinking, leaning up on one elbow.

'What in the devil's name is it?' he snapped.

'Peter Fairley, my lord. We've urgent news from the West. Scurriers rode in during the night and—'

'Very well.' Martyn was instantly awake. 'I'll be down in the hall within minutes. Come to my ante-room and help me dress.'

He bent and kissed Cressida's tousled hair. 'I don't know if I can breakfast with you today, my love.'

'You will let me know?'

'Aye, as soon as I'm sure the King is informed and everything put in hand that is needful.'

She watched anxiously as he pulled the cord of his bedgown tightly round him and moved into the small room nearby that he used as a dressing room. She could hear him talking to Peter, but could not distinguish what was said. Sighing, she rang the small silver bell which brought Alice to her side, knowing it would be useless to try to sleep any longer.

'Well?' the Earl said as he struggled into hose and shirt.

Peter bent to help tie the points. 'It's come, my lord.

The Tudor has landed at Milford Haven. The King has already been told and summons you to Council.'

Lord Martyn grunted. 'Good. Who is with him, Peter?'

'Sir Richard Ratcliffe, my lord. Lord Lovell is still in the south. Some of the northern knights—Sir Dominick Allard, Sir Guy Jarvis. . .'

'Jarvis? So he has ridden south, has he?' Martyn's tone was harsh. 'I want you to send a messenger in haste to Master Standish. Tell him I wish him to question Lord Strange. He is not to hesitate; he has the King's authority through me. Instruct him to get Sir James Tyrell to act with him.'

'Yes, my lord.'

Peter completed his work of dressing his master and exited as Martyn waved at him impatiently. Martyn then plunged his face into a bowl of cold water poured from the huge earthern jug by his squire and towelled himself dry. Feeling more wide awake now, he hastened below to the great hall.

The King greeted him cheerfully. 'I see you've been informed, Martyn. Wales, eh? I had expected the landing to come in the south. Your lady spoke of the possibility of Wales, I believe?'

'Only because there had been some coming and going of messengers and neighbours at Gretton. She assures me her father is totally loyal, Your Grace.'

'I received a courier sent on from Sir Daniel informing me that he intended to join me with a force of some one hundred and fifty men.'

'God grant he is not prevented by Henry's advance,' Martyn murmured.

'I shall summon Norfolk north with Surrey and Brackenbury. Comissions of array have been sent to Northumberland. I have assurances from Sir Thomas Bouchier and Sir Walter Hungerford that they intend to ride north also.'

Sir Richard Ratcliffe looked up with a grim smile from the vellum map the household gentlemen had been examining.

'His Grace thinks it best to make for Watling Street. Undoubtedly Henry Tudor will attempt to reach London, more than likely by that route, and he must be cut off.'

Martyn nodded in agreement. The King joined them after giving some instruction to his squire.

'I cannot say I'm disturbed by this news, Martyn. I've been spoiling for battle long enough. We are in the hand of God now, my friend.'

'Aye, my lord.'

'You look concerned. We have taken all precautions. . .'

'True, Your Grace. I've no lack of confidence in our ability to meet this challenge. My concern was personal. I fear for the safety of my lady. I had wished to send her home. Now that appears impossbile.'

The King's eyes twinkled. 'She must ride out with us, Martyn. I shall go to Leicester. I am informed the castle hall roof is in some state of disrepair but, in all events, I shall not remain in the town long. Accommodation should be available for Lady Wroxeter in the castle gatehouse. See to it when we arrive.'

He placed a hand on Martyn's arm. 'I know how you feel, old friend, but she should be safe enough there.' His grey eyes looked into the far distance as he added, 'Anne would have wished to be near me at such a time.'

Cressida rode beside Martyn in the army which set out for Leicester on August the sixteenth, the day following the Feast of the Assumption. She marvelled at the imposing war panoply and was not surprised by the crowds of curious townsfolk and peasants who flocked to see the King ride south.

Richard was mounted upon his favourite white charger, White Surrey, and attired in the armour which Martyn had told her he had worn at Tewkesbury, when scarce eighteen years of age. His body had thickened little since that time. Cressida had not seen her husband armoured since that first time in the tilt-yard, and then it had been in jousting armour. Peter Fairley, grave-faced, rode behind.

Through the Nottinghamshire countryside the army progressed, marching four abreast, the baggage train in the centre. The King himself with his household knights followed, Martyn and Cressida within that company, protected by the wings of mounted cavalrymen.

Cressida's heart was thumping hard against her rib-cage, yet she was in no way afraid for her own safety, only for Martyn and the success of the King's righteous cause. She had received a message from her father that he would await the King in Leicester, so she would see him then. She had also received, stoically enough, Martyn's grave command that she should remain within the town when the royal army marched out.

These, then, were the last days she would spend with her husband before the battle. She wondered, fleetingly, if Howell Prosser was in the rebel army with Henry Tudor, marching relentlessly through Wales.

On the last night of the march Cressida slept cradled in her husband's arms in a curtained-off corner of the hall of some Leicestershire manor whose squire had agreed to accommodate members of the King's household. Martyn was very tender and loving with her and it was all she could do to hold back her tears. She had a terrible presentiment that all was not well.

Martyn bent to kiss away a solitary tear. 'Be brave, my love. This business will take only days and soon we shall be back together in the Strand house in London.'

'I have had you for such a short time, discovered my love, and now—' she gulped helplessly '—I am so afraid for you. You said yourself that there are traitors abroad. When Lord Strange tried to escape from house arrest and was recaptured he admitted that his uncle, Sir William Stanley, and Sir John Savage have declared for Henry Tudor. Can his father, Lord Thomas, be trusted?'

Martyn's voice was falsely cheerful. 'I have had my doubts about the man, but Strange swears his father is still loyal and the King refuses to believe ill of him. Despite these few traitors the King has many true friends and his army well outnumbers that of the Tudor.' He bent and nuzzled her ear.

'Have you no confidence in your husband's warlike skills? I'm an experienced warrior, I assure you, and too much in love with my wife to take undue risks. That is never good battle strategy in any case.'

She forced a smile then for his benefit and again when they rode into Leciester town to be met by open-mouthed townsfolk and yokels who had come to see the King ride up the high street by the swine market and take up accommodation in the inn of the White Boar.

The landlord came out sweating, agitatedly wiping his greasy hands upon his apron and anxious to please his sovereign and oversee the positioning of the great bed, which the King took upon his travels, in his finest bedroom.

The town was already packed to overflowing by the supporting forces of John, Duke of Norfolk, and his son, the Earl of Surrey, Sir Robert Brackenbury, the King's Constable of the Tower and many other lords with their men-at-arms who had come to defeat the traitorous Welshman who dared to challenge Richard for the crown of England.

The King's officers were already established in the inn, ready to receive instructions and offer advice about the order of march in the morning, for the King intended no delay. Martyn excused himself and obtained permission to accompany Cressida to the castle gatehouse. The King, despite his urgent business, called her to him before she departed with Martyn.

'You will be reasonably comfortable, my Lady Cressida, until that fine husband of yours comes again to claim you. I'll send him as soon as I can. Be very sure of that.'

He looked confident but tired, and Cressida glimpsed the marks of suffering on his clever features. She bent to kiss his hand.

'God guard you, Your Grace.'

He stooped and dropped a light kiss upon her bright hair where the hood of her travelling cloak had fallen back.

'Thank you, my child. I know that you were not pleased at first by the marriage I made for you, but I shall pray for your happiness. Pray for me, Cressida, and for all of us.'

'I will, sire.'

She was determined not to give way to tears when Martyn left her in the capable hands of one of the harassed castle serving women. He had left her with two grizzled veterans who had served at Barnet and Tewkesbury and Towton before that. They were not pleased to be left behind in this decisive battle, but knew they must obey their orders and guard their lord's lady with their very lives.

Philip was with her, and Alice, and she waved to Martyn cheerfully, though her heart misgave her as he strode off to return to the council of war at the White Boar with the rest of the King's commanders.

Lord Martyn stood a little apart from the group of household knights and lords who surrounded the King on the ridge above the village of Sutton Cheney. From here he could see the countryside for miles around,

green, uncultivated land, marshy in places, especially
on the edges of the ridge and near the spring behind
them where his squire, Peter Fairley, was even now
watering Martyn's courser and his own mount.

The King had camped near the village overnight and
Martyn had emerged from his tent during the evening
to see the fires of the royal camp and those of the
opposing army in the distance. Jack Wainwright, who
had insisted on marching with the army and abandon-
ing his kitchen, had told him that the enemy was
camped near Dadlington. Jack had kin in the nearby
town of Leicester and others in Shenton near here, and
had some knowledge of the lie of land.

It was still early in the morning of August the twenty-
second, and the heat mist was now just dissolving, so
that Martyn could again glimpse the enemy men-at-
arms massing for battle formation.

He glanced round doubtfully at the forces of the Earl
of Northumberland drawn up close to Sutton village, a
reserve force to be called on to reinforce the two main
battle formations, Norfolk's in the van and the King's
main force behind, as had been decided at last night's
battle conference. Martyn would fight beside the King
in the company of his former companions from the
days of the border campaigns.

He was glad to recognise the friendly faces of Sir
Richard Ratcliffe and Sir Robert Percy with the Lord
Chamberlain, Lord Lovell, who was at this moment
talking animatedly to Richard, who leaned close to
listen. Also there was Sir Robert Brackenbury, Lord
Ferrers of Chartley and other, lesser knights who had
served Richard well in the past—men like Sir Dominick
Allard and Sir Guy Jarvis.

William Catesby, a lawyer who had once been in
service to Lord Hastings and was now deep in the
King's confidence, was nervously fiddling with his mail
gauntlet as he talked with the King's secretary, the

bluff John Kendall. These two were not experienced knights yet both had taken up arms to be with their sovereign on this momentous day, as Wainwright had insisted he be by Martyn's side as he had been on other campaigns.

The King had heard mass in the little plain church at Sutton and Martyn had knelt on the hard floor and prayed not only for victory but also for the safety of his beloved wife, Cressida.

He fingered the small reliquary which hung by a fine chain around his neck. Cressida had placed it there after she had helped Peter with the refractory buckles on his vambrace when he had gone back to her after the war council at the White Boar in the early hours of August the twenty-first. She had risen and come to him at once when he was announced just before dawn and he had held her so tight to his body that he had feared afterwards that he had cracked her ribs.

She had kissed him hungrily and laughed at his fears for her comfort.

'What are a few bruises? Oh, my love, I thought never to see you again when you went off to the inn.'

'Are you comfortable here?'

'Yes, well cared for by Alice, and young Philip is keen to serve me and rouse the slow servants, though he would have loved to go with you. The castle servants are all bewildered by events, poor souls. Martyn, how is the King?'

'Cheerful and confident, outwardly at least.'

'Was Northumberland at the conference? I know you were concerned about his slowness to comply with the commission of array.'

'Yes, not pleased, but there, and agreeable to what was decided. Lovell is here. The king was delighted to see him. Francis had to ride hard to reach us in time.' He had bent closer, his hands urgently squeezing her shoulders as he had stared, bewitched, at the glorious hair which streamed below her shoulders to her slim waist. 'Have you had news of your father?'

She had shaken her head. 'No, no word. He was riding through the border. I pray he has not been attacked by rebel outriders.'

'He may well have been delayed,' he had comforted. 'Whatever happens, whatever you hear, remain in the safety of the castle environs until I come or send you word.'

He had seen alarm reveal itself in her widened eyes and had quickly kissed her soundly. 'Just a precaution. Trust no one with information about the battle but those you know well.'

She had nodded silently and two tears had rolled down onto her pale cheeks. 'I shall go to the chapel and pray continually. Oh, take care, my love, for I do not think I could live on without you.'

Then it was that she had given him the relinquary. 'It has an enamelled likeness of St Martin of Tours. I meant it for your birthday in October but I want its added protection for you now.' And she had slipped it over his mailed shoulders. The chain was long and fine and he had thought it needed to be stronger for such duty, but he would not have left it off for anything in the world.

She had clung to him then, desperately, until he had gently put her aside as the dawn light grew stronger. He had turned once at the door to fill his eyes with one last sight of her, then had gone hurriedly from the room.

Trumpets sounded shrilly and destriers behind the line neighed and pawed the ground restlessly. Martyn saw men round him hastily cross themselves and did likewise. He saw the banner of the lion stream in the wind as Norfolk began the march down Ambien Hill, named, so Wainwright had said, for its single tree, to take up his position. He wondered if the message pinned to the Duke's tent flap warning him of betrayal disturbed him.

'Jockey of Norfolk be not too bold
For Dickon, thy master, he bought and sold.'

Martyn approved of the King's decision to take command of the high ground. In the distance he saw a blur of green jacks as Henry's advance battle formation began also to advance under the command of the Earl of Oxford. Martyn could just distinguish the Earl's banner of the star with its streaming lines. He turned to look for the King who had now assumed his battle helmet, round which glinted the crown of England.

Martyn grunted his disapproval. Repeatedly he had argued in company with Francis Lovell that Richard should not so openly mark himself a target for the enemy. But he knew his sovereign. Richard's obstinacy was well known in the household. On occasions he could display a burst of Plantagenet temper worthy of the famed King Henry II. He fought for England, for the realm itself, and he was its anointed king. His men must see that circlet proudly marking him as the focus for their loyalty.

As yet Martyn could not see the Tudor's banner of the red dragon, but the King's personal standard of the white boar was held over his head by his standard bearer and another flaunted the royal standard of England with its leopards and fleur-de-lys. Martyn signalled for Peter to unfurl his own standard of the saltire argent over the field vert, glad this day to be identified with the family of the dead Queen Anne, the Nevilles.

'Peter, stay by me unless I give you a command to withdraw to the horse lines. Then you will obey me at once.'

His squire opened his mouth to protest, then, seeing

his lord's grim expression, he held his tongue and handed him his battle helm.

Oxford's men had wheeled round slightly to avoid the marshy ground round the foot of the hill and now faced Norfolk's van, which he had drawn up in the shape of a bent bow. Cannons thundered from Henry's position and the weird silence, previously only punctuated by the neighing of horses and the tramp of booted feet, was broken. A man screamed in agony as a stone ball found its mark and felled him and jeers, oaths and furious war cries came from the waiting foot soldiers.

The heavy guns appeared to have done little real damage and soon hand-to-hand fighting began in earnest. The former quiet of the countryside was now shattered by the screams and oaths, the clanging and thuds of bills and pikes, the splintering of wood as men savagely thrust and stabbed at each other. Sweat and dust from the combatants half blinded the commanders upon Ambien, preventing them from seeing much of the carnage, but Martyn had seen such sights before and hardened his heart against pity for the lives spent and bodies shattered by the brutal business taking place below him.

He heard Peter give a sudden gasp as an agonised scream sounded too near for comfort. He reached out a gauntled hand to steady the boy's shoulder.

It was a relatively short time, though it seemed hours, while they waited for further commands from the King, then suddenly a shout went up which struck them all to the depths of their courage.

'Norfolk is down. The good Duke is slain.'

Martyn could see the King turn agitatedly to his close companions but could not hear what was said.

A royal pursuivant raced by him to the horse lines and Catesby walked towards him, awkwardly clumsy in unfamiliar mail.

'The King has summoned Northumberland to bring up reinforcements.'

Martyn nodded tersely. It was difficult to bellow over the noise of combat and helmed as he now was. He saw men carrying the body of the stricken Duke back towards the horse lines. Norfolk was a stalwart and experienced campaigner, a good friend to the King, and this was a severe blow to the royalist cause.

Martyn was not surprised when the pursuivant returned alone from Northumberland's camp. He sensed that the man he had long suspected of petty jealousy towards Richard during their earlier joint rulership in the north had given some excuse for yet holding back his force.

Still the furious fighting continued and the stinks of gunpowder and fresh spilt blood drifted back to the commanders watching grimly upon the hilltop.

Another pursuivant rode a lathered horse up to the command post and dismounted. Martyn watched intently. The man had been sent earlier to order Lord Thomas Stanley to come to the King's support and he guessed by the rigidity of the King's head and shoulder posture that Lord Thomas had refused to obey.

Ratcliffe turned and bellowed, 'My Lord Wroxeter, the King would speak with you.'

Hurriedly he moved to the King's side. The royal visor was up and Martyn saw the signs of one of Richard's royal rages in the hectic spots which marked the normally pale cheeks and the hard-held line of his mouth.

'Martyn, you were right. Lord Stanley refuses to join us. I have threatened to execute my hostage, his son, Lord Strange. Send one of the squires to see to it immediately.'

Yes, Your Grace.' Martyn was about to step aside when, just as quickly, he was recalled.

'No, stay, Martyn; let us await the outcome. What

point to vent my fury on Strange? He is not to blame for his father's perfidy.'

Martyn was glad of the King's change of heart. He had no stomach for executions when the terrible carnage below was exacting its full toll of dead and wounded. He knew now, as he was sure the King did, that this battle was lost. Northumberland and the Stanleys were intent on treason and though the King's force had outnumbered the rebels when they had arrived at Redmoor the combined forces of Henry's with the Stanleys', especially if Northumberland joined the fray on the rebel side, would give this victory to Henry.

Catesby was murmuring urgently that the King should fly the field and fight another day. Reason told Martyn that the man's advice was sensible and should be heeded but, wearily, he knew that no one would convince Richard of the practical good sense of it.

Already he saw squires dispatched to bring up the destriers and the King's voice carried to the household.

'Gentlemen, it seems we are bedevilled by treachery. There can be one way to end this business and one way only. A scout has informed me that, at last, Henry has joined his force. I intend to charge full into the enemy lines and confront him. I order no man to ride with me, but those who do know they ride to defend the realm and the honour of their King.'

Martyn snapped an order to Peter as the lad brought up his destrier.

'I ride with the King. Get back to the spring near the horse lines.'

'But, my lord—'

'Obey me, Peter. You have your Countess to consider. See to it that she is informed of whatever happens now and—lad—tell her of my undying love.'

Peter, wide-eyed and frightened, held Martyn's destrier steady as he mounted, then stood away from its plunging hooves. The highly trained animal had scented blood and was as eager for the fray as his master.

There was no fear in Martyn's heart, only a calm acceptance. There was still a chance. Richard was a doughty fighter and could save the day, but many of them would die on this final charge; he knew that. The household knights grouped together around their sovereign. The horses moved in a slow walk down from the summit, then, as the steepness of the ground lessened, momentum carried them into a gallop.

Martyn could see the white boar banner streaming in the wind above the King's mount and spurred his own destrier to the gallop. They were flying now into the full might of Henry's cavalry.

A giant mounted figure loomed ahead—Sir William Brandon, Henry's standard bearer. As if berserk, like his Viking ancestors, Richard cut him down with his battleaxe and the giant toppled, dragging the red dragon banner in the dust where it was trampled underfoot.

Martyn charged on, oblivious of the shouts of the men around him, determined to stay near the King, as battle-crazed now as those with him. He wielded his own broadsword vigorously from side to side, ignoring the thuds and clangs of weapon against armour, his eyes half-blinded by his visor and the flying clods of earth and grass tussocks thrown up by the destriers' hooves.

A savage blow toppled the King from his courser but he fought on valiantly on foot. Men shouted hoarsely for someone to bring the King a fresh mount and Martyn strove desperately to reach Richard's side.

He saw a sudden sun flash on red jacks and yelled a warning as Sir William Stanley's men streamed ahead of them, joining Henry's force. The King was surrounded, but still fought on doggedly.

Martyn felt a jarring crash upon his helm which

paralysed him arm, still upheld to strike his opponent. For moments he remained upright in the saddle, bemused. His last thought, in the moments before the red mist hampered his vision and then the blackness engulfed him finally, was of Cressida, leaning down from the chamber window at Nottingham to smell the climbing white rose, then he lurched sideways from the saddle before the hooves of the oncoming coursers.

CHAPTER TEN

CRESSIDA could hear the growing buzz of noise in the street as she returned to her apartment in the gatehouse from praying in the church of St Mary's within the castle walls. She paused for a moment in the courtyard, her hand on her heart. Was there news of the battle already? She hastened inside, her anxiety conveying itself to Alice who was close behind her.

Alice said softly, 'It may be nothing, child. Crowds gather for any reason which offers some excitement. It could be some dishonest baker being carted through the streets for punishment.'

Cressida nodded abstractedly. She wanted news desperately but feared to receive it when it came. She remembered Martyn's last advice to her.

'Trust no one with information about the battle but those you know well.'

Philip, white-faced, was waiting for her at the door to her chamber.

'My lady, they're saying in the streets that the battle is lost to the King and Henry Tudor has been crowned on the field with the golden circlet which fell from the King's helm when he was cut down and slain.'

Alice gave a little growl of warning but the boy rushed on.

'Lord Thomas Stanley had a stool brought for the Earl of Richmond to sit on and crowned him himself. The circlet was found under a thorn bush and a soldier brought it to Lord Stanley.'

Cressida drew the boy within the chamber and signalled to Alice to bar the door. 'They are saying the King is dead?'

'Yes, my lady.' The boy blinked unhappily. 'I heard one man say it was the Stanley brothers who won the day for the Tudor. They waited till the last minute and then brought their forces to cut off King Richard's men and—and the King was killed fighting on foot. . .'

'Then the royalist forces are in retreat?'

The boy swallowed hard and avoided her eyes. 'It—it would seem so, my lady. I—I didn't wait to hear more, but came back to tell you.'

Cressida sank down heavily upon the bed while Alice came to her side and put a reassuring hand on her shoulder.

'You must not give up hope. The Earl may well have escaped the field.'

'My father told me of the pursuit after Tewkesbury,' Cressida said woodenly. 'It was more bloody than the battle itself, he said, and every man in Lancastrian livery was rounded up and—and the ringleaders executed. . .'

There was a terrible numbness within her which would not allow her the solace of tears. She had feared this for so long, during those last, poignantly sweet days with Martyn. Where was he now? Had he perished on the field or was he, even now, being hunted down like some animal?

She could not take it in. Martyn had kept on assuring her that the King's forces were superior to those of the Tudor, that King Richard was far more experienced a commander than Henry Tudor or any of his supporters, yet here was Philip telling her of this disastrous defeat.

The King had been despicably betrayed. In his heart Martyn had known this was likely, yet he had kept up a brave front before her. She turned a frightened face towards her nurse, made a little anguished sound and buried her head in the folds of Alice's skirts.

Alice said gruffly to the boy, 'Take yourself off for a while. Do not go into the streets again but keep your

ears open for talk from the castle servants. Say nothing
about the Earl, nor are you to remind anyone, for the
moment, about the presence of your mistress here in
the castle.'

'But—but how are we to be served?' he stammered
fearfully.

'I will see to that personally. And, before you come
in again with more distressing tidings, speak to me
first.' These last words were uttered in a threatening
hiss.

The boy nodded dumbly and scrambled out of the
room.

Still Cressida could not cry. At last she sat upright,
one hand still clinging to her old nurse's skirt. 'What
are we to do? What will become of us? I will not be
moved from here until—' Cressida's lips trembled
'—until I hear word of Lord Martyn.' She broke down
finally and whimpered, 'Oh, Alice, how could he have
escaped? He would have fought near to his King, I
know it.'

Alice pursed her lips. 'We know nothing of the sort.
You've just said yourself your father escaped after
Tewkesbury.'

'He was taken prisoner and it was only by the mercy
of the Duke of Gloucester.' The last words were jerked
out brokenly as she thought of the bleakest of Philip's
tidings—that Richard, who had been Duke of
Gloucester then and spared her father, was now dead
on the battlefield himself—if the rumours were true.
Wearily she faced facts. The news *had* to be true. Why
else was there so much commotion in the streets? She
had heard it in the distance and dreaded knowing the
outcome, even then.

Cressida refused a late dinner which an excited
serving man brought to her chamber. In spite of her
charge's protests Alice took the laden tray from him
and placed it on a fald table within the chamber. She

questioned the man as to further news of the battle. Wearily Cressida climbed to her feet from the prie-dieu where she had been praying for the repose of the dead King's soul.

The man glanced shiftily towards the Countess. 'The new King is to enter the town within the next hour and—' he shifted awkwardly from one foot to the other '—some man-at-arms riding in shouted that they be bringing in the late King's—that is the usurper's—body for public view.'

Alice dismissed the fellow quickly and came back to Cressida, who had turned a horrified face towards them both.

'No, no, they cannot do that,' she raged. 'It is not decent. It—'

Alice drew her down onto the bed. 'My lady, it is customary. The new King must let the people see King Richard is truly dead. It was so with the late King Henry VI, and King Edward lay in state for his subjects to view the body.'

Cressida covered her face with her hands. She had been present at the obsequies of the dead Queen, had seen how reverently things had been done, and now the King she had come to like and admire was to be the object of curiosity for every townsman or beggar in this town to come and stare at in vulgar and idle speculation.

'I must go and see.' She spoke with cold determination, knowing that Alice would protest vehemently. 'At least there will be two or three souls there who will mourn him in honour.'

Alice offered no objections, knowing it would be pointless to do so, but summoned the two men-at-arms whom Lord Martyn had left to guard them to accompany their mistress into the crowded streets of Leicester town. Philip refused to be parted from his mistress and, wearing a dark gown and simple cap, and a lightweight grey cloak, for the afternoon was sultry, Cressida left the castle ward. Her guards made way for her through the avidly curious and whispering townsfolk onto the high street near to its junction with the road which led westward to the little town of Market Bosworth.

The King's party rode in soon after. Cressida caught only a glimpse of the man who had been a thorn in King Richard's side for so long and who would shortly be crowned more ceremoniously in London as King Henry VII of England. He was closely hemmed in by a bodyguard of men wearing green jacks with his device of the red dragon.

Beside him and behind him rode those lords who had helped him to the crown, two of them, at least, by treachery, she thought bitterly. She saw only a tall, slim man dressed very soberly, with lank brown hair, his face shaded by a black velvet low-crowned hat. The standards of the Stanley brothers and that of the Earl of Oxford were borne triumphantly by.

Cressida could not believe she was seeing what followed. There had been ragged cheers of welcome from the crowds lining the street which the new King did not acknowledge, then the people fell strangely silent and looked back to the rear of the procession, craning their necks and whispering awkwardly.

A lone white horse was ridden by a solitary pursuivant. Cressida's mouth went oddly dry as she recognised Richard's favourite courser, White Surrey, his head hanging low as if for very shame at the proceedings he was forced to take part in. The pursuivant, too, she knew; it was the youthful herald Blanc Sanglier, the man who had proudly carried Richard's banner of the white boar in the royal army which had set out from Nottingham.

He sat upright in the saddle, his youthful face set into a mask of seeming stone, and behind him the body of the dead King was slung ignominiously, stripped of

his armour and clothing, naked, bloodstained, and
wearing a halter like a common felon, the dark head
lolling grotesquely downwards, as if bowing to the
watching subjects.

Cressida made as if to step forward to make a public
protest at this gross indignity but Alice caught her and
held her forcibly back. Her own face expressed total
horror and she motioned to their two veteran guards to
prevent their mistress from making any further move.

Tears streamed down Cressida's cheeks and she
knew she was sobbing. People near her turned to stare
but she was beyond caring. No one was making any
comment. One or two had the decency to turn away
and one old grizzled townsman who might have been a
butcher, judging from his bloodstained apron, murmured brokenly, 'It ain't right. 'E was the Lord's
anointed.' He was hastily and nervously shushed by a
fat woman near him.

Alice whispered urgently, 'It cannot matter, my little
darling. He feels and sees nothing. Please, you must
not make a scene.'

Cressida gave an anguished cry despite the grim
warning when the courser approached the bridge over
the River Soar and the lolling head struck one of the
coping stones in passing and a concerted cry went up
from the watching townsfolk. Still wary, the townsfolk
continued to watch as the white courser passed onward,
bearing its horrifying burden towards the castle and the
church of St Mary, known as the lesser, to distinguish
it from St Mary's within the castle precincts.

There Richard's body would lie for some days,
exposed to public view as Alice had predicted. The
news of the King's death would be carried from
Leicester town by the new King's messengers and by
the gossip of these witnesses. Soon all England would
be made aware that a new king had won the crown.

Cressida was almost fainting and Alice was forced to

hold her upright. They were compelled to remain where they were for some time for the crowd dispersed slowly and uneasily, muttering amongst themselves as mounted knights rode in at the rear and behind them, wearily, men-at-arms on foot. Finally came the baggage train and, with it, a pathetic group of pinioned prisoners.

At last it was possible to return to the castle and Alice was relieved to have Cressida safely behind the locked door of her own chamber, for she was afraid that her mistress would continue to speak our fiercely about the irreverent way the body of the fallen King had been treated.

Alice was not sure if the new King Henry was even now accommodated within the royal apartments of the castle, but she knew that the great hall roof was still being repaired so he could not be installed with any degree of state.

Cressida refused to eat at supper and spent the rest of the evening in St Mary's in prayer. Later Alice insisted on her retiring to bed and watched until Cressida fell into an exhausted sleep.

The next morning Cressida agreed that it would be better to remain in her chamber and Alice herself went down to the castle kitchens for food for her mistress, herself and Philip. The men, she knew, would forage for themselves, and it was of those two that Cressida spoke, after breaking a frugal fast.

'They should leave here, Alice. Ask them to come to me. I shall send them home. They must not remain here wearing Lord Martyn's livery. Best that they should set off immediately for Wroxeter.'

'But we do not know yet what news they should carry of their lord's fate.'

Cressida's expression was set but calm. 'Whatever it may be, he will be unlikely to return to his manor and his servants should be informed. These men could be arrested. You saw those wretches in the procession. These men are my responsibility now and I must think of their safety.'

Alice looked at her charge keenly. Cressida was scarcely seventeen—only a year ago she had been castigating her for childish follies. Now, already, Cressida was taking on the role of sole arbiter of her husband's estates. She had grown up far too quickly for Alice's liking.

Just before Alice set off in search of dinner, Philip came to the door of the chamber, his face grave, and stammered that there were visitors for his mistress.

Cressida was talking to the two men-at-arms who were arguing, though respectfully, that their master had charged them with her protection and how could she be left alone within this now hostile castle? She lifted a hand to quell further objections to her orders, then turned and nodded to Philip to admit the newcomers.

Her heart was beating so fast that she thought it would burst free from the restraining ribs and she had to force her trembling limbs to hold still and support her.

She gave a little sob of surprise and relieved joy as Sir Daniel Gretton walked in briskly and waited for no greeting but came hurriedly to her and embraced her in a bear hug. She allowed her tears full rein then and sobbed against his shoulder.

'There, there, lass,' he said gruffly, patting her shoulder in awkward sympathy. 'Thank the Virgin I am here now. You can rely on me to see to your interests.'

She lifted her head and stared beyond him to where Howell Prosser stood silently near the chamber door, and behind him she glimpsed a dust-stained, white-faced Peter Fairley. She gave a little choked cry and stood fully upright, putting an arm out to withdraw herself from her father's protective embrace.

'What is this traitor doing in my presence?' she said

haughtily. 'Isn't it enough that you betray your anointed King, but you must come and mock at me also?'

Howell bowed, his brown eyes imploring, but he did not attempt to come any nearer.

'God knows I would not hurt you by any action or words of mine, Cressida,' he said quietly. 'I shall not try to excuse myself. You know well my sympathies have always been with the House of Lancaster. I have served *my* King to the best of my abilities and can only rejoice that he is triumphant, but I regret that his victory causes you pain. It is ever so in war.'

Cressida suddenly turned angrily to her father. 'And what are you doing in this man's company? Have you too turned your coat, after King Richard honoured you so recently?'

'No, Cressida,' he returned mildly. 'I was on my way to join the late King's force at Leicester, but our way was blocked by the Tudor army. It was impossible to proceed. I took no part in the battle.' He hesitated then added, 'Perhaps it is just as well I was prevented, since I will be in a better position to protect you and guard your rights. I met up with Howell here in Leicester when I rode in with my men following King Henry's force.'

Her blue eyes were blazing and he stepped back a little from such passionate fury.

She ignored both men and held out a hand to Peter. 'What news do you bring me, Peter?' she said at last, very softly.

He opened his mouth as if to try to speak and then turned away brokenly. Howell then advanced further into the chamber.

'I was aware how much you would wish to know of— Lord Martyn's fate after the battle. Fortunately, I encountered Wroxeter's squire with some of the other

squires and pages, near the spring. As soon as it was
fully light I took him to search the field.'

He cleared his throat. 'We concluded that—that
Lord Martyn would be found, if still on the field, with
those who died near the King at the foot of Ambien
Hill. There were enemy bodies. . .'

He paused and swallowed as Cressida continued to
look intently at him, her blue eyes now sparkling with
restrained tears. He pressed on, turning slightly as if to
avoid the full stare of those accusing eyes.

'We searched those. Finally we came upon the body
of a tall knight—it was impossible to be sure, for most
had been half stripped of their armour and armorial
bearings. Already the bodies had been despoiled in the
night by those ghouls who prey on the dead and prosper
after battles.'

'Yes?' The single whisper was a determined command for him to continue.

'Peter here thought—that is, he identified his master.
The Earl was wearing this, though how in God's name
it escaped the thieving hands of the robbers I cannot
say—possibly they left it for very shame, knowing it to
be a sacred reliquary or fearing it would be noted and
recognised later.' He shook his head.

He was holding out to her the reliquary of St Martin
which she had given to Martyn the morning he had
ridden out from Leicester with the King's force. She
gave an anguished little sob and wonderingly took it
from him.

'Your squire said he was wearing it when he charged
down the hill with the King's company.'

Cressida's eyes met the sorrowful eyes of Peter
Fairley. She said very softly, 'Is he truly dead, Peter?'

The squire could not answer. He nodded dumbly.

Cressida said woodenly, 'Thank you, Master Prosser.
I—I have been very anxious to know—the worst.
What—what is to be done? My husband's body must

be brought from the field and tended. If he could be brought here. . .'

'No, no, Cressida, I'm sorry.' Howell's voice was harsh with embarrassment. 'That won't be possible. The King has commanded that those enemy dead are to be buried near the field. Trust me to see to it that— that the Earl is interred with honour.'

'Unlike his sovereign,' Cressida said in a brittle voice and he winced slightly.

'You must realise, Cressida, that these things are necessary and—afterwards—I am sure that the King will arrange for—'

'I trust he will do so,' Cressida said icily, 'for other-wise his subjects will surely cry shame on him as a dishonourable victor.'

Her father said weakly, 'Cressida, child, I beg you to have a care. . .'

She turned from him back to Howell Prosser. 'Am I not to have an opportunity to see my husband's body and mourn him in honour?'

He drew a hard breath and looked to Sir Daniel for support. 'Believe me, it is best that you do not, Cressida. He—he was badly disfigured in the charge. The following destriers must have—he must have been unhorsed early—and—'

Still she did not weep, though her mind took the full pain of the picture his words had conjured however he had sought to hide the truth from her.

'I see,' she said coldly. 'Thank you again, Master Prosser. And now—now, if you please, I would like to be alone for a while with Alice.'

Sir Daniel drew Howell to the door after dismissing the two men-at-arms, who were round-eyed with horror.

He spoke to Alice. 'We are lodged at an inn in the town. I will come back when your mistress is less distraught.' Peter trailed miserably after them.

Cressida stood staring into space until Alice came to her and gathered her close to her heart. The tears came then and she sobbed as if her heart would break. Afterwards she drew away and said briskly, 'I must not give way, for there is much to be done. See to it that those men are provided with coin and send them off to Wroxeter. There is no need now for them to remain at risk here, since my father's men will escort me when it is time for me to leave. I will go to St Mary's and have masses said for Martyn's soul.'

Alice nodded and went off to do her bidding. Cressida summoned Philip and set off for the church. Even now, though she had feared the worst, she could not fully take in the fact that she would never see Martyn again, never lie with him, her head pillowed on his shoulder after the delight of lovemaking, never see those sleepy lids sweep back to reveal those dark eyes smouldering with desire for her, never hear his half-humorous rebuke— 'Cressida, you have always been difficult.'

There was a terrible ache at the back of her throat which she knew was caused by the tears she must not shed. If she stopped to weep now she would not be able to do what must be done. There must be masses said. In spite of Howell's promise of honourable burial, she must insist that her father accompany her to the churchyard where Martyn would be laid. Later she must arrange for mourning black to be doled out to all their servants. . .

She was thankful that the church was deserted. As yet there was no priest in attendance. He must be summoned and given instructions for the requiem masses. She knelt alone before the altar, Philip, at her command, remaining at the rear of the nave, her lips murmuring intercessions to the Virgin and St Martin that her husband's soul would not suffer too long in purgatory.

She was sure that he must have been in a state of grace. The King, known to be pious, would have had mass said before the battle. She continued to intercede for him too. Kings had much to atone for. It was necessary that they be ruthless. Martyn had assured her that the King had done no murder, that his nephews had not suffered at his hands, but there were others who had suffered in order for King Richard to take the throne and keep the peace in England—and Martyn had been in his councils, worked with him.

She closed her eyes and prayed fervently for all those brave men, on both sides, who had fallen that day.

She knew she was still numb, that true realisation would come soon and, with it, increased suffering, but for the moment she forced herself to think only of Martyn's soul's salvation.

She was half-distressed and half-annoyed to hear booted feet approach. She desperately needed to be alone with her grief. Deliberately she did not turn, hoping that the newcomer would see her need and leave the church quickly, but she heard a rustle of movement as the intruder knelt some paces behind her. Clutching her beads determinedly, she continued to pray.

Then it was that she heard the whisper from the shadowed gloom of the nave.

'My lady, do not despair. Lord Martyn lives.'

She thought at first that she was experiencing a hallucination of her own desperate longing and shut her eyes fast. She must address herself to God and not allow false hopes to weaken her purpose.

Again came the whisper, this time even closer to her ear, as if the speaker had leaned forward eagerly to speak secretly to her.

'I have waited to find you alone, my lady. He was badly wounded.' It was undoubtedly Peter Fairley's voice. She half turned but he warned her hastily, 'Do not turn round, my lady; just listen to what I say. You must not acknowledge me in case someone enters.

'We searched for him last night as soon as the pursuit was well in progress and Henry's men had left the field to the despoilers of the dead.' He sounded bitter. 'Jack Wainwright and I, we were hardly noticed in such a company and we had both torn our Wroxeter devices from our jacks.

'We found him, more dead than alive. He wasn't conscious and Master Wainwright said that as the helm was badly dented he must have taken a blow to the head from a mace or battleaxe. His arm was broken. We feared for his life, but he was breathing, though very shallowly.

'We—stripped him of his armour, as others had been so despoiled, and found some other poor soul about his height and put some of it on him—the dented breastplate and part of the vambrace—and—and I put the reliquary round the stranger's neck. Master Wainwright, he—' Peter gave a shuddering breath '—he saw to it that the other man would not be recognised. He was past heeding, mistress, so it was no sin, though I—baulked at it.

'We managed to carry Lord Martyn from the field and hid him in a ditch near the marsh. I stayed with him till Master Wainwright came back with a cart and we managed to get him away.'

Again there was a hard swallow which told Cressida of the terrible horror and fear which had haunted the boy throughout all this and she clutched at her beads until the knuckles of her hand whitened with strain. Still she did not turn, obeying Peter's strictures, though her heart was pounding and her whole soul longed to cry out questions.

He gulped and continued. 'We piled straw over him, and the dung, and we got him clear of the field. There were some of Lord Stanley's men drinking near one of the baggage waggons, but they did not question us, thank the Virgin. My lord moaned, but did not come to consciousness. We thanked God for that at the time. Then I went back. Jack said that would be less suspicious.'

'Where is he now?' Cressida asked urgently. Hope was flooding back into her numbed being—yet he was sore hurt, Peter had said—and a head wound—

'In the house of Master Wainwright's cousin, here in Leicester. We dared not summon a physician but Master Wainwright tended him. He has cared many times for sorely wounded men on other campaigns, my lady. We feared—brain damage, but once or twice Lord Martyn half came to and seemed sensible. He knew us but he kept falling off again, but Master Jack says that is just nature's way. We have hopes of full recovery, but he may not get back the full use of his sword arm. Master—'

'You must take me to him.'

'No, mistress. You must not go near him, not until the King's men have left the town—not even then until we are sure there will not be searches made for fugitives.'

She drew a hard breath. He was so tantalisingly near and yet she saw the sense of it. She must not endanger him, nor those who gave him shelter, but, sweet Virgin, even now he might die and she not at his side.

Peter explained. 'Master Wainwright says that—that because of the work my lord did for the King the Tudor would never pardon him. Already there is talk that Master Catesby must die.'

She said as calmly as she could, 'What must I do, then, Peter? Oh, Peter, take him my love. . .'

'He knows he has that, my lady. In his delirium he speaks your name.'

She swallowed back tears of joy and newly roused fear for his safety.

'You must continue to mourn him, my lady. Not even your father must know and certainly not Master Prosser. When it is safe I will bring you news again.'

She heard the rustle of his garments as he stood up and moved away down the length of the nave. She remained where she was until she heard the heavy door close and then fell forward, face down, upon the hard stone and whispered her heartfelt paean of praise to God, the Virgin and all the Saints that they had heard her prayers and granted her the life of the man she loved.

Cressida shifted awkwardly upon the hard bench where she waited in the ante-room to the late Queen's chamber while a page carried her request to the Lady Elizabeth Plantagenet for an audience. It was three weeks since she had heard the heart-stopping news that her husband had escaped Redmoor field. Now she had arrived at Westminster and was fervently praying that she would be received by her friend, for only the Lady Elizabeth could offer her any hope of pardon for Lord Martyn.

Henry Tudor was already England's acknowledged King, and on his accession he had declared his intention of honouring his pledged word to the Lady Elizabeth that he would take her to wife. Elizabeth would be the new Queen and cement the union of the houses of York and Lancaster, thus making it more probable that the common folk of England would accept without protest his claim to the English throne. They had all had enough of the wars; Londoners had loved her father; they would greet this promised union with glad hearts.

Cressida could only hope that Elizabeth would still look with pleasure on their erstwhile friendship and grant her request.

She had done what Peter had told her—returned to

her apartment in the castle gatehouse, outwardly the grieving widow. Her father had called several times in the days which followed to offer her clumsy attempts at sympathy. He had wanted her to return at once with him to Gretton but she had determinedly refused, knowing she could not leave Leciester until she had managed to glean further news of Martyn's recovery.

Only one person had she trusted with her wonderful secret—Alice. Her maid must know, for if there was the remotest hope of seeing Martyn Alice would insist on accompanying her.

Alice had been totally dumbfounded, but had rejoiced as her mistress had done. She was utterly trustworthy yet capable of duplicity while secrecy was so desperately needed. She had laid out the black silk mourning gown Cressida had worn at Court for Queen Anne's obsequies and continued to play the supportive role expected of her to the young widow.

Determined to play her part to the end, Cressida had pleaded to go to the churchyard near the village of Daddlington where the bodies of the royalist dead had been laid to rest. Howell had gently but firmly prevented her, explaining that any outward show of sympathy for the late King's cause could only exacerbate the King's enmity towards the families of the fallen royalist knights. Her father had also reminded her that Lord Martyn would have wished her to salvage what she could from the ruin of the Wroxeter fortunes.

'It is fortunate that the Prossers have always been supporters of the new King,' he declared. 'Howell will use his best efforts on your behalf to see to it that your dower rights are protected.'

Because it served her purpose, Cressida had reluctantly acceded to their wishes. The unknown knight who was buried as the Earl of Wroxeter had been interred quietly but decently and Cressida had sent gold to the priest at Daddlington to say continual

masses for his soul. She had prayed privately for this
unknown man in his own right.

Howell had been proved right. Henry had shown
ruthlessness in his determination to heap infamy upon
the memory of the dead King. A proclamation was
issued accusing him of many crimes against humanity,
one unspecified, pertaining to shedding of infant blood,
but Cressida noted that the new King had not dared
openly to accuse King Richard of the murder of his
nephews.

She wondered why that was. Was Henry himself
unaware of their fate and feared that one or both of
them might one day appear to dispute his own claim—
or, worse, was he guilty of ordering the murder of the
boys himself? That question she was unwilling to dwell
on.

King Richard's body had finally been laid to rest in
the church of the Grey Friars. Cressida had heard of
the execution of William Catesby, though of what the
man was guilty, other than loyally serving his sovereign,
she did not know. Two other men had been hanged in
Leicester town, but she knew of no other noble prisoners who had suffered so.,

She was told that Norfolk's son, the Earl of Surrey,
and the Earl of Northumberland, who, astonishingly,
had taken no part in the battle, were to be imprisoned
in the Tower. Of Lord Lovell's fate there were no
tidings and she assumed that he had managed to flee
the battlefield.

With the King on Ambien had died Sir Richard
Ratcliffe, Sir Robert Brackenbury, Sir Robert Percy,
even John Kendall, the King's secretary. She had
known them all and grieved for them.

During those terrible days Cressida had grimly hung
on, hoping against hope that Peter Fairley would be
able to contact her again in secret. He had come to her

at her apartments frequently, but there had never been any opportunity for them to speak together alone.

She had been returning from one of her usual visits to the church one day when a lanky boy, most likely one of the kitchen scullions, had come across the court then stumbled and almost fallen into their path. Alice had scolded him roundly for his carelessness but Cressida had heard to her utter astonishment, a whispered message.

'Mistress, if you would see my lord, dress in plain attire and wait for me tonight by the church lych-gate. Bring only your maid.'

The boy got to his feet, apologised gruffly, and was off before Alice could cuff him about the ears. Cressida stared after him in wonder.

After supper she informed Alice, who was equally bewildered and more than a little alarmed.

'Are you sure you can trust this messenger?'

'Alice, I must. How else will I ever know how my lord Martyn is? Can you lend me a wollen gown of yours and a simple cap?'

'Aye, of course I can, but I'll come with you, even if I have to wait outside the house. We must give it out that you are unwell—a headache has come on through overmuch weeping. Philip will stand guard outside your sleeping chamber until we return.'

'What shall we tell the boy?'

Alice pursed her lips. 'Tell him we are going to keep a night vigil in the church. To tell truth I think he may well suspect, but he's loyal to the core. He'll do what you command without question.'

Alice was right. Philip made no objection to his mistress leaving the castle court without him, nor did he comment when he saw Cressida emerge from her chamber with Alice dressed in a skirt of brown fustian and white linen blouse. Her bright hair was thrust well under a concealing linen cap. Alice had given her a basket to carry.

Though the hour was late and most of the castle servants were engaged in serving those supporters of the new King who had remained after Henry had set out for the capital, Alice assured her that many women went out to buy cheese and bread from one or two shops which stayed open.

'The poorer folk shop when the food is less fresh and it costs less at these late hours. We will not be noticed.'

They waited by the church gate, anxiously scanning the deserted street. The same lanky boy who had accosted them earlier sidled into view and beckoned. Cressida hastened to catch up with him as he set off. It was evident that he did not wish to be associated with the two women and they must simply follow and keep him in sight.

They reached the high street with its cross and then passed the inn where Richard's officers had spent that last night before the battle in conference. Cressida caught her breath as she recalled the King's last kindly words to her. The innkeeper had decided to play safe and had already painted the white boar device on the inn sign blue.

Their guide plunged down an alley nearby. The light was beginning to fade now and Cressida had difficulty in picking out his outline but at last, near an old house whose upper storey was leaning crazily towards the house opposite, she saw that the lad was waiting for her. A torch flared on one of the nearby houses and, as he faced her, she thought she half recognised the boy. Could it be the ill-used scullion she had tried to rescue from dire punishment at the hands of their cook in the Strand house?

He knocked upon the badly warped door and turned to face them again, signalling them to enter as the door was opened.

The familiar bulky figure of Jack Wainwright almost filled the small room into which they were ushered. Cressida gave a relieved gasp at sight of him.

'Master Wainwright, where is Lord Martyn? He is not worse...?'

He shook his head decisively. 'We have him in a room above stairs. We must move him soon, so I thought this your best opportunity to see him.'

Alice opted to remain with their guide in the downstairs room. From the kitchen a woman emerged and curtsied.

'Welcome to our house, my lady Countess. I will bring you ale and meats...'

'No, no,' Cressida said agitatedly. 'Do not put yourself out. You have done more than enough in risking yourselves for my lord Earl.'

Wainwright nodded towards the plump, smiling woman who was plainly but respectably clad. 'My cousin, Mistress Joan Wainwright. Her man, Dick, is a groom in service at the Blue Boar, as we must call it now. Come upstairs, my lady. Tread carefully; the light is dim here in the shadows.'

Heart in her mouth and winded, for she was too eager to see Martyn and climbed too hurriedly, Cressida was also too breathless to question Jack Wainwright.

He moved through an upper sleeping chamber where two pallets gave evidence of occupation by his cousin and wife. He stooped at a low door at the rear and pushed it open, revealing a room behind, more than likely usually used to store apples or barrels of salted meat. The light was dim, but Cressida could just distinguish a pallet on which a man lay. The unshuttered window gave her light enough to approach and kneel by her husband's side. Wainwright stood waiting near the doorway.

Martyn was half turned from her. He was dressed

like their scullion, in brown hose and a torn fustian
tunic of some indeterminate colour. He had not been
shaved and there was dark stubble upon his chin and
cheeks, though she could detect no rank odour from
his body, so he had been cleansed and tended well. A
linen bandage about his head was marked with a
seepage of blood. He was breathing steadily and
appeared to be sleeping normally.

She bent and kissed his cheek. He had not lost his
normal tan, for he had spent the summer at Bestwood,
often in the chase, but there were dark bruises about
his eyes which spoke to her of suffering. She whispered
his name very softly.

'Martyn, my dear lord.'

He moved restlessly and, at length, at the touch of
her hand on his, he opened his eyes and blinked at her
owlishly. She was fearful that the blow he had taken to
his head had rendered him witless, but at last recognition dawned and the hooded lids swept fully back.
Joy lit up those dark brown eyes and he struggled
weakly to turn and rise up against the straw pillow.

'Cressida, can it really be you?'

'Yes, my love. I am here. You must not try to talk
too much if you are still weak.'

He grinned at her mischievously. 'As the proverbial
kitten. They tell me I've been here for days.'

'Yes, my love, you know where you are?'

He nodded. 'Aye, in Leicester.'

She said with a little catch to her voice, 'You know—
about the King?'

The dark eyes clouded and he nodded again. 'Aye,
God rest his soul.'

She stroked his face, then traced the beloved lines of
eyes, nose and chin with one questing finger. 'You have
much to thank Master Wainwright for. You must be
guided by his advice now.'

She turned to their erstwhile cook. 'You say you must move him. Is there still danger?'

The burly giant frowned. 'Who knows? Few have been executed so far, but my lord Earl is a special case. Many of Henry's supporters have suffered because of him.'

Martyn's fingers tightened suddenly upon Cressida's hand.

'You should go home to Gretton soon now. You must not be involved in any plan to get me from here.'

'Hush, hush. We shall all be very careful, I promise. Rest now.' Worriedly, she saw how the least movement tired him.

'Kiss me again before you leave me.' The command was almost imperative, as she remembered, and she stooped, her lashes wet with tears, to kiss him full on the mouth then on the eyes and chin.

'See her safe to the castle, Jack. Let your parents go on thinking me dead, Cressida. Do not worry about me. I'll manage to stay hidden. Jack will send you news when it's safe to do so.'

Cressida was unwilling to leave him so soon, but she dared not be too long away from her chamber at the castle. She moved back to the storeroom door and turned for a last look at him, then she hastened back again and pressed into his hand the reliquary. 'Keep it safe. It helped to save your life.'

He coughed weakly and bent to kiss her fingers, then she hurried out with Jack Wainwright.

She conferred with him below. 'How well is he really?'

'He is still weak. At first he rarely remained conscious for long, but he is much better already. He lost a great deal of blood, but his arm is mending and soon we must try to reach the coast. He is not safe within the realm.'

'But I hear Henry is anxious to appear merciful and will pardon many who fought for King Richard.'

Wainwright's bulbous eyes narrowed warily. 'Believe me, my lady, he will not pardon my lord Earl. There is too much between them.'

'Where will you take him?'

'Eventually to Burgundy, if we can make it, but the ports are watched. Travellers need licences to take ship.'

Grimly she recalled the licence she had stolen for Howell. How could she obtain one for Martyn? Dared she trust Howell? But immediately she knew she could not. Only one person could possibly help her now. The Lady Elizabeth was to be the new King's bride. Martyn had shown her some hostility. Would she, for the sake of the friendship she and Cressida had shared, be willing to help him now?

Her father had made no objection to her avowed intention to travel to Westminster and had provided her with an escort of Gretton men.

'Go by all means, daughter. Your friendship with the Princess should influence King Henry in any decision he makes concerning the possible sequestration of your husband's estates. Your dower rights must be protected.'

He had not added that possibly, in time, the new King would provide the widowed Cressida with a new husband.

So now she waited, hoping that the Princess would see her and remember the hours they had spent together in amity. Her fingers surreptitiously touched the modesty vest of her gown where Elizabeth's letter to her, written from Sheriff Hutton, was hidden.

The door to the Princess's chamber was opened and a page called haughtily, 'The Countess of Wroxeter?'

Cressida rose hastily and he beckoned her forward.

Elizabeth was seated in a padded armchair, wearing

a gown of deep purple. She rose at once, hands outstretched graciously, to greet her friend.

'Cressida, how glad I am to see you here.' She glanced pointedly and imperiously towards two elderly attendants who sat stitching industriously in the window seat. 'You may all leave me. Go, I say.'

They moved reluctantly but the Princess stared at them coldly and at last they backed from her presence, pulling the doors to after them.

Elizabeth drew Cressida to a seat by her chair. 'I'm sorry I kept you waiting. Lady Stanley has been to see me, as she does most days, and it is difficult for me to be alone, as you saw.' She looked towards the closed door and Cressida realised that, like her late uncle, she had already discovered how a monarch was denied privacy, especially the privacy to grieve.

Elizabeth looked down at Cressida's mourning garb and sighed heavily.

'How can I say how sorry I am that you have lost Martyn on that terrible Leciestershire field?' She turned away momentarily as if she did not wish Cressida to gauge her expression. 'At least you have the right to grieve. I dare not.'

The whispered words were anguished and Cressida reached out and touched her friend gently on the arm. Elizabeth swung back to her briskly.

'You know I am to be King Henry's wife?'

'And England's Queen. Yes, my lady, and all England will rejoice on your marriage day. I wish you all happiness.'

'Do you?' Elizabeth's question was brittle. 'I shall do what is necessary, as other members of my family have done. The King honours me with this proposal and— and I must be humbly grateful.' Then she said quickly, 'I shall be a queen in name only, unlike my aunt, whose husband listened to her advice at least, even when he could not always, for the sake of the realm, accede to her wishes.'

Cressida was silent. Uncomfortably she knew that Elizabeth was trusting her with a confidence she could share with no other. Looking up fully into the Princess's blue eyes, she read the truth at last. Elizabeth had truly loved her uncle as a woman loved a man, knowing that that love was not returned, yet having no regrets, only, now, the terrible knowledge that she could never acknowledge it to a living soul.

Elizabeth said softly, 'Can I help you in any way, Cressida? I can still expedite matters of a personal nature. Do you wish to return to Court when your mourning is over? I should be glad to have you with me.'

Cressida shook her head very slowly, her eyes filling with tears. How lonely Elizabeth was to be in the years ahead.

'No, my lady, I. . .' She hesitated, not knowing, even now, if she dared to trust this woman, then plunged on determinedly. 'I came to beg you—that is, to ask if you could obtain for me—a licence to travel overseas.'

Elizabeth stared at her intently. 'For yourself?' Cressida swallowed painfully then again shook her head. Elizabeth leaned towards her eagerly. 'You need to help someone to flee the realm?'

'Yes, my lady, unless there could be hope of pardon from the King. . .'

Elizabeth was still staring at her, so hard that Cressida thought she could read her very soul, then at last she whispered incredulously, 'For Martyn?'

Cressida inclined her head.

Elizabeth sat back in her chair and Cressida could almost see the thoughts racing through her brain, then she said very determinedly, 'You could never hope for pardon, Cressida. Never allow King Henry to know your husband lives, or anyone else at this Court. No, do not tell me where he is. Even that would not be wise.' One hand went to her lips as she stared across at the oriel window. 'He must be got to Burgundy, to my aunt Margaret.'

'But how, my lady?' Cressida murmured urgently. 'I hoped—prayed that you might be able to help me. I know he was—distant in his attitude towards you, but—'

'He had his reasons, and though I was angered at the time I understood them.' Elizabeth rose and moved to the window, where she stared down into the pleasance below. 'I think there might be one way. Was he injured?'

'Yes, my lady. He—he received a blow to the head, otherwise I think he would have ridden on to his death with—with the King. . .'

'Yes.' The voice was a little hoarse with unshed tears. 'Is he fit to travel, sit a horse?'

'I think so, now.'

'I am soon to travel to the shrine of Our Lady of Walsingham in Norfolk. I shall pray there for a child—Henry's heir. We shall not be far from the port of Lynn. If he could be disguised he could ride in my company as one of my grooms.' She hesitated. 'There are men in Lynn whom—whom my uncle trusted to do very special secret work for him, men with ships who sailed privily to France and on to Burgundy. Somehow Lord Martyn could be smuggled on board one of those vessels. Can you get a message to him?'

'Yes, my lady. My page is with me and some of my father's men, but they know nothing of— My father is unaware that Martyn lives.'

'And should remain that way. Cressida, I shall take you with me. How natural that I should. You will need comfort from Our Lady of Walsingham as I need the great boon I pray for. It has already been arranged for me to leave in one week.'

She sighed. 'It will be a relief to be away from the prying eyes of Lady Margaret, Henry's mother, even from the vigilance of my own mother. I shall rest one night at St Edmund's shrine in Bury. Send to Martyn to join my train there. My captain of escort is trustworthy and will arrange for him to replace one of my servants and travel on with us. That way he will be able to approach the coast without undue notice.'

Cressida was summoned to the stable of the convent where the Princess had elected to stay for the night. It had fallen out as Elizabeth had promised and easier than Cressida could ever have hoped. They had set out from Westminster escorted by twenty men-at-arms, most of whom wore the livery of the dead King Edward, Elizabeth's father, the sun in splendour badge ornamenting their jacks.

Six wore Henry's badge of the red dragon and Cressida knew they must be wary of these men, obviously set to spy upon the Princess while she was away from the King's eyes. Elizabeth appeared unperturbed by their presence, however, apparently putting her trust in her elderly captain of escort, who, she assured Cressida, was totally loyal to her.

On this, the third night of the journey, they had arrived at the shrine of St Edmund in Bury and Cressida and Alice had stayed within the little cell-like room assigned to them, Cressida's heart beating fast in anticipation and alarm.

She had dispatched young Philip to the house in Leicester. The boy had been overjoyed at her news and, despite his extreme youth, she knew she could trust him with his master's very life. He would not join her on this journey. She had sent him on to Gretton with news to her parents that she had undertaken this service to attend the Princess.

They had had no tidings. Of course, she had expected

none, but now she feared that Philip had failed in his mission, or, worse, that Martyn would not be well enough to travel. Fear touched her heart at the thought that he might be recognised and arrested leaving Leciester or at any place along the route to Bury.

When Peter Fairley tapped on her door she almost threw herself into his arms at her relief on seeing him. He was dressed like a servant, his brown hair tousled as if it had not seen a comb for weeks, but his eyes were shining triumphantly.

'My lord is here in the stables. If you would see him you must come now, while the men of the escort are at their meal in the convent kitchen and the sisters are at their devotions.'

She had already donned one of Alice's fustian cloaks and went with him instantly. Jack Wainwright was standing at the stable door with the boy, Wat Forrester, beside him.

'All is well, my lady. He is in there. This meeting must be brief. You understand that?'

She nodded and waited no more but hastened into the gloom. The stable smelled sweetly of straw and hay and horses—even the familiar sharp scents of horse urine and more pungent dung could not disturb her.

At first she could not see him, deep in the shadows, then he had enfolded her in his arms in the old masterful way and kissed her hard, hungrily, demandingly. She responded eagerly, her arms reaching up round his neck to pull his head down even closer to hers.

'Oh, my darling, darling Cressida.' He sounded like a man who had hungered for weeks and just now had had delicious food placed before him. She murmured incoherently of her love and he strained her body to him yet tighter.

'Come,' he whispered hoarsely. 'Here, down on the

hay. Jack will keep guard and God knows how soon it will be before we meet again.'

She could not even see him clearly, but she knew every part of his dear body that was hidden from her by the unfamiliar fustian tunic and coarse woollen hose. She protested when his chin rubbed against her cheek raspingly and she realised, laughingly, that he had grown a full beard.

She surrendered to him joyfully, feeling his own shuddering delight in her nearness, his desperate longing to possess her. Death had been so close and could even now draw near again. She was here within his arms and he took full advantage of her presence. But afterwards, as she lay spent in his arms, he bent to smooth down her disordered clothing and whispered a hasty apology for his urgent roughness.

'Don't,' she whispered softly. 'Don't even speak of it. I have needed you quite as desperately as you have wanted me. Oh, Martyn—Martyn, I thought I had lost you—and then Peter came—and I dared not believe him. My joy was too great. . .'

He nuzzled his bearded cheek against her nose and then her hair.

'I could hardly believe it myself when I came to in that upstairs room in Leicester. I had to feel myself all over to be sure I was no revenant.'

'Will you be safe—even now? Oh, Martyn, I could not bear it if. . .'

'We have come so far safely, my heart, with the care and help of these three good men. Peter has had to grow up very quickly and as for Jack—' he drew a hard breath '—he is tried gold indeed and always has been. But for his quick thinking I would certainly be languishing in one of Henry's dungeons now, awaiting—who knows?'

He bent and kissed her again as he felt her shudder with fear beside him. He gave a bark of a laugh. 'As for Wat, well, his knowledge of the underworld of society stands us in good stead now. Bless the boy, he knows I saved his life and has proved a willing messenger, guide—aye, and scavenger. He says he will go with me and God knows we need his special skills.'

'The Princess says you will make for Burgundy.'

'Yes, to the Court of the Duchess Margaret at Malines if God is with us.'

'You will be very careful?'

'I swear it, my love.'

Jack Wainwright's warning whisper reached them from the doorway. 'There are sounds from the kitchen that tell us the men will be coming out soon, my lord.'

'I must go. I must not endanger you.' She rose immediately. 'Oh, Martyn, it will be so hard not to acknowledge you when I see you in the Princess's train.'

'I know, my love. I shall hardly dare to look your way.'

He drew her close again and she felt his body go rigid with the strain of this parting, then, gently, he set her from him and she moved to the stable door. A horse whinnied and moved restlessly and she turned.

A shaft of moonlight from the open door illuminated him for her. She saw his tall, erect figure crowned with a mass of dark hair that, like Peter's, had grown over-long and was in disarray from their tumble in the hay. His eyes were shining and his bearded mouth was parted in a reluctant smile. He lifted one hand in farewell and then she stepped out into the cold, moonlit court.

Later that night the Lady Elizabeth sent for her. She had dismissed her elderly attendant and was alone with Cressida. 'He is recovered?'

'It would seem so, my lady.' Cressida blushed hotly and Elizabeth laughed.

'I am relieved to hear that, and now, Cressida, you should go early tomorrow back to your father at Gretton. It will be hard for both of you to remain in my train and avoid looking with such obvious love at each other.'

Cressida's heart turned over. 'So soon? Oh, my lady, why cannot I go with him? I did not speak of it in the stable for I knew he would object, but—'

'No, Cressida; he would never manage to board that ship with you. For his sake, you must let him go alone.'

'But I must see him again, just once more—please. . .'

'Would you make the parting harder for him to bear? He loses everything—title, home, friends and, most of all you—but his very survival now depends on the fact that everyone continues to believe he is dead. Believe me, Cressida, I know how hard it is for you to accept that premise. I too must forgo any contact with—with someone I love—for his chance of life.'

Cressida stared at her hard but Elizabeth shook her head decisively. 'You must let Martyn go. If he is taken, he will endanger more than his own life.'

'But will I ever see him again—and won't he look for me at least to say goodbye? He will think I have deserted him for my own comfort, knowing he has nothing to offer me in exile but a life of hardship.'

Elizabeth did not answer. Her eyes glittered oddly and Cressida was not sure if that was due to unshed tears or steely determination. Cressida sighed, curtsied, and made to withdraw.

Elizabeth said softly, 'I will send my new groom on some errand. He will not see you ride out early. Trust me. My friends will see him safe, at risk to their own lives.'

Next morning, when Cressida rode out early with Alice and two of the men from Elizabeth's own trusted escort, she looked back once towards the stable, busy now with grooms and ostlers preparing mounts for the

Princess's departure for Walsingham. There was no sign of Martyn. She rode forward towards the convent gate feeling as if her heart would break and die within her living breast.

Martyn of Wroxeter looked up at his friend, Lord Lovell, with a wistful smile.

'I wish I were going with you, Frank,' he said.

Lovell drained his wine goblet and rose to his feet. 'You will be considerably more useful to the cause here in Malines,' he replied. 'Your collation of information gathered from all sources will be invaluable. The Duchess Margaret needs you and there is the boy to think of.'

Martyn shook his head. 'I know it, but I hate to skulk here in safety while you risk your life in England to sound out the northern lords for rebellion. Henry will have spies everywhere.'

Lovell smiled grimly. 'The Staffords are still free and I too have my companions who are ready to lay down their lives to bring Henry Tudor down.'

He took his leave after the two grasped hands. Halfway down the stair he said, 'Do you wish me to have someone contact the Lady Cressida?'

Again Martyn shook his head regretfully. 'No, I will do nothing that could endanger her. Keep well away, my lord.'

He returned to his seat near the window and looked down over the street below. His lodging was not large but it was comfortable and conveniently placed for his work at the palace of the Duchess Margaret of Burgundy.

He had come here with scarcely more than the clothes he stood up in, but Richard's sister, Margaret, had welcomed him warmly as she had other survivors of that débâcle on Ambien. As Lovell had said, he had soon slipped into the work he had done for King

Richard, acting as the Duchess's spymaster and collecting all information which came to Malines which could help in the cause of dealing Henry Tudor a blow mighty enough to topple him from the English throne he had usurped.

Martyn had never needed luxurious accommodation; he had rooms on this second floor which served for his use and that of his squire, Peter Fairley. Below in the kitchen Jack Wainwright ruled benignly over the serving and kitchen wenches. Wat Forrester slept with Wainwright in the attic rooms at the top of the house and, for the most part, went his own way about the town, though he too had his uses. He met English and Burgundian merchants in taverns and brought back a wealth of information.

Martyn gazed about the room thoughtfully. The furniture and hangings were somewhat spartan, but he had been far less comfortable many times in his life on campaign. No, it was not concern for his bodily ease which brought the hint of brooding sadness to his dark brown eyes or the wistful downward turn of his lips.

It would soon be the Holy Season of Christmas. Last year at this time he had not met the fairy child whom he had made his beloved bride. She had been the King's pawn, wed to weld her father's allegiance to King Richard, and though the ploy had been successful it had all come to naught in the end with the fall of the King at Redmoor.

Martyn had not thought then that he could come to love that exquisitely beautiful child with all the passion and devotion of his heart. He missed her desperately, knew she was secure upon her father's manor at Gretton, but longed with all his being to have her her with him now.

He had little to offer. His title meant nothing here and he had no fine town house nor rich estates on the Welsh border. Despite all their intended efforts to dislodge Henry from the royal seat, Martyn could not dispel the thought from his mind that he would never have those things again.

No, Cressida was best in England. Her parents considered her a virgin still. It might yet be possible for her to obtain a dispensation and wed again, some man Henry favoured. He ground his teeth in bitter desperation at the thought.

A knock came at his door and he called for Peter Fairley to enter.

He did not look up at once and wondered why the boy remained in the doorway and did not state his errand. Then he turned.

She stood, framed against the lintel, the formidable form of Alice Croft beside her, and behind them, shuffling uncomfortably in the confined space of the landing, young Philip Kenton and the stolid frame of his former captain of escort at Wroxeter, the redoubtable Sergeant Chubb.

At first he thought he must be hallucinating, then she gave a little inarticulate cry and moved towards him. Alice shooed away the others and withdrew herself, leaving them alone.

She was real; he could feel her close to his heart. He pressed passionate kisses upon the top of her head, then pushed back her hood, tilted up her chin and kissed her again on her mouth, cheeks damp with happy tears, eyes, chin again. At last he drew away to arm's length, holding her hands still, and took in his full sight of her.

He said, hoarse with emotion, 'I—I cannot believe you are real. If I continue to look, will you disappear from view like the fairy you are?'

She laughed merrily. 'I am very solid indeed, my lord, more so than usual for—for I bring you an heir.' She was blushing rosily in shy embarrassment.

Again he stared at her, then abruptly enclosed her in

his arms again. This time he could not hold back a sob of amazed joy.

'I had meant to be more decorous than that and tell you more gently,' she confessed, 'but—oh, Martyn, I have waited so long to see you that it could not wait.'

She stared back at him now wonderingly. He was again the elegant courtier she had known at Westminster. His beard was gone, his cheeks smooth-shaven, and his dark hair was combed back from his face in sleek waves and fell to his shoulders. She drew a hard breath and laughed again in sheer delight at reaching him at last.

He drew her to the chair and, sitting her down, knelt before her.

'I think either the Virgin has answered my prayers or you yourself, with your magic, heard me call to you across the sea. Oh, my darling. How is it possible you are here?'

'The Princess convinced me that I must not leave with you. It would endanger you, she said, and I must return to Gretton and pretend you were indeed killed, so I did.' It was so simply said, with no mention of the immense difficulty of accomplishing that, that he had to laugh aloud.

'It had its problems,' she confided, 'especially when I discovered that I—was to bear your child. I told Alice, of course.' Her expression sobered. 'I could not even tell my mother.'

'And then Howell came to Gretton.' Her clear blue eyes looked deep into his. 'Howell loves me. He believed I was a widow and—and he proposed to me—after my period of mourning was over, of course.'

'And you said?'

'I told him that could never be and—and he guessed, because he loves me, I think. He said we could still get a dispensation if it was believed I had been no true wife—and—and that he would say the child was his.'

Martyn gave a little hiss of protest.

'I had to tell him then how dearly I loved you—that even if you were dead I could never give my heart to another man.' She was silent for a moment, then said, 'He is a very honourable man, Howell, even though he supported the Tudor. His allegiance was given there, as yours was to Richard. At last he said he would help me to come to you if I truly wished it. Oh, Martyn, how much I wanted that.'

He sat back, regarding her with a little crooked smile. 'And so you came. You never let little difficulties prevent you from doing what you wished, did you, my wife?'

'Never.' She reached down and kissed him. 'Alice had to come, of course, and Philip. I could not ask my father, so—Sergeant Chubb insisted that he could not let his Countess embark upon the high seas without her sergeant-at-escort. Besides, he wants to be with you.'

He stood up and held out his hand to her to rise, then took from her her cloak and looked hungrily at her beauty again. As yet there was no sign of impending motherhood. She was, as ever, tiny, resolute, holding herself with the grace of a queen, and her blue eyes shone with love for him. Suddenly her expression clouded. 'You will not send me away?'

His voice was almsot choked with tears as he said, 'Never, never, my darling.'

She looked round anxiously. 'You are happy here? The Princess indicated that you would work for the Duchess Margaret.' She hesitated. 'She also said you would endanger more lives than your own if caught. Did she—did she mean one of her brothers, Martyn?'

He nodded slowly. 'Richard of York has been here in Burgundy for almost two years. It will be my duty to serve him.'

'And the other Prince?'

He shook his head regretfully. 'I do not know.

Edward was sent north to Barnard Castle with Sir Guy Jarvis. Guy came south to fight at Redmoor. I cannot say what has happened to the boy since then. I hear Jarvis and Allard both survived and have paid heavy fines and returned to their manors.' He did not add that he believed both would be active in Lovell's proposed rising against Henry.

Cressida said quietly, 'Elizabeth saved your life. Martyn, I believe she truly loved Richard.'

'I know. In that lay the danger.'

She sighed again. 'How lonely and unhappy she will be in the coming years. She is to marry Henry in January. We shall all grieve for the death of the King. I have a Book of Hours he gave me and will treasure it for ever.'

'We must pray he has his wish and he and his beloved Anne are reunited. He would have wished to die like that, fighting gallantly for the realm.' He was gently stroking the palm of her hand. 'You do not mention the problems of your journey.'

'Howell found us a ship sailing from Milford Haven—ironical, wasn't it?' She dimpled. 'It was very uncomfortable. We were all sick, then the journey was hard. Alice said I must travel slowly because of the child.'

'And now you are here and there will be eons of time to hear all about the long days we have been separated, but for now we must think of our happiness together. My darling Cressida, I have little to offer you but a life lived in the Duchess's favour, for which I am grateful. I brought little coin and no treasure from England.'

'But I did,' she said happily. 'Alice and I sewed jewels into our clothing and they will keep us remarkably comfortable for a while, at least.'

He threw back his head and laughed aloud. 'Truly

you are a redoubtable Countess of Wroxeter and will always be the love of my life.'

She offered herself for his embrace and he drew her into his arms. Christmas would come here at Malines and he would rejoice with his lovely bride by his side.

Historical Romance™

Coming next month

EMMA AND THE EARL
Paula Marshall
REGENCY ENGLAND

Miss Emma Lawrence was badly in need of a new job, and
had no choice about accepting the post of governess to
Lady Letitia Hastings, young daughter of Dominic
Hastings, the Earl of Chard. What unkind twist of fate had
brought her to this, working for the man she might have
married when she was the rich Miss Emilia Lincoln?
And—more worrying—would he recognise her? In ten
years they had both changed out of all recognition—but
what had not changed was Emma's abiding love for
Dominic...

SEAFIRE
Sarah Westleigh
REGENCY 1814/15

Having finished school, Miss Miranda Dawson was on her
way to Barbados to join her family. But the uncomfortable
relations between America and England landed her in
trouble when the American ship Seafire attacked. Taken
prisoner of war by the Captain, Adam York, Miranda was
determined not to be cowed, and her defiant attitude
earned the admiration of Adam. But with their two
countries virtually at war, what future did they have?

One to Another

A year's supply of Mills & Boon® novels— absolutely FREE!

Would you like to win a year's supply of heartwarming and passionate romances? Well, you can and they're FREE! Simply complete the missing word competition below and send it to us by 28th February 1997. The first 5 correct entries picked after the closing date will win a year's supply of Mills & Boon romance novels (six books every month—worth over £150). What could be easier?

PAPER	B A C K	WARDS
ARM		MAN
PAIN		ON
SHOE		TOP
FIRE		MAT
WAIST		HANGER
BED		BOX
BACK		AGE
RAIN		FALL
CHOPPING		ROOM

Please turn over for details of how to enter ☞

How to enter...

There are ten missing words in our grid overleaf.
Each of the missing words must connect up with the
words on either side to make a new word—e.g.
PAPER-BACK-WARDS. As you find each one, write it in
the space provided, we've done the first one for you!

When you have found all the words, don't forget to fill in
your name and address in the space provided below and
pop this page into an envelope (you don't even need a
stamp) and post it today. Hurry—competition ends
28th February 1997.

Mills & Boon® One to Another
FREEPOST
Croydon
Surrey
CR9 3WZ

Are you a Reader Service Subscriber?   Yes ❑   No ❑

Ms/Mrs/Miss/Mr   _____

Address   _____

_____

_____ Postcode _____

One application per household.

You may be mailed with other offers from other reputable companies as a
result of this application. If you would prefer not to receive such offers,
please tick box.   ❑

mps
MAILING
PREFERENCE
SERVICE   **DMA**

C496
A